COVEN COVE

The Shape of Things to Come

David Clark

1

Ever notice the switch to turn on your nerves was someone telling you not to be nervous? That was the on switch for mine, and Mrs. Saxon threw it into the on position when she told me the Council of Mages would be visiting tomorrow. She told me several times to not be nervous, which, of course, caused me to worry like hell about what I had to be nervous about. Yes, our coven had been attacked by some two hundred-year-old vampires, and yes, technically, it was my fault… and that was where my mind stopped, and the mental gymnastics took over.

I spent the rest of the day asking anyone I could find about the council. My mind had already created an image of twelve people walking in wearing black robes with their noses held high, ready to pass judgement, and sentence me to some horrific magical punishment. None of the other students had ever met or seen them. Not even Gwen, and even she seemed concerned when I mentioned they were coming for a visit, but I couldn't be sure that she wasn't just messing with me. We had a rather tenuous but unspoken truce since Reginald Von Bell's attack. She had stepped in during the attack and defended me, and even called me sister, something that I thought of a few days later while watching over Nathan. Was it just a comment or exclamation, or was she referring to me as a sister witch? I never asked. I didn't want to push things and threaten our peace. There were still the little jabs here and there, but no more than anyone else, and she no longer tortured me during our classes. Well, at least not as much as before. We even sparred once in Mr. Helms' class, and it never became heated or out of control. There was a still an icy glare from her when she saw me with Nathan, but I didn't let that bother me. Why should I?

"Oh dear, you have nothing to worry about," Mrs. Tenderschott said when I asked her about the council.

"I really wish people would stop telling me that. It makes me think I have something to worry about." I let my head collapse down on the table with a thud.

"Nonsense. I have met with them many times. A few of them are full of hot air that they like to blow around to make themselves seem important, but the rest are just like us. Nothing to worry your pretty little head about." She reached over and gave the back of my head a soothing rub.

"But you once called them witch hunters." I said muffled, and then picked my head up to see her response.

A nervous smile crept across her face, and her eyes ran away from mine. "Don't worry about that. That is old history."

The lack of conviction in her voice sent my head back to the table with a thud. "What do they want?" I asked, muffled against the tabletop.

"I imagine they want to make sure everyone is okay and find out everything they can about what happened." I felt her hand on my head again. She stroked my hair first and then gave it a little tug. I lifted it off the table and looked up at her. "That means they will want to talk to you. Just tell them what you know, and tell them clearly what you don't know. You will be fine. Now, are you ready to try again?"

I rolled my black eyes up to the ceiling and sat back in my chair. Another day, another potion. "Sure, let's do this." I held out my hand, and Mrs. Tenderschott handed me a vial of green liquid that had flecks of orange in it. I made the mistake of asking a few times what the contents were. Something I instantly regretted. Now I don't ask. I just down the concoction and hope it doesn't kill me or cause my body to grow hair all over the place. I wasn't ready to become a part of the dog pack.

It tasted worse than it looked. The orange specks were chunky and hard; and they scraped my throat on the way down. If this were meant for witches, I wasn't sure how their sensitive human systems would be able to handle it. Like every time before, the room dripped away, leaving me in darkness before that dripped away too. What appeared were the steps leading up to the front porch of my childhood home. I went in and immediately headed to the kitchen. My mother was there. She wasn't sitting at the table like she was the first time. This time she was at the sink, washing dishes while looking out the window. The sunlight that came in the window caught her red hair just right, making it almost glow around her. She turned when I stepped in and caused the floor to creak.

"Larissa!" She rushed and hugged me. I hugged her back. "You are still so cold."

"It's fine, mom." My voice still sounded like a much younger version of myself. I still didn't want to discuss what I really was, not yet. It was something I knew I would have to tell her. How? Now that was the big question. I was still getting to know my mother. I wasn't ready to break her heart yet. Not that anytime would really be the right time to tell her.

She let go of our embrace, but grabbed my hand and led me over to the kitchen table. I sat down while she took off her white apron and folded it neatly over the back of her chair before she sat. For someone that was washing the dishes, she was dressed rather well. White short-sleeve shirt, grey skirt, and wide black belt. "I am glad you came back to see me."

"I promise I will make more of an effort to visit often. There has been a lot going on, and right now I still have to use a potion to come see you."

"Because you still can't remember your life here? I see." My mother's brow furrowed as she looked down at the table in front of her. "And you can only do one potion a day. Even that frequently can have side effects."

"No kidding," I muttered, causing my mother to cover her mouth with her hand as she let out a reserved giggle.

"Enjoying the nightmares?"

"Not really." I gave her my best face of dismay. I remembered the nightmares from when I was human again, but since the antidote had worn off, I hadn't slept, so no more nightmares. Having to explain that to my mother would mean explaining the other detail I didn't want her to know about yet. To me they were, I guess, daymares. Little flashes of hell while I was wide awake.

"There are various spells that can create a memory block. Unfortunately, breaking them is not as easy as putting them on. Is that wise witch that showed you how to visit me the first time still around?"

"Yes ma'am. In fact, there are many wise witches around me. I am part of a coven up in the northeast. They are teaching me all the things I need to know." Hearing this appeared to bring a smile to my mother's face. At least I was able to give her some good news. "I know we were part of the Orleans' Coven. I have been reading through some of their records to learn about our family. Things are coming back to me." I lied. Nothing was coming back to me. Not yet. Mrs. Tenderschott and Mrs. Saxon had already tried a few reversals for memory blocks, and every cleaning spell they knew. Neither were hopeful they would make a difference. Memory loss wasn't common in the turning process, but it happened, and at the moment that was the leading theory of what my problem was. The best I could do was read the records, which I had, and come back to visit my mother. If something clicked, I could handle these trips all on my own.

"In fact, mom, there was something I read about, a party, my debutante ball."

"Oh my," her hand again went up in front of her mouth, but I could still see the edges of her wide smile on either side of it. "I hadn't thought about that in years. You were so beautiful in that light blue dress." Her voice cooed.

"Yea, I read about that."

"I still remember you dancing with Todd Grainger. He was in a tuxedo with a bow tie, and you wore that dress. You both made such a cute couple. Have you seen him recently?"

"No ma'am. Not in a few years." *Try about eighty years.*

"I had so hoped you would have stayed in touch with him, but you didn't really seem to enjoy yourself dancing with him. He was such a nice boy, and his family..."

"I am sure they were a fine family. He just wasn't my type." I wasn't sure if he was or wasn't. By now, he would be long in the ground and definitely not into dating. Not to mention I had Nathan, I hoped. "Mom, do you remember anyone with the last name Norton?"

I watched my mother pinch her lips together and her eyes searched her memories as they floated by, giving a little shake of her head. Then it became more pronounced. "No, that name is not familiar. Why do you ask?"

"It's just a name that keeps coming up in the research of our family. I was trying to understand the significance." I watched my mother again, as she pinched her face and appeared lost in thought. Maybe I was reading too much into her expression, but to me, it looked like more than just someone trying to remember something. Did she know the name? She had to. If Jean St. Claire were as much of a nuisance in the New Orleans area as I had been told, and my parents were who I heard they were, there was a good chance she would have known members of his coven.

"No. That's not a name I am familiar with," she answered. Her voice wavered. There was a question in there, maybe to ask why I was asking about them, but I wasn't ready to open that can of worms yet. Of course, it could just be my mind playing with her response. I knew the truth of who they were and what happened, and I didn't doubt my mother still viewed me as her little girl and might hold something frightful back.

"Okay," I answered, letting it drop. "I do have another question for you, more on the magic side."

She sat up straight, but still not as straight as Jennifer Bolden. That was a vampire thing. "That I can handle. What is it?"

"Two actually. You said there was a way for me to come back and visit you on my own. That I could just drift back and forth. Can you show me how to do that?"

"I can tell you, and then you can try later. You need to focus on memory that you have of this place, but you have to more than see it. You have to feel it, like you are there in that moment-" Her voice trailed off as my mood declined. I had to assume I projected that depression on my face.

"That's the problem. I remember nothing, so there is nothing to focus on. I tried remembering back to the first time I came here, but that didn't work."

"No, it wouldn't," agreed my mother. "It has to be a real memory. That is why they need to work on breaking through that memory block. Once that is gone, you will have what you need to come back to see me anytime you want. No more yucky potions." She said as if she were talking to a six-year-old who just took her last spoonful of medicine. "What's the second question?"

"This one, I hope, is easier. Did I have good control of my magic when you were—alive?" I gulped.

"Oh yes," she beamed. "The best of anyone your age. You developed superb control at an early age and progressed beyond simple to complex spells before anyone else. Why?"

"I have been all over the place lately. For a while, anything I tried to move either didn't move or flew across the room violently, almost killing someone. I was told it was a question of focus and that I needed to concentrate everything on something the size of the head of a pin, but that is exhausting to have to remember to do each and every time."

"But it is good advice." My mother pointed at me when she said it like a lecturing parent. "You have a powerful gift, always have. That requires a stronger focus to control. That rule applies to everything from moving objects to even your spells and potions. Most think the potion is really just the combination of ingredients, but it is much more than that. We are the ones responsible for enabling the potion with our gift. The words we say, the thought we have in our head when we say it, give the potion the power to do what we want. The ingredients are just vehicles for our magic. It's not the other way around. Not having good control and focus then can lead to disastrous outcomes."

"Gotcha." I tried my best to sound sure of myself while inside I was again realizing how dangerous I really was.

"How much time do you have?" she asked hopefully.

I looked down at my watch, which wasn't there. What I saw beyond my arm was the edge of the straight black skirt I was wearing. My hand slipped down under the table and explored the fabric up to my waist, where I found the texture of a thick leather belt, much like my mom's, bordering a white blouse. This must be one of the last outfits my mother remembered me in. I thought about it, and knew I hadn't been here too long, maybe twenty minutes, and had a couple of hours until my date with Nathan. "I have a bit. Why?"

"Let me show you a few things."

2

"So, she didn't remember the Nortons?" Nathan asked.

"No, and yes. She said she didn't, but there was something about how she said it that makes me question that. Remember who my parents were. They would have known them, or at least heard of them. She just didn't want to tell me." The more I had thought about the look on my mother's face, the more I was convincing myself that I was right. Of course, I understood. I would have done the same if I were in her place.

"I am surprised. You have lived here all your life and have never been out here."

"I didn't say I have never been out here before. Let me recap your suggestion and my response for clarity." Nathan coughed and released my hand. There goes my comfort. His hands met up around his collar and adjusted the invisible tie he wore that would have looked rather funny over his t-shirt. "You said, 'tonight, since we aren't allowed to leave the coven just yet, why don't we walk out to the cove? It is a beautiful sight at night.' To which my response was, 'Sounds great, I have never seen *IT*.' Meaning, I have never seen it at night." He smiled, and I slugged him in the arm for being such a smartass. He whimpered before he admitted, "I have been out here many times, just only during the day. The woods are…"

I interrupted, "Spooky? Scary? Do the deep dark woods scare the big … strong … man?"

"Forbidden," he shot back.

"Oh," I said, stunned by both the harshness of the word and the realization that I had become a bit of a rebel. Here I was, breaking another rule. I looked up at his face to see if he was just making a joke, but the absence of his world stopping smile gave me my answer. "Is it really?" I asked, watching his response.

"Kind of," he answered. "The woods are considered off limits at night unless you are a werewolf or shifter out checking the grounds or Friday night for you guys. Other than that, no one is really supposed to be out here, and especially not alone."

"Oh." I leaned into him. "I guess we should head back." I hoped he wouldn't take that suggestion, but I didn't want either of us to get into any trouble; something I had caused enough of already. I felt Mrs. Saxon was taking a leap of faith by letting whatever this was Nathan and I had continue. Though her nervous twitches and looks told me she still wasn't completely comfortable with it. Add another moment of me putting Nathan in some kind of harm's way, and I was sure there would be some backtracking on that faith.

"Nah, it's not really night. I can still see some of the light. The dog pack won't be out here for a few hours still. We have time. Plus, I am not alone." His arm gave me another squeeze. "How much further is it?"

"Not far." I grabbed his hand, and we continued walking through the woods as the sky took on a purplish hue as dusk settled in.

We pushed through the edge of the woods and the world opened up before us. Nathan stopped there at the top of the bluff and let out a "Wow!"

I said it too, but kept it quiet. I had been there a few times, mostly after one of our hunting sessions, but I had never seen it like this before. Magical was the only word I could use, and I felt bad that Nathan would never see it as I did, though I could feel the beauty of the moment had affected him. Colors and sounds were more vibrant after you were turned. Combine that with walking upon this sight at the golden hour. The soft light of the setting sun wasn't robbing objects of their natural richness. The dark blue of the water, and the white spray of the waves crashing against the craggy rocks. They were works of art all on their own. Brown and hard, with pits of character all over them. Above, the first stars of the night were twinkling into view to the east. I could still see a few of them above us just before the purple faded into an orangish red that continued to the western horizon.

I walked him by the hand down to the sandy cove just short of the outgoing tide and sat down on the cool, wet sand. A steady, salty breeze blew my hair away from me. He finally joined me and sat down, putting his arm around me as he did. I leaned into him as I had seen in the movies, and for the second time in just a few weeks, we had one of those Hollywood moments. This time, there was no cheesy dialogue, just us and the magic of the moment. It was just what I wanted it to be.

I felt him laugh, and asked softly, "what?"

"Just thinking," Nathan sighed.

"About what?" I looked up at him. He was staring out at the water. A blissful smile consumed his face.

"This. This moment. It's both absurd and beautiful all at the same time. I am sitting here staring out at one of nature's true wonders, while also holding another of its wonders."

Oh my god. Did he really just drop that cheesy line on me? I didn't care, and I wasn't about to bust him for it. Hearing it touched that soft and cheesy spot that I had, which I never let anyone know existed, and I melted back into him, and felt both of his arms wrap around me.

"Are you nervous about tomorrow?"

"The council?," I clarified. "Everyone says I have nothing to worry about."

"So, are you worried?"

I looked straight ahead out at the water, and watched the chaos of the crashing waves, and appreciated the great forces at work. Force and resistance. A simple pattern to life. Something happens, and something resists. As much as the rocks resist, the water will eventually win. The force and determination of the waves making their assault day after day will wear the rock down little by little, but it will take thousands of years before it shows any real wear, unless a crack opens up. I hadn't decided if I really had anything to worry about, but I knew the challenges would keep coming. I couldn't let a crack show and instead would be the rock and just deal with whatever the council brought.

"Concerned yes, worried no. I am sure they will have a lot of questions about what happened, which other than what everyone else saw too, I can't really add anything. Who and what I am will probably be a topic for discussion." Mrs. Tenderschott seemed to think so when I spoke to her about the council's visit. "This is who and what I am. I can't change it, and I will be like this forever, so I better learn to accept it and deal with it."

"I am sure they won't be too hard on you, and will see you for the wonderful person you are, like I do."

He did it again, and again I didn't mind. I turned my head and snuggled the side of my cheek against his chest. The warmth and that familiar beat pushed any doubts and concerns I had away.

"So forever. I hadn't really thought about that before, but you will be like this forever?" There was a concerned tone in his voice.

That wasn't a word I had thought about much either. I knew we were immortal, and I was already ninety-eight years old. The passage of that time seemed short, though there was some part of it I still didn't remember. Would I be who I was at this moment forever? There was the corny answer, and what I felt was a sophisticated answer. I went with the latter. "I hope so. I am sure in some ways over time I will grow as a person, but I will still be me."

"And when I am thirty, you will still look like, what... sixteen or seventeen?"

"Yes."

"When I am fifty, you will look like someone old enough to be my daughter, or maybe even my granddaughter?"

"I guess." It was a fact I hadn't really thought about, but the vacant stare I looked into told me Nathan had. His eyes had lost the sparkle, and that light-up-the-world smile was hidden behind a frown. "Look, don't even think about that stuff, okay?" My voice shook. My hands did too, and this wasn't me imitating how a human might react. Two emotions battled for control in my head. The depression of what our future together would mean tried to douse the flame that was fueled by knowing he thought about a future with me.

"Just don't." I reached up with my hand and caressed his warm cheek. He didn't, and never had backed away from my cold touch, but when I didn't see the light return to his expression, I took a more drastic step and squirmed free of his grasp, and sat up right in front of him face to face.

"Just don't." I whispered again, and then gripped both sides of his face and pulled him in close. I bathed in his warm breath and moved in closer, letting my cold lips meet his warm ones, and I felt the light return. The light lasted until a distant scream forced us to break our embrace.

3

I didn't want to let go, but I needed to. With what had happened, the concern that Jean St. Clair, or one of his stooges, would show up again, was a constant threat. They knew where I was. What was stopping them? I jumped to my feet and grabbed Nathan by the hand and rushed back through the woods while paying attention to everything around us. If something or someone was in the woods, I wanted to know before they found us. The one creature I wasn't paying attention to was the one behind me that I was now dragging at a speed he struggled to keep up with. Despite his cries of "Wait!," I continued forward a few hundred yards.

"Oh God. I'm sorry," I gushed apologetically. My cold hands worked to soothe the shoulder his own hands were nursing. "I panicked."

"I didn't think you felt emotions," he complained, grimacing as he rolled his shoulder in an attempt to work out the pain. I was surprised, and happy, he could even do that. With how fast I was pulling him, I was worried I had pulled it out of the socket all together.

"Uh yeah, we do. We just don't have the same physical reactions. Are you okay? We need to get back. I think someone is here."

"I need a moment." He shook his arm and then pulled on his wrist with his other hand.

"We don't have a moment," I urged. My arms swinging in the direction of the coven to convey our need to get moving. "Nathan, they might be here again. You heard that scream."

"I know." His voice and expression were pained.

"I could..."

"Absolutely not." He interrupted gruffly before the suggestion even made it out of my mouth. It had barely crossed my brain. I knew it was his machismo talking here. The voice of his ego, but this was no time to listen to it. We needed to get back to safety.

"No time." Before he could object, I gathered his large muscular frame in my arms and took off, carrying him in a full out run. At this speed, we would be out of the woods before we knew it.

"Not a word to anyone," he conceded into my ear. "Not a word."

I felt no one other than Nathan the whole trek back. Then I realized I was being really stupid. I wouldn't feel them. They were like me. No pulse. No blood that I would be able to taste from a quarter of a mile away. If I could have let out a heavy sigh of relief, I would have when I saw the edge of the pool deck, but couldn't, so I didn't. Nathan let out one deep enough for both of us when I put him down on his own two feet. We were safer, but not completely safe until we were back inside, behind the doors and the runes that Mr. Demius and Mrs. Saxon had put across the entrances after the building repaired the damage.

We were just about at the door, walking hand in hand again, when we heard the scream again. This time, louder and closer. It came from inside, and we both dropped each other's hand and reached for the door. We weren't the only ones that heard it. The stairs were lined with others staring in one direction. Even Jennifer Bolden and Mr. Markinson were out on their respective landings. From the clueless looks on their faces I knew they knew no more about what was going on than we did. The painful cry filled the halls again, and I saw Apryl point to the hall that led to Mrs. Saxon's residence. My mind flashed back to when I heard Robert's painful cries coming down the same hallway and the scene I found when I followed it.

Nathan was already on his way, and I followed cautiously. Jennifer wasn't far behind. I heard Mr. Markinson's voice instruct everyone else back to their halls, followed by a few moans of those obviously wanting to see what was happening.

Mrs. Saxon's door was already open when we arrived and inside there was a gathering of instructors. Mr. Helms and the blonde I had first seen when Edward dumped who I was on me. I had asked around and found out her name was Mrs. Parrish, and my suspicions were correct. She was a shapeshifter. I had developed a kind of a sixth, or seventh, sense about these things. Their hearts beat slower than humans, and a lot slower than werewolves. That was why I started looking around as soon as we stepped in. There was something, or someone else, in there.

"Mom, is everything okay? We heard the screaming." Nathan asked, concerned.

Mrs. Saxon turned toward us, giving us an unobstructed view of who, or what, was behind her, and said, "Everything is just fine. We have a new..."

"A shapeshifter," I whispered or thought I did. Everyone looked right at me. Including two bright green eyes that were surrounded by patches of red brought on by crying. A horrible contrast to the angelic face they were set in underneath a mane of blonde hair. The girl couldn't be any older than nine or ten, and she sat there on the couch where I sat and cried just a few weeks ago, probably feeling just as confused as I was.

She let out another ear shattering scream with both fists clinched and pounding on her own legs. I had to wonder if I was the cause. Me and my black eyes could be enough to give anyone who had never seen one of us a nightmare. I stepped forward and knelt in front of her. "Hi, there. I'm Larissa. What's your name?"

Again, another scream that even made me flinch, but it was shorter this time and ended with a sniffle. Then weakly, and hoarse, probably from all the screaming, she looked up and said, "Amy."

"Well Amy. It's nice to meet you." I held out my hand and watched as she held out her hand tentatively. It shook the whole way. When she finally took mine, the contact was momentary before she pulled back and slid back hard against the back cushion of the sofa. "It's cold, is it?"

She nodded. Her eyes were huge, and her lips clamped tight. I was afraid there was another scream building up behind them, and I wasn't sure if anyone's ears could take another blast. I was sure mine couldn't. "Yeah, it's all right. I get that a lot, but he doesn't mind." I looked back over my shoulder at Nathan. He had moved forward a little closer to me. Her fear had thawed enough to allow her eyes to glance around the room at everyone. I didn't know her whole story, but I recognized that look. "Lots of unfamiliar faces. It's kind of scary, isn't it?"

There was another nod and a weak, "Uh, huh." Her arms were trying to give herself the world's biggest bear hug, and seeing her there, with that look on her face, I knew what was missing. "I will be right back."

I sprinted up the stairs to the room I called my own for those two days. Before opening the door, I tried to envision one thing. Something I cared for deeply that always sat on the windowsill in my room. Yes, I was sixteen, but that didn't mean there were still parts of me that didn't still want to be a little girl, even though I didn't remember ever being one. When I opened the door, I saw my old room just like I had left it, and over in the window was what I wanted. My stuffed animals. A bear, Mr. Snuggles, an elephant I never named, and a big old tabby cat. I remembered the day Mr. Norton brought that home. I wanted a real cat as a pet, but there were obvious reasons that wouldn't have worked out. A stuffed one was the safer option for that cat, not me.

I rushed back downstairs where I saw in my absence Amy's guard had gone up even more. She had backed up as far as she could get on the sofa, and her hold on herself was so tight, her hands were turning white. She never heard me coming and jerked when I sprang back in front of her. *Nice going Larissa, scare the girl more with pop-up vampire.*

It was a good thing I had brought a peace offering. "I want you to have this." I held out the sandy colored stuffed bear. "His name is Mr. Snuggles. He always brought me a lot of comfort, and now it's your turn." Her attention was fully on the bear that danced in front of her. "I was new here, like you, not that long ago, but I have to tell you everyone is super nice, and they will take good care of you." I looked up at Mrs. Saxon, who had a pleasant look on her face.

Finally, Amy let down her guard and reached out for the bear. She snatched it and pulled it in close. If it had been a real animal, she would have crushed it, but I had done that to him more than a few times before. Then, right before all of our eyes, the ratty old sandy bear changed to a dark brown bear with a light blue bow tie. Amy didn't notice. She held it too tightly to her body to see it, but then I heard it. A sigh as her cheek pressed against the top of its head.

I stood up and watched her. What was next for her? I didn't know. It was probably similar to what I went through. A period of acclimation and then school. I almost laughed at how simple I made that sound, but I knew she was in good hands, and I looked at Mrs. Saxon again. This was a time she and Mrs. Parrish were better suited for. It's what they did. I bent down close to Amy. Her eyes were closed as she snuggled her bear. "Well Amy, I am going to leave you with these nice people, but I will see you around. I promise." Her eyes popped open as I was telling Mrs. Parrish and Mrs. Saxon goodbye and walked toward the door with Nathan.

I hadn't reached the door before I felt Amy latching hold of my leg. Nothing would have prepared me for the look on that precious child's face when I glanced down. Two big eyes staring up at me, and a grin displaying two missing baby teeth. "Don't go Larissa," she begged.

"I will still be here. My room is just down the hall. Trust me, you will see me." I brushed her golden bangs out of her eyes and tucked the longer ones behind her ear.

"You promise?"

"I promise," I said with an over-exaggerated head nod. She let go and let Mrs. Saxon lead her back to the sofa.

At the door, I gave Nathan a hug and a quick kiss, which was something we hadn't really done publicly yet, and I didn't realize we had an audience that was left gawking. Luckily Mrs. Saxon wasn't part of them. She had her back turned and was walking in with Amy. To say she was still on the fence with Nathan and my little social experiment would be putting it lightly. She had already caught us kissing once, and it was only after that time that she agreed to allow us to spend some time together, alone. I wasn't sure how she would react to see how close we were now.

"You were a natural with her," Jennifer said while we walked down the hall toward the stairs. "So good, one might think you had kids of your own."

"Shut your mouth." I gave her a light bump with my elbow, but inside I was wondering. Could I have? I didn't know. I was almost a hundred. I just can't remember most of it.

"Larissa?" Mrs. Saxon called from behind. I turned, concerned she had seen our little display. She stood in the open door of her residence. "Remember, the council will be here tomorrow morning at nine sharp. Make sure you get a good night's sle...." She caught herself before she even finished it. Her chin dipped and her hands fidgeted with one another in front of her. "Right, just relax tonight, and I will see you in the morning."

"I will," I replied before she ducked back into her residence.

"You really have nothing to worry about tomorrow," Jennifer said as we resumed our walk to our area.

"I wish people would stop telling me that."

4

After a night of being told there was nothing for me to worry about, I felt I had a lot to worry about. A group of vampires telling me not to worry about meeting with the Council of Mages, when not a single one of them had ever even met a single member of the council or was a witch, seemed to lack even a touch of credibility. I didn't have a clue how it would go or what they would ask me about, but that didn't stop me from trying to rehearse every question and answer in my head all night long. This did nothing but make me the most nervous person in the coven that night. Well, make that the second. I had a feeling Amy was probably more nervous.

I found my thoughts drifting to Amy off and on all night. I had been there, but I was luckier than her. I was older, and I felt that gave me an advantage in dealing with, well, everything. The waves of my own worry parted to allow in worry for her. I hoped she was asleep, enjoying some kind of pleasant dream. Yes, she would eventually wake up and find herself back in a very confusing world, but it was a break, a sanctuary for her to find some sort of comfort. Twice I walked over to the railing and leaned to see if I could see Mrs. Saxon's light still on, something I often did to see if Nathan were still up. It was dark tonight.

Perhaps it was the stress of my own internal interrogation I put myself through, or the worry I felt for Amy, or the other several dozen concerns and worries that occupied my thoughts that allowed it to happen, but it happened again. I was vulnerable, and Jean St. Clarie opened the door. His dark eyes leered at me from above his pointed nose. Always a smile on his face. Not a pleasant or happy one, but a devious and menacing one. Often he spoke to me, repeating the same warning, like a broken record. Other times, he just hovered there in my thoughts. This wasn't a case of my mind playing tricks on me. With all the messing around in my memories and trying to establish connections with my mother and Mrs. Norton, we had created an opening. One that, with the help of what Mrs. Tenderschott thought was voodoo, he came knocking on whenever he wanted. Most of the time I could feel the dark weight of his arrival and fight it off, but in my current state, my system was open and vulnerable, and he used both handles to yank it wide open and walk right in, and stand front and center on the stage that was my thoughts.

"Larissa, I can see you. Your destiny is here. Why fight it?" Each message he delivered was oddly respectful and dignified. Like I was a visitor in his estate. Here for tea or a formal dinner. Never threatening in tone. Even his touch. It wasn't the violent chokes of Reginald. More graceful movements; gentle while violating. His fascination was with the charm, and me. He caressed it as much as he did my shoulders and chin as he moved around and admired me. I wasn't able to stop him during these visits. I was nothing more than a guest, forced to endure. Where his tone and actions lacked their usual vile nature, the presence that was around him made up for that. It was dank and full of death. Yet, oddly familiar. A sensation that worried me at times more than his message.

Tonight's visit was not much different from any of the others. His eyes drilled through me. The weight of knowing who he was, what he had done, and what he wanted to do pushed me down to the depths of despair. A thin, white-gloved finger chased across my cheek and under my chin while he smiled that wide toothy grin, pushing me even deeper. "Larissa, my dear. It's time you should come home." I felt what I shouldn't be able to. Cold and clammy. Beads of sweat formed on my skin, fueled by the reservoir of panic underneath. I wanted to be angry, to strike out, but he played my fear like a maestro.

A knock on the door pulled me out of his grasp and sent me jumping from where I sat on my bed. My hands searched for evidence of what I was feeling, but only found my own cold and dry skin. The weight of the visit still pressed down on me as I walked to the door. I opened it and found Mrs. Saxon standing there in a long grey pencil dress with no sign of makeup or jewelry. Her white hair tightly pulled behind her head. "Ready?"

This was not a question she would entertain the answer of no to, but I was not ready. I was dressed for it. Forgoing my normal jeans for black slacks and a long sleeve white silk shirt. None of which I had ever owned or had been in my closet before, but I knew I would need it for today, and there it was. My external appearance was all that was ready for this, but again, I didn't have a choice.

"Yep." I stepped out, closing the door behind me. There was no good morning or normal chit chat that Mrs. Saxon normally attempted to start. Not that I was complaining. I could sense something was on her mind. Something was on my mind too; lots of things were. There was only one question that bubbled up to the top that I felt I could ask, "How's Amy this morning?"

"She is fine. Mrs. Parrish is with her," she said tersely. The normal light click of her heels on the marble floor was replaced by a thudding that resembled the drumbeat of someone heading to the gallows.

"Did she sleep okay?"

"The important thing to remember this morning is to just answer their questions truthfully and honestly." Her hands were animated with every word, and she stared straight ahead. "There is nothing to worry about. Nothing you can say would be wrong. Understand?"

"Yes ma'am."

"Don't let their appearance or presence get to you. They enjoy putting on airs for the show of it. Very old school vibe. Their bark is far worse than their bite," she rambled while her hands swatted at imaginary bugs. "Be respectful though. These are not people you want to get on the bad side of. They can make your life exceedingly difficult, if not impossible. You need them as allies, or at the very least, not enemies." Her hands only stopped to grab the door handle, where she paused and appeared to take a breath before pulling it open. "You ready?"

I nodded, though a night of being told to not worry about it, and the walk down which was full of well… warnings. Not to mention my visit. I was anything but sure. If I could have sighed to release some tension, I would have.

Mrs. Saxon led the way through the dark black curtain of the ritual room, the same one Lisa's accession ceremony was held in. As shocking as it might sound, the room was creepier with daylight shining in from above. At night, I didn't notice all the demonic cherub looking figures up high on the wall. There are those statues and pictures that are created with certain angles that make you feel the eyes are following you. In this instance, it wasn't an optical illusion. Their eyes were following us, along with their heads and hands that pointed at me as Mrs. Saxon led me to a chair in the center of the room, the very spot Lisa had knelt during her ceremony.

"Sit!" a voice commanded, echoing from in front of me where a veil of darkness hid the source from my view. Not wanting to give them a reason to not like me right off the bat, I did as I was asked and had a seat.

"Miss Larissa Dubois, is that correct?" asked the voice.

"Yes," I said. My voice shook.

The lights in the room sprang to life. An event that was both a blessing and a curse. I could now see the areas the daylight from above couldn't reach. Eerie shadows ran everywhere. If the cherub statues didn't look evil before, they sure did with shadows accentuating their features. Especially the fat one with the huge belly and chubby cheeks. It had a smile on its face like a fat kid eyeing an unwrapped chocolate bar.

From the darkness ahead of me emerged the council of twelve seated up high on some sort of ceremonial stage behind a large bench. Like twelve judges, positioned to look down on me, down here in the pit. Each glared at me from their perch. Each unique and odd in their own right, if odd was even a strong enough word to describe it. One wore a wig you might see in court in England. A few others resembled Mr. Demius with dark hair dangling in front of their pale faces while wearing dark suits. The woman directly in front of me was the oddest of them all. I believed a Shakespeare festival somewhere was missing its Queen. She even wore a crown atop her scowling face.

"Miss Dubois," the misplaced queen began. "I am sure Mrs. Saxon has filled you in on who we are, so there is no need for introductions. They are unnecessary anyway. You do know why we are here?" Her voice echoed across the room. Above me the statues took notice and looked in her direction as she sat back in her chair waiting for my response.

"Yes, the incident two weeks ago," I replied, and attempted to make eye contact with each and every one of them.

The twelve exploded into a raucous laughter. Even the statues above joined in. Several of them exchanged looks and tried as much as they could to speak to one another in between their laughs. Two even appeared to be out of breath. I knew I was at the center of the joke. I just didn't know what the joke was, except possibly that it was me, and that started a fire deep inside.

I glanced over at Mrs. Saxon, who held her palms up and mouthed, "relax." This was not the place to lose control, and I knew it. That didn't mean it would stop me. My control was better, but not perfect, and I hadn't been tested emotionally in the last two weeks. Above me, the stupid little cherub statues that glared down on me had stopped laughing. I had started formulating a plan for how to remove them using some of my newly found gifts, and I think they knew it. A few of the council members may have noticed or sensed something as well. *Crap.* I forgot some, or all, of them could be like Jack, and they would feel my emotional energy building up. One of the Mr. Demius impersonators coughed and attempted to refocus the others' attention.

"Child, we don't need to hear about that. The building"—her long-nailed fingers motioned around her — "told us all we needed to know. That is not our problem or our query. It is you. We are here to talk about you."

"Me?" I asked. There was an edge to my voice that even I heard and recognized. I knew I needed to control it, but hearing me called a problem made that out of the question. Of course, I ignored that I could just be their query.

"Yes. You are the daughter of Susan and Maxwell Dubois of the Orleans' Coven. Both witches who were more than just in high standing within your coven. Your father had served as a member of this very council until his capture and then death. Your bloodline is one of the longest of our type, which we had thought ended with your father's death. Your mother was dead, and you were missing, but presumed dead even though you were never found. The coven assumed your remains were dragged away by the savages that killed you, or wildlife in the area, being that you were smaller than your mother. Yet, after eighty years, you turn up here, not aware you were a witch, which in factbl you are, and a vampire too. An extremely dangerous combination, I am sure you understand that. As the council, we need to interview and get to know you to find out which you prefer to be so we can take actions for protection."

"Protection of who?" I asked, possibly interrupting her monologue of details that I already knew.

"The world Miss Norton, or is it Miss Dubois, which ever you might be now. A bloodthirsty vampire that can use magic would be a menace in the world and virtually uncontrollable." She leaned forward against the bench and glared right down at me. The rest stayed sitting back in their chairs. Some rested their chins on the tips of their fingers, which they had pressed together at their chest. "I am sure you realize that. Why else would Jean St. Claire have wanted your father and now you?"

Now a few others, a couple of the Mr. Demius look-a-likes and a blonde with more make-up on than all of Hollywood put together, had leaned forward waiting for my reply. I wanted to reply, I really did, in so many ways. None of which were going to be pleasant for them or me. If anything, it would help them make their case, and that I didn't want to do. Not for the harm it could cause me, becaus I didn't want to give them the satisfaction of being right. So, I just sat there, and while I didn't smile, I didn't grimace or frown either. I just sat and observed, raising my shoulders up and down at regular intervals to show calm breathing. Now if I had really breathed, those would be seething between my teeth right now.

"One of the great many things we need to figure out is how you were influenced during your captivity. It is rather obvious that the Nortons knew what Jean St. Claire wanted your father for, and they wanted you to try themselves. It is really rather amazing you survived as long as you did."

I felt it. Right up at the top. As much as I tried, I couldn't keep my hands from balling up into fists and then releasing before squeezing them shut again. They took notice. I am sure the cherubs did too, and if any of them knew what I was thinking, they would have taken cover. I felt the last bubble pop on the top of my boiling psyche, but even then I didn't let it out. I couldn't. All I could do was let a simple response fly, "You're wrong." My tone cut through the room.

No one flinched. No one leaned back. Instead, the rest leaned forward to observe me, the freak show they all came to see. Were they testing me on purpose? Just to see how I would respond?

"Then, Miss Norton, why do you think they did what they did?" The man third from the right asked. A rather interesting looking fellow, bean pole skinny with a handlebar mustache that appeared to weigh more than he did. While his frame was not imposing, his eyes were. There was a great weight behind his gaze, and flames burned in his eyes. The black top hat he wore appeared to tower over my head.

"To protect me. That is what I believe."

"To protect you?" he scoffed. "Miss Norton, you will have us believe that they killed your mother, mortally wounded you, and turned you into a vampire to protect you. What kind of sense does that make?"

"They didn't kill my mother," I exploded. "They didn't attack me. They saved me and treated me as if I were their own."

"Miss Norton, it is a logical leap, don't you agree? They are vampires. Vampires attacked your mother and you, and you end up with them, and became a vampire yourself. What other alternative is there?"

I steadied myself for a moment. My legs wanted to explode up out of the chair, but I knew I needed to try to at least give the appearance of calm. This wasn't the first time I had heard that argument. It was just the first time I heard it in someone else's voice. This argument had ransacked my head throughout the last three weeks. Try after try with Mrs. Tenderschott to go back to a memory that would shed some light on this, or provide a way to contact Mrs. Norton if she were still alive, and nothing worked. Everything led right back to the same conclusion. I didn't know, but I hoped. "There are many alternatives. Unfortunately, no one knows the truth except the Nortons, and Mr. Norton is dead, and I don't know how to contact Mrs. Norton. I have tried with the help of others here."

"How did they raise you?" asked the blonde make-up counter.

"It wasn't what you think. I have been told and read about the horrible treatment of my father by Jean St. Claire. All of his attempts to take my father's power and merge with his. They did nothing like that. Nothing. Not once." I felt myself getting emotional again, and my words were moving about as fast as I could run. I forced myself to slow down, so they could understand me and wouldn't see me as some sort of raving lunatic. "They treated me as a daughter, and it was only a few weeks ago that I found out I wasn't." I felt a lump of sorrow in my head.

"But they raised you as a vampire—," the slim man reminded me.

"Yes, they did. That is because I was, I am, a vampire."

"You were also a witch," the woman with the crown pointed out. Again, another reminder that I didn't need.

"I didn't know I was."

My reply seemed to have caught the council off guard. There was a loud gasp in the room, followed by a stunned silence as they all looked back and forth at each other. Finally, a blonde haired male, much younger than the others on the council, leaned even further. As he moved, the shadows behind him appeared to follow. I hadn't noticed him before. I wasn't sure why not though. He had dark make-up around his eyes and as he slowly moved his hands and fingers before he spoke, I spied black nail polish on each finger. "You didn't know you were a witch?" His voice moved around the room like a serpent. In and out of every corner and crevice. Its great coils surrounded me and squeezed. "There are no vampires with the ability to wipe one's mind." The statement dripped in accusation while his tone squeezed me further.

"I must agree," came from the corner. Mrs. Saxon stepped forward out of the darkness of the corner she had made her place during what I felt was a crucifixion. "Master Thomas, I would agree no vampire can wipe one's memory, but memory loss can be a side-effect of the process of turning."

"That might be so, Mrs. Saxon, but they had a responsibility to tell her who and what she was."

"I don't disagree, but I am sure they had their reasons." Mrs. Saxon looked at me after her rebuttal. I hope they had their reasons too, and those reasons weren't what the council was hinting at.

"Being that as it may. We have to consider where their allegiance lay, where they came from, and most concerning, what they are," responded the one Mrs. Saxon referred to as Master Thomas.

"Excuse me," I blurted out. I really need to work on my filter, but since I had already opened my mouth, might as well go ahead, and let the rest spill out. "What does that mean, what they are? Does being a vampire make someone more deceitful?"

"Madame Dubois. Forgive me if my bluntness implied anything of the sort. I think I speak for all when I say nothing of the sort can be applied to all vampires, but there are factors that WE," he looked up and down the table at his colleagues, "have to consider. While you are relatively young, even at what you might perceive as an old age, let me explain. Being immortal gives one time to think of things in a way a normal person never does nor has the time to. We live our lives, hope to make an impact, and leave a legacy behind us. Imagine, though, if you never died. Never worried about the legacy you leave. Never feeling the clicking clock of your life counting down the moments. This creates a sense of arrogance and superiority in some of your kind. No matter how content you are in life, after hundreds of years, the questions and desires of power and conquest are harder and harder to ignore. Usually fueled by a single thought, that with all your acquired knowledge and experience, and in your case your ability, you could do it better. While they may have stopped Jean St. Claire and his coven from having you, that doesn't mean they didn't want you for themselves to either take your ability, or groom you, to challenge Jean or to obtain a position of power themselves. He has been a powerful force in your world for hundreds and hundreds of years, unchecked and unrivaled. The decades you spent with them are just seconds in the grand scheme of the immortal."

"I was not groomed to be anything but a teenager," I countered with my mind spinning. I certainly had never had any thoughts of *conquest*, but there was something about the thought of living forever that was truly daunting. Never being able to leave a set of pearls behind that grandchildren would refer to as grandmother's pearls. Instead, wanting to rule the world. Would I ever succumb to those kinds of thoughts? They were the furthest from my mind right now, and I am sure the Nortons were the same. "They taught me to be an honest and compassionate person. Mrs. Norton gave me her love of reading, and Mr. Norton gave me his sense of self control. I will admit I am still working on holding my opinions to myself. Both explained to me what life was like as a vampire," I thought back on them and what our life was with a smile, "but that is not how we lived. We lived as people. The only thing that separated us and how others lived was we didn't sleep, we never aged, and we fed, and even then, I was taught to control and do that responsibly. As a family, we isolated ourselves from others to avoid detection, but we were around humans, and there were never any problems or temptations, or desire to manipulate or strike fear or whatever you think we would do to them. That is not how I was raised. They raised me as a person first, and a vampire second. Definitely not as a weapon."

"Possibly they hadn't yet, and there is a possibility they never had. Another possibility we must consider is it happened without you even knowing it."

I shook my head violently, probably too fast for them to even see it. I walked in here expecting to talk about what happened the day his goons tracked me down and attacked the coven. Not be grilled about what and who I was, with concerns that I was some sort of weapon. I knew I could bolt out of here and there probably wasn't anything they could do to me, but I wouldn't do that. The warnings of Mrs. Saxon and Mrs. Tenderschott played in my head. "I can assure you I am not a weapon."

"But child," stated the self-crowned queen, "oh, but you are. You are an immensely powerful, yet undisciplined witch and with your augmented physical abilities and immortality you are a threat to everyone. I am not sure if our role in this world was explained. As witches, we are to live our lives the best we can as who we are, but we are never to interfere in the world of humans. Never use our abilities against them or to help them. This council monitors this and step in when someone needs a reminder or correction. You are a threat to that balance we fight to keep."

Then it hit me. They feared me. Either of whom the Nortons groomed to be, or who I could become because they, the Council of Mages, didn't believe they could keep me in check if needed.

"I can assure you, she is not a threat," protested Mrs. Saxon. She had left her corner and walked to the center of the room. "She has been with us for the past several weeks and I can attest to her character. She is not a concern for you in those matters, and we are still working with her on her control of her abilities. I believe they turned her to save her life, and they hid her to protect her from Jean St. Claire."

"Mrs. Saxon, we understand that, and that is why we put you in charge of teaching her and helping to evaluate her as we continue to observe this matter. You could be correct, but you could be incorrect."

She regarded her fellow members of the council. "Are there any other questions?" They each answered with silence. "Then, at this moment, we have no final judgement to make, but will continue our investigation and will be in constant contact regarding Miss Norton."

I was stunned. The words final judgment slapped, and before I could recover came the word investigation. This had been nothing but an accusatory monologue by the entire council. Mrs. Saxon had given me the impression that this would be more of a question-and-answer session. They hadn't really given me any opportunity to speak and tell my side. They hadn't asked me anything. I began to protest, "But, I haven't..."

"Oh, but you have Miss Norton. You spoke quite a lot, and we have other ways of continuing this." With that, the lights fell again, sending shadows back over where the council had sat.

Mrs. Saxon walked over and gathered me, "Let's go," and I followed her out.

"That didn't go too badly," she said with a sigh of relief once we were outside the door. I had to wonder what it would have been like if it had gone badly.

5

"Larissa, weapon of mass confusion," chuckled Martin. His comment seemed to amuse Doug and Rob. Even Nathan stifled a laugh as he poked at the fire in the fire pit behind the pool. He mouthed "sorry," in my direction as I pouted.

Nathan had invited me to come hang out with the dog pack for a little while to relax and blow off some steam, but when I tried to follow him through the door, I found the answer to a question I had wondered about a few weeks earlier. What happened when someone that wasn't the right type tried to cross through those magically charmed doors? It bounced your ass to the floor with a thud, that's what. My foot never crossed the threshold. It only attempted to. That was when the universe's biggest rubber band snapped back and sent me down to the floor with a huge "Thou shall not pass" boom. At first, I wasn't sure that sound was my body hitting the floor or the door itself. That put any idea of hanging out in what Nathan had described as their little clubhouse out of my head and left only one option. The pool deck.

"It's not funny guys. They really think of me as some kind of weapon." I sounded a bit whiney for my taste, but I felt it was warranted. No one on the council had ever met me before today, yet they had already passed judgement on me. They wouldn't have been here if they hadn't.

"Maybe you are. We all saw what you did to Jack that day." Rob added, and seemed rather proud of himself.

"Guys, cut it out," Nathan warned. "This is really bothering her." He sat down next to me by the fire and put his arm around me, giving me all the comfort I needed and leaving the fire to be just atmosphere in the cold fall night air.

"Sorry," Rob said sheepishly. Martin stopped laughing too. Even Doug went silent. Which was his natural state when he wasn't laughing at something one of the other boys said.

"So, what's next?" asked Nathan.

"I don't know." Which I didn't. "They said they would stay in contact and observe. It makes me feel like some kind of damn lab rat. They had it all wrong. The Nortons never tried to groom me, or whatever they think that was. We were just a family. A mother and a father, with me the daughter. Yes, we were vampires, but that wasn't the most important part of our lives. Our family was." I looked around at each of them. There was no other way to say it. "I don't really see how we were different from any other family."

"That is probably so..." Nathan started.

"It is so. There is no probably about it." I interrupted to make sure there was no doubt about the facts. To complete my point, I even shook Nathan's arm off my shoulders. Something I regretted as soon as I felt the real world hit me without the warmth of his touch.

"Okay, it is so. The way I see it, you need to do two things. Don't cause any issues and show them you can be just like everyone else, which shouldn't be hard. You are one of the best people I know." Doug and Rob sat on the other side of the fire making mock puking sounds. Nathan tried to ignore them, but I felt a little flutter in his pulse. "Let them see that side of you. Then we need to make sure they hear the truth about the Nortons."

"I tried to tell them." I interjected when Nathan stopped to breathe.

"I know you did. We need to find someone who isn't you."

"A witness," added Rob.

"Yep, a witness," continued Nathan. "Someone from the outside, who wasn't part of your actual family. Maybe a relative or a friend of the family. Can you think of anyone like that? An aunt or uncle?"

I shook my head. This was going to be a problem. There was nobody. No aunts. No uncles. That was if you don't count the ones I created in my mind. "No, not even a neighbor." The next closest one was a mile or so down the road, and we never saw them. My father, Mr. Norton, didn't even have a regular job. He was a carpenter who built cabinets, which he always delivered and never had anyone over to his workshop. Even the few trips we made to the coast were by ourselves. We stayed by ourselves and kept to ourselves the entire time. Our solitude was our defense; now it was a penalty.

"Then there has to be another way." Nathan put his arm back around me and pulled me in. I didn't resist, but quickly sprang from his embrace up to my feet, just a few inches from the fire.

"Edward!" I yelled, and stood there waiting for him to appear in front of me. Of course, that would be in the middle of the fire.

"That doesn't work out here. You have to be inside the Coven," Rob reminded me.

"Oh yeah." I settled back down, and pulled Nathan's arm back around my shoulders and snuggled up against him, resting my head on his chest. When we went back in, I would make my request for Edward. I only hoped he could help.

"There are two other options," suggested Nathan. The vibration of his voice in his chest was a perfect symphony to my ears.

"What are those?" I asked.

"You can recover your memory of them and think of something that might help, or..." His voice trailed off just before it hesitated.

"Or what?" I prompted for him to continue, but knowing what his suggestion would be.

"Find Mrs. Norton. Have her come talk to the council."

I stood up, pulling away from Nathan's embrace, then started a very exaggerated pacing. I could feel the dog pack watching me, almost nervous. I wasn't sure if they could pick up on my moods. Some animals could read humans. I stopped and put on my best act as I stared at the ground, a finger over my lips while I stood there and pondered what had to be one of the dumbest suggestions I had ever heard. Nathan meant well, I knew that, but what have I been trying to do since I arrived here, and so far nothing. "Why didn't I think of that?," I asked rhetorically. Sarcasm dripped from each word. "I could just call her up and ask her. That would solve everything."

"Sorry, I know you have been try..." Nathan started, but I cut him off with a raise of my hand. It wasn't that I didn't want to hear his apology, and definitely not a desire to not hear his voice. That desire didn't exist, and as far as I was concerned, it never would. What prompted me to cut him off was the realization that maybe I was one of the dumbest people on the planet. I have spent weeks drinking different potions and going through various incantations, and nothing has worked. I missed the most obvious of all.

Nathan stood up and walked over as he attempted to apologize again. "Larissa, I'm sorry."

I spun around and met his lips with a simple kiss just after he finished. I felt the surprise in their touch and heard the gasp from the others. "I know," accepting his apology, even though he didn't have to. My hands wrapped around his back and fell down to his butt. They wanted to linger longer, but I felt that might be an unwise public display of affection, plus I had a mission and groping a butt cheek wasn't it. Nathan's body tensed up and his pulse raced. It went up another notch when I reached around and explored his front pockets. I was afraid the old boy might have a heart attack before I let go. He, on the other hand, held me tighter, which meant I needed to push back a little firmer. "Nathan, where is your phone?" I whispered.

"Huh, my phone?" He stumbled through the words as blood returned to his brain.

"Yes, your phone. That thing you make phone calls with and watch cat videos on."

"Back in my room. Why?" he asked, still confused and maybe suffering the aftereffects of my rather aggressive groping.

"Larissa, here." I turned before Robert's phone hit me. My quick reactions snatched it from the air. "Nice catch. I have never made a call on it, just used it for the internet. I really don't have anyone I would call."

I held the device, actually stunned and not sure how to use it. There was never a need for me to have a phone, but both my mother and father, the Nortons, did. Mr. Norton would call us often while he was out gathering supplies for another project. Just to let us know he was safe and on the way home. Not like he needed to gather a grocery list from us. Mrs. Norton did the same when she was out running errands, mostly clothes shopping for something new for us to wear. We never outgrew anything, but we sure outlasted them.

I think Nathan understood the confused look on my face, and finally got what I was going after. He grabbed the phone, brought up the keypad, and handed it to me. I quickly dialed the number, which I must have dialed dozens of times when she was out, and I had become worried about her. My fingers shook over the numbers as they dialed. Just hearing a ring would have brought me some level of comfort, and knowing her and the precautions we all took, I knew she wouldn't answer. She never answered any unknown numbers. There was a long pause of dead air before a pleasant sounding recording said, "The customer you are trying to reach is unavailable." My hand dropped to my side while the recording replayed through the speaker. Everyone heard it.

"You didn't dial it right. You should have heard her voicemail," Doug suggested.

"She never set it up. We needed to stay hidden," I said absently to no one in particular, and handed the phone back to Rob without ever taking my stare off the darkness out in the woods that looked just like I felt, empty.

"Well, it was a good idea," said Rob.

"It was," agreed Nathan, and he wrapped me in his warmth to block out the cold, cruel reality. "It's getting late. Why don't we go back in?"

I nodded my agreement, not really caring how late it was, but I had had my fill, and to be honest, I just wanted to be alone. Even if that meant being without Nathan for a bit. The cruel reality that was life. As nightfall brought darkness, my one source of light had to retire too, but like the day he would be up with the sun to bring it back to me.

He walked me in, like we had done many times now, and my mind wandered to something he mentioned out at the cove before the scream of a lifetime. The future. What kind of future was ahead for us? Would there be a time when my light never left me? A shiver went through my mind with the answer. It was yes and no. If it were meant to be, we would be together, spending every moment of every day with each other. Whether that was life outside the coven or even still here. Jennifer had mentioned the possibility of living here to me, it would be what it was, heaven on earth. But all things, bad and good, come to pass, and that shiver was the harsh reality that one day he would leave me, and as I was so reminded during that accusatory interrogation I had been put through earlier, I was immortal and in the grand scheme of things, our life together would be nothing more than a flash.

"Larissa!"

I turned around just in time to brace myself before Amy attempted to take my legs out from under me with a hug of a lifetime. She might be small, her head not even reaching my waist, but she packed a punch when she hit me. "Hey squirt."

She looked up at me with a gapped grin as my hand brushed the hair out of her face. "I missed you," she cooed.

"I missed you too." I really did. There was something refreshing about her, and seeing her there, smiling like someone her own age, was a relief after what I had witnessed last night.

"Hey, what about me?" Nathan protested.

"Well, I was just with you a second ago," I stated, smiling sarcastically. I knew what he meant, and Amy let go of me and rushed over to where Nathan had bent down to meet her hug. The little girl wrapped her arms around him, and I watched as she latched hold. I couldn't blame her. I knew that feeling well. I also knew the spark I saw in her eyes. A little case of puppy love. Who could blame her?

"Remember, best three out of five. I can still catch up." Nathan said, evoking that little girl laugh that could brighten any room. Just seeing her brightened my mood, and hearing that sent it up to another level. I had almost forgotten all about the council, almost.

"You won't win," Amy announced.

"We've been playing board games. Amy's rather good."

"I see." I bent down. "Have you been beating Nathan?"

She beamed that smile at me with the little girl giggle escaping through her teeth. "We can play again later tonight. Right now, Mrs. Parrish is taking me to my room."

I looked up and saw Mrs. Parrish emerging from the hallway. She glided toward us, and didn't say a word as she extended her hand toward Amy. She took it and the two of them headed for the stairs.

"Second floor for you. I am just three flights up," I said when they hit the bottom step.

"That's right Miss Norton. She is on the second floor, and you are on the fifth. Remember, the doors are charmed," Mrs. Parrish reminded me with all the warmth of an artic winter, never stopping her march up the stairs.

"I'll stop by for a rematch later," Nathan called up the stairs after causing Amy to look back and wave. "I can get through all the doors," he whispered into my ear from behind. An elbow to his side thanked him for rubbing it in.

We stood there and watched as Mrs. Parrish and Amy walked up to the first landing and then went in through the door. Nathan was still trying to gasp for breath when I went off. "What the hell was that? Did you see how she treated me?"

"Yes," he croaked.

"Is she normally like that?" I asked, not having any real experiences with her.

"No," Nathan said, now with more air in his lungs and able to stand up.

"Jesus. Am I going to have to put up with that from everyone around here? I guess what happened with the council got around." My gaze jumped back and forth between the door they disappeared through and Nathan. There was a question in what I had said, and when he didn't answer, the steely stare of my black eyes focused right in on Nathan.

He just shrugged with a deer-caught-in-the-headlights look. He kept that look while I stomped around the entry a few laps attempting to cool off. When I came back past him for the third time, he finally spoke. "She isn't the warmest person in the world, but she usually isn't that rude."

He gave me a quirky little smile that I echoed back at him, scrunching my face just like he did.

"Just give her time. All she may know of you is what she has heard. She just needs to get to know you."

That was what I was worried about. It meant someone was talking. That sent me on a fourth lap around. This time, he caught me in his arms, and hung on while I faux-struggled to get away. I could have pulled away with no effort at all, but this was a little game I allowed myself to play, always finally submitting to his embrace. "Just give her time to get to know you. Once she sees the *you* that me and the others do, she will come around. Plus, Amy seems to love you."

"Is she the only one?" I fished.

And there it was. The heart flutter I could always produce. The first time I made that kind of comment to him, it fluttered on for a few minutes, and his skin went clammy. Now it was just a flutter, but still, that was something.

"Possibly." He danced around it, and then spun me around, kissing me before *he* knew it. I usually made the first move, but he never knew that. It was one of those kisses that made the world pause around us. My eyes were closed, like they always were, but there was no empty darkness there. A world of colors and warmth danced through me. It almost felt like I had a soul again.

Nathan pulled back and then pulled me in for a hug. "I need to go grab a board game. There is no way I am going to stand for her getting the better of me."

"You do that. I should probably head up to the deck, see what the others are doing."

"See you tomorrow?" Nathan asked. Which was the same dumb question he asked every time we parted.

"You know it." He drifted back away from me. My hands tracing the muscles of his arms until my fingers caught his hands. They hung on until the tips of my fingers hit the end of his, and then they pulled apart as Nathan walked backwards toward the hallway, and I stood there watching until he disappeared around the corner.

With no other reason to stand there, I headed upstairs and tried to remember what night this was. Movie, music, or board game. I couldn't remember, but I knew I would find out the minute I hit the stairs in my closet.

"Pssst, Larissa." I heard on the third landing. Marcia stood there at the door.

"Hey Marcia," I replied.

Instead of replying, she lunged at me and yanked me through the door, using a little more than just her strength to move me. I spun around inside the hall, and up against the door and found myself face to face with Gwen. *Oh, happy day.*

"Spill it," she commanded. "What was it like meeting with the council?"

The others were gathered on either side of her. Each looked at me with eager anticipation. It was like I just met their favorite pop star or something. If I had told them I had shaken one of the council member's hand, they may want to touch it before demanding I never wash it again.

"Uncomfortable." That was the best word that I could think of. Seeing Gwen deflate before my eyes made me wish I had said it earlier.

"Uncomfortable?" she asked, bleakly. "It wasn't... well... at least interesting." The normal perkiness quickly evacuated from her expression.

"Oh, it was interesting. Interestingly intimidating. Interestingly horrible."

Gwen dropped her shoulders and sulked down the hall away from me. I watched as she entered the room I knew to be their common room. Why I followed with the others I didn't know, and I didn't like the feel of it. I wasn't one of her court. I slowed just enough to put a larger gap between Lisa and myself, so it wouldn't seem as if I were one of them. Lisa seemed to know what I was doing.

When we entered, Gwen was slumped down on the sofa against the wall. I didn't take a seat. I didn't intend to be here that long, but I did walk over to her. "What did I say?"

"Oh nothing," she replied morosely.

"No one but the teachers have ever met anyone from the council, and Gwen has a little case of admiration where they are concerned," Lisa said.

"More than that. She wants to be the Council Supreme one day." Tera added just before Gwen fired a pillow in her direction as her reply.

"So, none of you have ever met them?" I asked, surveying everyone in the room.

"Never," mumbled Gwen.

"But we do know all about them. Names, what they look like, their specialty. Even various decisions they have made," replied Tera.

"Gwen has studied each one of them. We hear about them so much we feel like we know them personally." Marcia raised a hand. "Don't even think about it,

Gwen," she warned. The green pillow next to Gwen settled back down on the cushion.

"Well, you aren't missing anything."

"How many are here?" Gwen asked. Her arms wrapped around her legs, pulling them close to her chest to create a platform for her chin to rest on.

"Twelve, I think." It was just a guess. I hadn't really taken the time to count. I was too busy being grilled.

"All of them?" Gwen's legs thrust out, breaking through her grasp, planting her pink socked feet on the floor with a thud.

"I guess." I chided, now taking a little pleasure in her reactions.

"What did they ask? Who did most of the speaking?" Gwen was now standing and walking toward me. I took a few steps back to keep some distance between us. We may have used the proverbial hatchet to kill a bunch of attacking vampires together, that didn't mean we had buried it yet.

"Some woman, she wore a crown. She was the one who talked the most, and..."

Gwen's eyes exploded open, and her voice cried, "The Council Supreme? Mrs. Wintercrest? You spoke to the Council Supreme?"

"I guess. It was mostly a one-sided conversation." Now the others had gathered around me, and I felt a little cornered. Enough to have to remind myself that I was still in friendly company and needed to tamp down some the impulses I felt.

"So, what did she say?" The hint of the eagerness I had detected in the hall had returned to Gwen's voice. "Did they congratulate the coven for how we defended ourselves?"

"Not exactly," I replied, and scrunched up my face, thinking about how far away from a congratulation the topic actually was. "They wanted to talk about me."

I saw her nose wrinkle and her mouth drop open before I heard the disgust in her voice. "*You?* They wanted to talk about *you?*"

"Well yeah. About what I am and the Nortons. Mostly about why they didn't tell me I was a witch." There was no way in hell I was going to tell Gwen they considered me a weapon and a threat. I would never hear the end of that if she knew.

With even just telling her they wanted to ask about me, and the Nortons I was expecting a shot or two from her, but her fandom took over. "Who else spoke?"

"I didn't get any other names, other than Master Thomas."

"Hold it right there. Master Benjamin Thomas?" Gwen lunged toward me and grabbed my shoulders. A move that I think shocked her more than it did me. She let go and stepped back. "Sorry," she nervously apologized. "He is just... well... rather," she stumbled through her words.

"Dreamy," spouted Tera, producing a giggle from everyone but Gwen.

"No, important," Gwen said with a look of admonishment at the others, and a hint of red in her cheeks. "He is one of a few on the council that continues to abide by the long-standing tradition of writing and instructing. His books are some of the best on spells and how to fine tune your gift."

"Even better than Mrs. Saxon's?" I just had to ask.

"Yes," Gwen answered immediately.

"Does she know that?"

"No," Gwen answered flatly. She looked around at the others and let out a deep sigh. I didn't know what was coming, but whatever it was, it appeared to be unpleasant to Gwen. "Will you stay for a few minutes, and tell us more. What they looked like? How they acted? For us, this is big. It's like a Catholic having an audience with the Pope."

I saw four sets of eyes beaming at me with anticipation, and that included Gwen. I didn't feel as conflicted as I expected I might. These were my sisters, or maybe half-sisters for my witch half. This was something I felt I needed to do to strengthen that bond, and learn more about that side of me.

6

When I finally emerged out on the deck – movie night – they greeted me like a regular walking into their favorite watering hole in any movie or show. "Larissa!" several voices cried up. As I joined them, I was greeted with several hugs. Jennifer was first, then Apryl, Laura, and Pam. When Mike got up from his seat and then awkwardly attempted to hug me, I got suspicious.

"Whoa," I backed up, and he looked relieved. "So, what is this all about?"

"Can't we just welcome a friend?" Apryl said, as she sat back down in the long outdoor sofa and patted the cushion next to her to encourage me to sit there.

I turned around to Jennifer. If there was ever a time I wished she were human, this would be it. I could have read her face if she were. Instead, she looked dead steady, but I knew. It was the only answer to how everyone was reacting. "You told them?"

She shook her head in denial, sending her raven hair whipping back and forth across her pale face. "I have nothing to tell. Mrs. Saxon didn't tell me anything about how things went. That's not how we work here."

"We just know you spent the morning in a room full of fancy witches." Mike faked a shiver. "That is bad enough." A few of the others laughed, including Brad and Mr. Bolden who tried to be rather sheepish about it. He even turned away from everyone to hide it.

I felt bad and didn't hesitate to turn and apologize to Jennifer. "Sorry." She was my advocate, my confidant, and I had just accused her of breaking a trust. She seemed unfazed as she accepted my apology, and for the second time, I wished she were human. Then maybe I could have been able to tell if she had really forgiven me. Of course, if I had Jack's gift, I would know. That thought sent a chill through me.

"Come sit with me," she said. I guess that was a good sign.

I joined her on the outdoor loveseat that was off to the side of the screen. From there, I could see the movie, but it wasn't the optimal angle to view it. Of course, I didn't really mind that. My mind toyed with the question, which of us would have picked an old black and white western? Looking at how intently Mr. Bolden was watching, I believed I had found the prime candidate. How old he really was under that late twenties or early thirties physique was a mystery. To be honest, age, our true age, was something no one really talked about. I assumed everyone who was considered a student was close to what they appeared to be. They were here as new vampires learning how to make it in the world of humans. It would be doubtful someone who was decades old would need such training, not to mention the normal high school curriculum, which I was finding out more and more I didn't really need. The witchcraft curriculum was a different story.

"So how was it?" Jennifer asked. There was the sound of general concern in her voice. It didn't come off so over the top as it did when someone did it for show.

"Brutal," I whispered back. "They didn't want to talk about what happened. Instead, they wanted to talk all about me and what I was. Which to them is a threat." I felt her body jerk beside me, and I knew that was real. "They believed the Nortons took me to groom me to challenge Jean St. Claire, or something like that."

"Is that so outrageous?" she asked.

"Yes," I shot back, louder than a whisper and causing a few of the others to turn quickly in our direction. I shooed them back to their movie.

"It really isn't. Jean St. Claire wants you for your blood because of the mix of what you are and what your power would give him. It only makes sense that if he wanted the power that badly, that someone else with that ability would be a threat to him." She turned and met my astonished gaze. Of all people to agree with the Council of Mages, I didn't expect it to be her, one of my own kind.

"They did nothing of the sort. I tend to think they took me to protect me. They were nurturing people, who taught me about life and were very caring. We were a family," I said staring deep into her black eyes.

"Grooming isn't always training a soldier or something bad. They groomed you to be a good person. Someone that would know the difference between right or wrong. Someone that would feel the obligation to act when she saw something wrong, and help others."

I turned back and let my eyes drift into the tumbling tumbleweeds of the screen. Things tumbling and spinning was a familiar sensation. My thoughts related to the Nortons hadn't stopped since I arrived. Now, there was a new possibility, which was harder to accept, but might have been closer to the truth than what I ever wanted to believe. "The truth is, we will never know for sure, and now I have to prove to the council that I was not made into a bad person. So, there is a lot to process. Let's change the topic. I saw Amy a little while ago. Mrs. Parrish was taking her to her room."

"That's great. I am a bit surprised. It's so soon considering…"

"Considering what?" I asked, curious about what Jennifer meant.

"Her circumstances," she stopped, and then mumbled, "the poor girl."

"What is it?" I asked concerned.

"Ms. Parrish rescued her from a small gypsy carnival sideshow attraction in Arkansas. She was kept in a cage and poked until she changed into anything."

I again turned around and looked at Jennifer. This time my action was more of a jerk. "You're joking. Please. Please, tell me you are joking," I pleaded.

"I'm serious," she said emotionless.

The thoughts of that poor innocent child being held in a cage and tortured to perform made me want to pay a visit to some Gypsies in Arkansas. She should be some place she could call home, with a loving family, passing the time playing with dolls and stuffed animals. Enjoying special times with her mother that were full of smiles and laughter. Things like playing dress up and singing silly songs to her cat who she gave a silly name like Socks. All the things a young child should be doing. All the things I cherished from my time with the Nortons. All the things I hope I had done when I was her age with my own mother.

Hearing what Amy had gone through explained how hysterical she had been that first night. She would have been wild, kind of like how Robert explained he was when they first brought him here. Of course, I didn't know if shapeshifter wild was the same as vampire wild, but I had to imagine we might be more animalistic. Now, I had joined Jennifer in her surprise that she had already become adjusted enough to be shown a room, but it also made me worried about the nightmares that would await her in the dark loneliness that everyone experiences around here, especially the first several nights. Motherly instincts didn't seem to exist in Mrs. Parrish, or maybe it was just me that brought the inner ice-queen out of her. A talent I seemed to have had with the council and others until they got to know me. Maybe Amy needed a big sister. She had Cynthia, Steve's younger sister, but she wasn't more than a year older, and I still hadn't seen her talk the whole time I had been here. Even though I wasn't the picture of stability, not by a long shot, there was something about that little girl, her smile, and what had to be hiding behind them, that pulled at me. "First nights are probably the roughest, but I can tell you the next few aren't much easier."

"You managed through a little better than most."

"I was..." I stopped before I finished the statement. My original reply sounded more than a little conceited in my mind. I wanted to say I was a little more refined, which I was.

"Stable." Jennifer finished my answer with a better choice of words than I was considering. "Your circumstances were different and came with challenges all on their own. Ones you are still working through, with all of our help." She threw her arm around me and pulled me in close and then pressed a kiss on my forehead. It lacked the warmth of Nathan's. "We didn't have to physically fight you like we usually do."

"I heard. Brad told me he was broken by Mr. Bolden like a horse."

Jennifer laughed. "That would be the best analogy. In a way, each of them had to be broken. Some were easier than others. Jeremy was the easiest by far. Most of the others were newborns. They were only a few weeks old. He wasn't. He had a few years under him, but not as many as you." She looked down at me, and I could hear the sarcasm in her voice. "We found him living alone in an old rusted grain silo in the middle of nowhere. Whoever turned him, left him to fend for himself like so many do."

"Is that how it happens? Someone turns someone and then just leaves?" That seemed so cold, almost evil to me. It was no wonder literature and popular culture always cast us as some kind of demonic monsters.

"Well now, it depends." Jennifer sat up straight and turned slightly in her seat to face me. It was almost as if she were entering instructor mode. She even crossed her hands on her lap like she did in the classroom. "Some hang around, or at least stay in contact from a distance, and then try to bring the person into their family, or coven. I would like to think that is how it works most of the time. My fear is it isn't the norm. There are rogue vampires that never got past their animalistic tendencies and roam the world looking for victims. To them, their victims are just food, and don't have any regard for what happens to the individual after they leave. I believe that happened to Jeremy, but like you, he doesn't have any memory of when he was turned."

"You said you found him in a silo. How did you even know he was there?"

"The internet." Jennifer said flatly, and I watched for any break in her expression to hint at the joke that I believe I was now part of. There couldn't be a vampire search engine, could there? She held her straight expression for a while, even as I appeared to be shocked. "Seriously. Stories of dead animals with strange bite marks on them started circulating around. None were really true news stories, just legends, social media posts that were shared. While most people dismiss those kinds of stories, and others believe they are evidence of otherworldly beasts, we use those stories as a map. In Jeremy's case, we started by identifying the closest city, which was Wichita. Then looking at posts and comments on the rumors and forum stories, we found a few that said they found those animal carcasses near them. That gave us an idea of where in Wichita to look. We looked at a map, found the fields the animals were most likely found, and then tagged spots for Kevin to check out. The next time one is on our radar, we will show you."

I nodded. I was curious about that. Not to mention, she was right about something else she had said earlier. Everyone here was helping me with my own challenges. Maybe this was a way I could pay them all back. Kind of earn my keep, even though no one had ever said anything to me about it. I felt I needed to contribute.

When daylight broke, we all headed back down, and it was back to class for me today. I had missed yesterday's thanks to the council visit. After my shower, and getting dressed I stood in the center of my room, about to gather the books to head downstairs when I eyed the stack of books Edward had placed next to my bed. The stack was about as thick as the warnings he delivered along with them. I knew those books held the way to find the answers I needed. Only one question was stopping me, did I understand enough of this magic stuff yet to try any of their contents safely?

7

My morning classes went on like normal. I still wasn't a fan of history. Yes, like Nathan had explained to me it was just reading, but I am sorry, I didn't feel engaged with the characters or the plot. This was no Bram Stoker's *Dracula*, something I had read over twenty times. A fact I wouldn't admit openly. The irony in that might be a little thick. Maybe if I were reading about my family's history I would be more interested.

After Edward provided me with the coven archive entries on my parents, my real parents, I asked him to go back and look for anything on my grandparents or great-grandparents. To know them would be better than nothing. He found a few entries on my grandfather's side. Nothing substantial, just a page or two. The house that I supposedly grew up in was my grandfather's. It was actually his grandfather's too. It was a working farm. Imagine that! We were farmers. Of what? I couldn't find a record of. We were also witches, not that it surprised me anymore, and just like my parents, my grandparents were well respected in the coven. His name was Claude Dubois and of all things, he was an instructor in the coven. I guess he did that when he wasn't farming whatever it was we farmed. He was considered one of the best in defensive spells and skills, like Mr. Helms. I wondered if he had a similar saying written in his classroom. I wondered what his classroom was even like.

The best I could tell from the timeline of his life, I might have known him. He didn't die until 1927; so, I would have been four. That was a bittersweet realization. I felt happy that I had a grandfather, and what appeared to be some semblance of a regular life, at least I did back then, but I didn't remember any of it. Memories, the ones I had, and the ones I didn't, had both become my tormentor.

I made it through my *normal* classes and found a few moments of happiness sitting there watching Nathan eat his lunch. Some of it was just sitting there with him, basking in the glow that was his presence. Another source was how I annoyed him by moving his french fries when he tried to grab one while explaining today's math lesson to him. He was usually fantastic at math, but he missed a key part of the geometric theorems that Mr. Markinson covered. I heard it clear, even though I was looking back at Nathan, who was looking at me. That was probably why he missed it.

Like most afternoons, he walked me to my magic classes, before heading to the gym. Today, we did something we had just started doing. Holding hands as he walked me to class. It drew some looks the first time a few saw us. Mostly from

Gwen and her followers, who had broken ranks more than once to almost become my followers. Not that I was trying to challenge her for the queen-b role. That was so not me. Gwen's looks were shorter, but more intense than any of the others. There was a flash of shock before her head turned. The others looked at us pleasantly.

My friends shared Gwen's reaction, but for a different reason, and I completely understood. The first time we held hands, it was more of a test. No matter how many times Nathan told me he trusted me, and that he felt I was different than the others, and how different and in control I felt, there was always something there. A tense moment of testing things out. Feeling the warmth of his skin, and the flow of the life giving fluid under the surface for a few moments was easy. I felt no urges, not even the smallest of burning. This was more than a few moments. This was minutes, close to a quarter of an hour, and it came with many check-ins by Nathan. "Doing okay with this?"

"Sure, doing just as well as I was five seconds ago." I think my responses got more annoyed sounding the more he asked. Okay, I wasn't just thinking they were, they absolutely had. I even reminded him a few times how he felt I was different and didn't need to worry about things.

When he asked again after I reminded him of that, I gave him a little warning accompanied with a squeeze. "Maybe you should stop reminding me that this could be a problem."

He stopped, in fact, he stopped everything. His fingers were almost limp, and the way his thumb caressed had ceased, and I really liked that feeling of the warmth moving over my skin. It almost made me feel like I had a pulse in my hand. So, I tried to reassure him by returning the favor, caressing his hand with my thumb. I wasn't sure if my frigid touch would have the same effect.

There was the normal gawking when we reached class, but it didn't last as long as it had during the first few days. A sign, I hoped, that things were becoming normal. Though, any sense of normal around here seemed to always be short-lived. This time it lasted only long enough for him to walk me into the room where some unexpected guests greeted us. My grip on Nathan's hand tightened, at the sight of them. Our three guests stood up front with Mrs. Saxon and Mrs. Tenderschott. None of the three looked pleased. Make that none of the four. Mrs. Saxon had her own scowl on her face, and I let go of Nathan's hand.

Our guests were from the night-of-the-walking-dead division of the Council of Mages. That was the name I gave them. The one benefit of being cornered by Gwen and her posse last night was her obsession of the council. She knew everything. I am not talking about a fascination, or an infatuation. This was pure on, almost stalker-ish, worthy of a restraining order, obsession. I was shocked she didn't sneak into the meeting with the council to be that much closer. Maybe they could have signed her council scrap book. Each member had a picture and biography in it with several pages dedicated to notes. I didn't even want to ask where she got the pictures from. For some reason I had a feeling Edward would not be pleased.

These three were ones I recognized from her pages. Each specialized in the dark arts, but I didn't really need her notes to guess that. Black and gray were their favorite colors. The men wore suits, one with a waistcoat that was all black with a black shirt underneath it. Their hair was stringy and black as well, with little bits of their bangs hanging down over pale faces, but who was I to comment on someone's complexion? The two men I knew were Mr. Juan Signorn of Peru, and the shorter version of him, Mr. Francis Davis of Utah. I would have never thought of witches being in Utah, but they were everywhere I guess.

Their traveling companion was Miss Sarah Julia Roberts from California who didn't resemble the glitz and glamour her name might hint at. Gwen even had a note about the name. It would seem her mother had a favorite actress. Miss Roberts was a gloomy thirty-two-year-old dark magic specialist. There were rumors she was more, but chose to hang around with those crowds. One look at her held-over-from-90's-grunge styling told me that choice was probably because she fit right in. Her dark hair wasn't stringy like the guys. Instead, it rose up high in a wave that crested at her front in a large pompadour do. Her makeup had two shades. Grey and red. It was grey around her eyes, but red rouge on her cheeks and her lips. My own trick. That in itself didn't make her striking, but her dress did. It was a black lace adorned garment that hung all the way to the floor with what looked like a hoop skirt standing out by a few feet all around. She had all the appearances of someone late for a prom, in hell. None of these three had said anything during my first meeting with the council. They didn't appear as interested as the others then, but it appeared something had changed, and I suspected it wouldn't take long before I knew what that was.

"Leave us!" barked Juan.

Nathan reached over and gripped my hand again, tighter this time.

"He's my son," announced Mrs. Saxon.

"So, he is aware of who and what she is?" asked Miss Roberts. Her voice trembled, and shock was plastered on her face.

"He is very aware, as is everyone here. She is a member of our family," responded Mrs. Saxon.

"Then close the door," barked Juan. When no one in the room moved, he awkwardly added, "Please." His tone more pleasant than before.

"I got it." Nathan said. I thought he was the one that was tightly holding on to me, but the opposite was the truth. My grip had become a death grip on his hand, and he yanked to get free. On his second less than subtle yank, I let go, and listened as his footsteps echoed on the tile floor back to the door which creaked closed before he returned to my side. His return wasn't as hasty as I would have liked, and my hand searched the empty space for a bit before I found him.

"Miss Norton..."

"Miss Dubois!" I corrected Juan forcibly enough to get his attention.

"Um, yes. There is a little matter we need to look into further. The council has discussed your circumstances and your lack of memory, and while most believe you, there are some that believe you are not being truthful in your current state."

"Ouch, you're hurting me," whispered Nathan. It was just above a breath, a trick I had taught him so he could talk to me with no one else hearing. Even that low I heard the pain. I hadn't realized I was squeezing his hand as tight as I was until that moment. What I did realize was how angry that accusation made me, but I decided to let it go, for now.

"The council has agreed to let us explore your memories and see for ourselves."

"Out of the question!" Mrs. Saxon objected. She stepped forward, putting herself between them and me. Something she had done once before, maybe more. "It is one thing to come in and ask the questions you have, but the accusations you have just made are offensive. I thought the council was better than that."

"Be careful there Rebecca." Miss Roberts spoke with a sneer. The valley girl accent put an edge on it. "You wouldn't want to question or interfere with a direct command from the council and the Council Supreme, now would you?"

A tension-filled silence ensued that even I could feel. Each time I thought Mrs. Saxon was going to respond she didn't. The weight of the threat was obviously holding her down.

"I didn't think so," she shot at Mrs. Saxon, and then stepped to the side so she could see around her and right at me. "Not to mention it's not your choice, it's hers. So, what will it be Miss Norton?"

"Larissa, you don't have to." Mrs. Saxon said weakly, still standing between us.

"If she doesn't, we all know what will happen," warned Juan.

"She doesn't know. We haven't covered any of that with her yet," Mrs. Tenderschott said worried.

"A shame." Miss Roberts' gaze was still locked on me. Her intensity only added fuel to the fire that started burning inside. One day my temper would be my downfall. Maybe that day was today.

"I'll do it." I fired back looking right at Miss Roberts and then looking around Mrs. Saxon at Juan, "I'll do it."

Mrs. Saxon turned around, her hands clasped together, and her eyes begged. "You don't have to do this."

"I have already done this a few dozen times with Mrs. Tenderschott, there is nothing to hide," I remarked. Then I stepped forward, letting go of Nathan's hand. He attempted to hang on, but couldn't. I wasn't going to back down and let their little threats and appearance intimidate me. I knew the truth and had nothing to hide. Not to mention, I was the one alpha predator in the room. A fact I knew, and so did they. Miss Roberts stepped back in line when I stepped closer to her. "Let's do this thing."

"Okay, we need to do this in the ritual chamber," announced Juan.

He pointed to the door, and I moved in that direction, but not without stopping to give Nathan a kiss goodbye. "I'll be back." I glanced backward at the three visitors. The horror of what they had just seen was painted clearly on their face. It was obvious these three were firmly in the camp of those afraid of me, and probably the main ones who believed I was lying about things. Why else would they be here? Mrs. Saxon didn't share their horror, but she had her own disdain. A price I would have to pay later for my little display for our visitors' benefit.

We walked down the hall to the room of my earlier inquisition. When we entered, it wasn't any less creepy with just us. The shadows still appeared to have occupants. Not to mention the odd little cherubs overhead that watched my very movement. That settled it. If I ever got the chance I was going to take care of those fat things.

"In the center," Juan directed.

When I tried to walk toward the spot in the center of the room, a hand grabbed my arm and yanked me backward with surprising force. I didn't think Mrs. Tenderschott had that in her. "Larissa, you don't have to go through this. You have nothing to prove to us, and I don't believe they could touch you if they wanted to."

I whispered back, "I have nothing to hide, and I have been through this several times with you already."

"This is different," she mouthed.

"Is there a problem?" Miss Sarah Roberts asked, moving a chair to the center. The spot where I watched Lisa kneel during her ascension, but that wasn't the only reminder of that occasion. Juan and Mr. Davis were drawing runes around the outer circle.

"No," I said. Then I moved to the center and sat in the chair. Miss Roberts had vacated the spot before I arrived. She seemed obsessed with keeping her physical distance from me. She stood on the outside as Juan and Mr. Davis completed the circle of runes. There was a brief conversation between the three until they parted, leaving Miss Roberts standing there on the outside of the circle staring at me.

"Sarah, are you sure?" asked Mr. Davis.

"Absolutely."

The two men walked around the circle, holding their hands over the runes. Slowly inch by inch a pile of dust or dirt gathered just inside. It was fine and grey. No particle bigger than a fine powder. It didn't have a smell other than old musky dust. They made several passes around the circle and gathered quite a pile of the substance all around me.

"Ready?" Miss Roberts asked, surlily.

She didn't give me a chance to respond before she started muttering something to herself. Then, for the first time in a few weeks something around here shocked me. I watched her eyes roll back leaving nothing but the blank whites showing. They were still focused on me though. Her lips moved, racing through words. The air in the room became heavy and above me in the skylight a storm developed. Rain pelted the glass while lightning flashed overhead. The walls shook with the distant rumble of thunder. I looked back at Miss Roberts, and she was still standing there muttering with those freaky white eyes. I couldn't make out any word she said, it was all too fast and something I didn't recognize.

The only sound I recognized was the silence when she stopped. Her white eyes remained locked on me as her ruby red lips puckered and she raised her palm up and blew a kiss in my direction. The kiss turned into a single flickering black flame a few inches away from her mouth. A trick I needed to learn. The flame I felt was heading for me, but it instead veered and slowly descended toward the floor and the piles of powder her partners had deposited.

On contact, a tower of black flames exploded up from the piles. There was an explosive whoosh as the column leapt upward from the floor. Their appearance and the speed at which the flames grew almost threw me off my chair. I had to grab hold of the seat to avoid falling into them. They billowed past me with a thunderous roar and closed in closer to me every second. I scooted my feet under the chair before realizing that wasn't going to be enough. The flames continued to move in. The only option was to climb up on the chair and stand there with my arms pulled in close to my body. I wondered if I could use a spell or magic, maybe the second trick I learned, to push them away. I attempted and saw nothing more than a small bubble form in the flames before everything snapped back. It reached the chair and continued to close in. Before now I hadn't really felt a panic; not expecting anything to be dangerous. Then I remembered how she leered at me before and then again through those white eyes just before she blew the flame. One thought accompanied my first scream. *That bitch had it out for me.*

The flames licked at my arms, and I pulled them back on instinct. Now the thought that I was being burned alive hit me. That was what they did to witches back in the old days. I was about to try another push, this time letting go of my rage when I realized something was missing, heat. These flames were cold, not hot, and their touch didn't cause any pain. Instead, it sent shivers through my naturally cold body. Inch by inch, the flames consumed me, sending more uncomfortable shivers through my flesh. I was no longer fearful for my life, but I was now freezing cold with goosebumps on my arms. I wasn't sure when the last time that had happened.

When it reached my shoulders, my fear and panic had melted away, and I just stood there shivering hoping this would be over soon. I needed to learn not to hope for things around here. My wishes and desires were usually provided sooner than I expected. The column consumed me, and I found myself falling in a dark vacuum down to a dark hard floor. When I landed, I smacked my cheek rather hard on the cold damp surface. I might have been wrong about the flames, but this time I was relatively sure that bitch had done that on purpose.

"Let's get on with this shall we?" Miss Sarah Julia Roberts sniped from behind me. I stood up and turned. She stood there, white eyes and all, holding a lantern, the only source of light in this place.

"Fine. Now what?" I asked.

"We go looking for what I believe is here." She held her hand out toward me and I watched another single flame escape from the end of her finger. It grew in size as it headed toward me, filling my sight. Then like a horrible cliché about dying, my life literally flashed before my eyes. Every moment sped past me in reverse. They were too fast to digest, but each recognizable as they were mine, and from my vantage points. It took seconds before I saw myself sitting next to Nathan's bed while he lay there and recovered. Then the entry way with broken glass and debris all around slid pass, as did my first week. The memories slowed, and one that was more painful to see again than I would have expected took center stage. It was me with my eyes barely open as my mother, Mrs. Norton, walked away. The very last time I was with her. Knowing that made the memory hurt more now than it did then. Like the others, this sped by, and what was the worst moment I ever remembered of my life flashed right by. The pain of it hit me like a bullet. Searing me as it passed through, and leaving both entry and exit wounds, just this time in reverse.

Life at home flashed through in reverse. I wasn't exactly sure what Miss Roberts was looking for, but she wasn't really stopping here. Which looking at things from this vantage point, I realized something that really wasn't much of a surprise. My life appeared rather mundane. Kitchen, yard, woods, library. Kitchen, yard, woods, library. Kitchen, yard, woods, library... Surprisingly I didn't see a groove worn in the floor. Then, it stopped, and held at one moment. It was another moment I knew quite well. The day I woke up in my bed.

The memories reversed and traveled in the correct direction for a few moments and then sped backwards again crashing into the moment I woke up in my bed again. Then it did it again. This time it appeared to slam into me waking up in my bed. Almost bouncing off that moment like a wall blocking any progression beyond that spot in time. I was glad someone else now knew what it felt like.

"Stop blocking me," Miss Roberts demanded. Her voice echoed all around me.

"I'm not," I tried to explain, but was cut off abruptly.

"You are. You know what I am after, and you're not letting me see it. It is obviously beyond this point."

"No. I'm not." I shot back. "I would give anything to remember anything before this point, but I can't. This is the moment I woke up like this."

"Or the moment they put a memory block in you."

My hands reached grasping for the air around me. They needed to squeeze something, hard. When they released the nothingness, my anger remained, and I attempted to throw it away when I threw my hands down to my sides in frustration. "Wrong!" I screamed. "This is the moment I woke up after I turned, and before you spout some crap about a memory block making me believe this is that moment, there is something you would never understand. That thirst. The thirst when you first wake up is insatiable. It burns in the back of your throat and only warm blood from a freshly killed human or animal will quench it. I felt that thirst then. The strongest I have ever felt it. A block of my memories doesn't explain that."

"Maybe," she said, sounding condescending.

"Maybe?" I asked.

The memories continued to bounce back and forth between just a few days after when I first woke up and back to that moment. Each time bouncing against the same exact moment. Me waking up in my bed. Miss Roberts walked around me, watching my memories. Her eyes became more focused, narrow, but still all white, and the time-slot that continued to bounce around us became a sliver of just a few minutes.

"Let it go Miss Norton." Miss Roberts demanded, and I complied, but not in the way she wanted. I let my rage out and without touching her, sent her flying through the memories and the black void, shattering it like glass. I expected to see her sliding across the floor, but as the shards of wherever we were finished crashing to the ground, Miss Roberts stood right where she had before this all began, and her eyes slowly rolled back to show the green of her irises. Her body collapsed slightly before she caught herself, and a hand roamed to her midsection probing for the source of some pain. A sight that gave me a slight reason to smile.

Mrs. Saxon walked me back toward my room and wasn't at all pleased at my little display. I tried to explain that no matter what I said or allowed her to see, Miss Roberts felt I was hiding something. It was true. Her and her two counterparts were convinced of what they believed to be the facts, long before they even started. I had even started to doubt the council had agreed to this action and appointed them to carry it out. A point that was met with harsh refute from Mrs. Saxon. "Questioning the council or their intention is not wise," she warned.

She didn't like it much when I sniped back, "And they think I am the dangerous one." It really felt they had already passed judgement without any of them really knowing any of the facts, and of course I had nothing to offer them that would sway their opinions. I needed more. Something concrete to convince them, and I knew a source to try.

8

It seemed it didn't matter who I let in my head for a little adventure, and how they did it, it always left me in a fog for the rest of the day. That mixed well with the tornado of thoughts that routinely circled my head, like water circling a drain. Well not exactly. The water would eventually go down the drain and leave the sink, my thoughts never did. They kept circling. Even when I felt like, well, a normal person, they were still there, circling, just an impulse from consuming my consciousness. Now the Council of Mages had added more to the debris that circled the drain in my head. They caused several doubts that I had pushed aside to come back to the forefront. As bad as that was, that wasn't the worst. Me, my own being, and motives were now under question. Like I was on trial for just being who I was. What really spun my world? I had no clue if there was a punishment if they were correct, and if there was, what it was. They were being tragically vague in that regard.

I had had an idea yesterday of where to possibly start the search for answers that may help, but I never actually took that step. As the saying goes, there was no time like the present, and hell I didn't know, maybe just taking this step would help slow the swirl. Of course, it didn't come without risk. No reward ever did, and I knew that. There was the chance something would be found, or nothing would be, and either way that could be a good or bad thing. Either it would give me answers, or lead to more questions.

I marched downstairs, hoping to not run into anyone. After my witch bonding session yesterday, I was a bit fearful that word of my latest encounter with the council had gotten around. Not that there needed to be a rumor mill for them to hear about it. Most of them were standing outside the door as I left with the three dark amigos. I actually found myself tip toeing past the door on the witches floor, ready to sprint if the door creaked open.

At the bottom I rounded the corner and headed down the hallway to my destination hoping not to run into anyone, anyone except the person I spied coming out of a door, just three doors down. She had her back to me as she closed the door, giving me the perfect opportunity to sneak up on her, something rather easy for us. I stood right behind her until she had the door closed and then wrapped my arms around her and asked, with a faked gruff voice, "What are you doing?"

She screamed and then spun around into my embrace. "Don't scare me like that."

I promised I wouldn't do it again through a laugh. It was a promise I had a feeling I wouldn't be able to keep, and one I didn't think she would mind if I didn't.

"I just finished dinner and had some ice cream. Are you coming down for dinner?"

"Nope, we don't eat." That comment drew a rather interested look. She was all of nine or ten, knowing the characteristics of a vampire was probably not high on her list of things she had learned in those years. "I was heading to the library, wanna come?"

"There's a library?" she asked.

"A magical library," I answered. She bounced up and down at hearing this. Any effects of my little fright or her first detail about life as a vampire were long gone.

I took her by the hand and led her to the library. When we entered I paid special attention to her face. Her reaction at seeing the towering shelves was just like mine, and I wasn't even sure if she had the same love for reading I did. Though I doubt she had access to many books in the cage they said she was kept in. I waited until I heard the first gasp at the sheer scale of it before walking her past the door. A "wow" followed it, just like I had said when I first experienced this place. Even having visited here half a dozen times since I had first seen it, the sheer wonder and scale of this room still took my breath away, just like it had for Amy, and I hadn't even shown her the best trick yet.

"Come have a seat with me at the table." She followed me over to a table, and I pulled out one of the wooden chairs for her. After she sat on it, I scooted her up to the table, and then took the seat next to her. "Are you sure no one has brought you here before?"

She shook her head back and forth.

"Well, this is the library. Obviously, the books, I know. Anything you need to know is here, or can be brought here for you. Now you are probably wondering like I was, how do you get anything down from up there?" I pointed straight up and watched Amy's eyes follow the bookcases up beyond our sight. "There is a librarian who can help. Would you like to meet him?"

"Is he nice?" she asked cautiously.

"He is very nice. You ready?"

She nodded eagerly.

"Here we go." I sat up right, and placed both arms on the table, and then summoned him, "Edward?"

No sooner had I called his name than he appeared, right above the table. Amy shrieked, and I felt the girl coming out of her seat and toward me. Her fingernails latched hold of my arm, and a pure look of terror covered her normally angelic face. It hadn't taken long for me to break that promise about not scaring her anymore. In truth, I'd never thought the image of a severed head floating above a table might be frightening. This place had probably desensitized me a little.

"Relax," I said in a soothing tone, but I let her come over into the chair with me and sat her on my lap. She buried her head into the side of my neck while I stroked her back.

"He don't got a body," her little girl voice whispered into my ear.

I gave a fake gasp, and turned and whispered into her ear, "You're right. I hadn't noticed yet." I winked at Edward who returned the same. "This is Edward, the librarian. He is our friend. He has been the librarian here for... I forgot, how long is it Edward?"

"Centuries, Miss Dubois," he announced. "It is very nice to make your acquaintance Miss O'Neil."

The girls eyes lit up at hearing his greeting. She looked back at me, and asked, "How does he know my name?" I didn't answer. Instead, I gently turned her back to face Edward and gave him a simple nod.

"Why, I know the name of everyone who is part of this coven, both past and present." Edward looked smug, or as smug as a floating head could.

"That isn't all he knows either. If you want to know anything, this is the man to come see. He can find you anything in this library, or any library in any of the other covens."

"Wow, you must be really smart." Amy was now warming up to Edward and now, with the curiosity of a child, leaned against the table to try to see what was underneath his head, something I had done once myself. I wasn't sure what I was expecting, and could even imagine what a ten-year-old's mind would expect.

"Let's just say, I know how to find information." Edward appeared to notice what Amy was attempting to do and moved back further from the edge of the table.

"All you have to do is ask, like this. Edward, I need some help. Can you please look through the archives for any mention of the Nortons?"

Edward gave me a curious look below his furrowed brow. "Can't let it go can you?"

"I need to find answers," I began my retort, but Edward interrupted me.

"I know, I know. The Council of Mages, and their questions. I can't promise you anything, but I will try to see what I can find. Vampire covens aren't as diligent at keeping records as others are, and I do need to warn you about what I might find. If there are any references to the Nortons in the records of those of us that keep records it is doubtful it will be flattering. If you catch my meaning?"

I caught it, right between the eyes. Its impact forced away some of the hope I had, but information was information, and something was better than nothing. Even if the information painted the picture that I didn't want to accept. I needed the truth, for them, for me. I just wasn't sure if I could handle the truth. "I understand. Just whatever you can find."

He tilted down and his eyes narrowed as they looked at me. "I feel I also have to warn you, whatever I research in the archives will be known to the council."

"You report back to them?" I hastily asked, feeling the urge to spring up from my chair, but I couldn't. A sweet precious child was on my lap.

"No Miss Dubois. It is not that. They can see anything I access in the archives. Since you are under the proverbial microscope, it would be safe to assume that they are watching, and will review anything I pull for you."

"I see," I said. This was just another detail of my plan I hadn't considered, and both revelations together were tragic. If there was something bad about them, I didn't need the council seeing it and then using it to further their persecution of the Nortons, and myself. I felt rather deflated, and it seemed someone else was picking up on it. I felt Amy settle back against my chest, and grab my hand pulling it around her. Nathan had similar reactions too. Little brushes of the back of my hands, or wrapping his arms around me. I wasn't consciously attempting to control how I reacted. There was no thought process around my physical reaction to how I felt. If I was giving out something externally, it was truly because that was how I felt.

"Understood, I need to think about it." The old saying 'the past should stay in the past,' flashed into my mind. The person who said it, probably didn't have their past trying to hunt them down on so many levels. "While you are here. Do you have any children's books in here? Maybe some nice stories for Amy?"

"I think I can find something. Maybe one with princesses and unicorns." Edward's smile matched the lighthearted request.

"And castles?" Amy asked.

"And castles," agreed Edward. "Shall I send them to her room?"

I had to think about that for a moment. I couldn't actually go to her room to read any of them with her, but that gave me an idea. "Yes, that would be fine." I looked down at Amy. "How about you and Nathan pick one out tomorrow night and we sit out around the fire outside and read it to you?" Her face lit up like the sky on the fourth of July, and she turned and wrapped both arms around my neck. I took that as a yes.

9

"So, what story shall we read next?" I wasn't waiting for anyone else to decide. With a little whimsical twist of my wrist the stack of children's books moved across the table to me. I could have just reached over and grabbed them, but Amy seemed to like it when I used magic to do something like that. "It is getting a little late young lady, and you have a bedtime that Mrs. Parrish made really clear."

"But it's a Friday," protested Amy.

"Even more of a reason," I said, not looking at her, but looking at Nathan. I wasn't ready for Amy to have to face what happens out in the woods every Friday night. "We have time for one more short one. So how about this one?" I pulled out a book that was a collection of shorter versions of some classic children's stories. Being out here with Amy, reading around the fire right up to her bedtime had become somewhat of habit for us. Not that any of us minded. The last three nights have been the most normal I could ever remember. It was like I had a little sister, or—this thought made me gulp every time I had it—a young daughter. We ended each night the same way, which was how I was trying to steer things tonight. One last story, out of this book of short stories, with Nathan doing the honors, then off to bed for her and homework for us. Of course, there was no homework on the menu for us tonight.

I handed the book over to Nathan, dismissing the normal 'who will read this' question. By now it was a given. When he opened it to the next story he laughed. This wasn't a little chuckle. It was a laugh that I hadn't heard or seen from him before. Amy looked up with a quizzical look that matched how I felt, but he kept laughing, even ignoring my attempts at less subtle clues to ask what was going on. Eventually I flat out asked him, "What's so funny?"

"You sure you don't want to read this story? It's Hansel and Gretel." He turned the book around and held it up so I could see the title on the page.

Now I got the joke. "Next story please."

"Why? What's this story about?," Amy asked, with a bit of a whine. I had hoped she wasn't going to ask that, but she did. There was no way to tell a girl that lived in the woods with a bunch of witches, about that story without causing some nightmares.

"It's a terrible story, not good at all. What's next?" I asked, then I saw Mrs. Parrish coming out the door, and felt a bit of relief. Not that I wanted it to end, but I didn't want her to ask about the last story.

"Amy, time for bed," she called from the door. Filing passed her were my friends, meaning it was a little later than I thought it was.

"One more story please?" Amy turned to me and begged with her gapped-tooth grin. It was a face that was hard to say no to, and if it were any other night, I would attempt to delay Mrs. Parrish a few more minutes, or offer to have Nathan take her up when we were done, but tonight was not any other night.

"I'm sorry Amy. Mrs. Parrish says it's bedtime, so it is, but remember I will see you in the morning."

She stared at me a few more moments with those innocent child eyes, and I knew she hoped it would change my mind. I felt it. The melting and wanting to stay in this moment longer, but I knew there was other business to be had, and she absolutely couldn't be here for this. When I didn't respond with anything but my natural stone-like expression, she conceded and gave Nathan a hug before she dragged herself over to me and hugged me around my neck.

I watched as she trudged her way to Mrs. Parrish passing a line of vampires on the way to do what nature intended. She didn't act scared of them; she had no reason to be. To her each of them were an older sister or brother. Ah, to be that innocent again.

"You have an enjoyable night with your mini-me?" Apryl asked as she filed past.

"My what?"

"Your mini-me. She is basically a little you. Attached at your hip every chance she can, and she has even changed how she dresses. Don't tell me you hadn't noticed."

I hadn't. I mean, I knew she wanted to be around me, and Nathan. I figured the first night had something to do with that, and the time we took to spend with her wasn't hurting. "Has she?" I asked in Nathan's direction.

"Yep," he answered sheepishly.

I hadn't realized it, and it made me feel a little, well, hard to explain. Surprised and upset that I hadn't noticed, and then worried that maybe I wasn't a good enough role model for her. I couldn't let the others know I had these self-doubts and just laughed it off. "At least she's not wearing pink."

That seemed to bring a round of hearty laughter from everyone. Even our monitors for the night Steve and Stan agreed. "All we need is another mini-Gwen," added Steve, but he barely finished his statement before he let out the biggest "Ha" I have ever heard. He was standing behind Nathan when he spoke. Following the outburst, he reached over him and grabbed the book of stories that was sitting open on the table. "Please tell me you didn't read her this story."

Now everyone else had gathered around Steve and were having their own laugh at the discovery. It was Laura who finally gained control of her laughter enough to ask what I believe everyone else was thinking. "So, you, a witch, sitting in here at a house in the woods was reading her the story of Hansel and Gretel?"

"No," I denied strongly. "That *was* the next one, but we were moving past it when she was called in for bed." I knew this wasn't going away anytime soon, and I couldn't blame them. I wouldn't let it go if the shoe were on the other foot. The jokes I could make were already rolling around inside, so I was ready for whatever they had to give.

"Poor girl," Pam said.

"She'll live. She survived seeing a floating head in the library." I brushed off their concern.

"Have you heard anything from Edward about his little –"

A quick slash by my hand across my throat cut Apryl off, or I hoped it had. The look Nathan shot at me dashed those hopes. Enough had leaked to do some damage, and I would now have to tap dance a bit to repair what it had caused. Why I kept my little task for Edward a secret from Nathan, I wasn't sure. All that mattered was that I did. When I told him about Edward's little warnings, Nathan added his own and asked me to let things be. I tried to explain to him that I couldn't, and then listed all the reasons why. The council, and my own need to know, but he was rather insistent that it wouldn't lead to anything but trouble and hurt, and begged me to just focus on the future. Which I felt he really meant the future with him, which I couldn't argue with. That was probably why I let it drop, and maybe why I let it sit in a way he thought he had won. I didn't think to mention it when I changed my mind the next day and asked Edward to go ahead.

Nathan stood up and reached his hand toward me. I knew what was coming, and I willingly gave him my hand and followed his lead away from the others to the other end of the pool. He was quiet, as we walked along the edge over the waterfall, escorted by the gaze of all our friends. Even I felt the awkwardness of this moment. Should I speak first, or let him? I mean I already knew what he was going to say.

"So, you talked to Edward?" Nathan asked, sounding brittle. What was even worse though was his lack of eye contact. The pool deck seemed to hold his attention.

"Yes, I did." No point in denying it now.

"I had hoped you were going to leave the past in the past, and just focus on what is ahead of you."

It made so much sense, and what he told me two nights ago was right. There was a better than fifty-fifty chance I was going to find more pain and hurt at the end of this. Well, that was his view, I still thought it was slightly worse than even odds, but that didn't change the need to know though. I needed him to understand one point.

"I am focused on what is ahead of us, but that doesn't change the need to find some answers." I sounded like a broken record from the last time he and I discussed this. I could tell from the shoulder slump that I wasn't winning any points. "I have to find out. Don't you understand? If I don't, there may be no future."

"The council," Nathan huffed, now firmly looking me right in the eyes. Disdain danced in the eyes that I usually found so dreamy. "You don't owe them anything. Let them think what they want, and just go on and live your life."

"You don't get it," I shouted back. Which I probably shouldn't have, but I did, startling Nathan. I couldn't help myself from reacting like that. There was a true fear inside me that was really in control at the moment. What they could do to me was still a mystery. Something terrifying they dangled over me.

"Why? Because I am not like you."

Don't say it. Don't say it. Please. "Yes." Damnit Larissa. I really needed to stop speaking my mind.

His eyes returned to the same spot on the pool deck that had now become more interesting than I was, and I felt a shiver move throughout my body. I didn't look at it to see if it was more attractive too. "Look, I am a witch, and from what I understand they can make my life uncomfortable if they want. Even your mother said so."

"How?"

"Well, I don't know," I conceded, but to Nathan the answer appeared to be a gut punch. He stayed there focused on the same spot on the ground and fidgeted backward creating a greater physical chasm between us. An exhausted sigh escaped through his mouth.

"You need to go do your thing," he told the ground as he turned and walked away from me and inside. At that moment, I didn't feel the urge that I should have been focused on. That was the farthest feeling from my mind. My only urge was to follow him, but I didn't. No matter how many times my brain told my legs to move, they didn't listen. Probably because I couldn't answer the next question. What would I do to fix things? I couldn't do what he was asking.

10

I stood in the shower for longer than I ever remembered doing before and let the hot water attempt to wash away the remnants of the night before. It may have removed the physical, evidenced by the red swirl around the drain, but the emotional debris was still there. That dreadful moment played over and over, which seemed to be a pattern in how my mind worked. Instead of playing a wondering memory over and over, it picked the worst to put on replay.

Inside I debated whether to rush right down to talk to Nathan or let things be and just see him later. Still in question was what would I say to him? To know that I would need to know what it was that I said that was wrong. It may have seemed obvious at first, but thanks to the multiple replays my brain had provided me every few minutes, other possibilities had popped up as potential sources.

Yes, I know he wanted me to stop dwelling on the past, and there was a part of me that wanted to, or would like to. There was actually nothing more I wanted than to leave all the pain behind and just get on with the future. One I hoped that Nathan would be part of. My past, so far, was nothing but a source of pain. Rather it was the pain of watching the man I loved like a father murdered, knowing that those that killed him were still after me, not knowing if the woman I believed was my mother was still alive, why they turned me, or all the unknown that existed about who I really was. They were all sources of despair that were sources of questions, and I wasn't even sure if finding the answers would lead to any relief. The truth could be worse than what I already knew. It was all the not knowing that ate me alive, and what used to be small bites were now large chunks of me taken with every chomp. The answers would at least fill those voids, even if they left me in a worse state than I already was. So, leaving the past behind was not something I could really consider. In a way, I owed it to my real mother to find out what I was and what happened to me.

Then there was the fact that I lied to him. Well, I didn't really lie, I just didn't tell him I changed my mind and decided to take the risk of having Edward look into things. I tried to dismiss this a few times, but it kept coming back up. As far as I knew, this was my first meaningful relationship. Of course, I could have had a boyfriend before and not remember him. A little voice reminded me of Todd Grainger, the one my mother told me about. I had to admit, I was a little curious what he looked like, but not curious enough to ask Edward. I could only imagine

Nathan's reaction if I did. From what I have seen in movies and shows, most people don't take someone looking up a past love too well.

What shocked me most was that I kept reminding myself to consider Nathan's feelings, not just mine. I might not consider asking Edward to by lying to him, or going behind his back, but he could. Especially if you considered point one, that he wanted me to leave the past alone. I felt rather proud of myself, that I was that mature. Not that I was giving myself a lot of credit. I seemed to have screwed things up so royally between us and didn't have a clue how to fix it. My mind also wondered why he was so insistent about leaving the past behind. Did he and the others know something?

It was a notion that I often discarded as preposterous as I walked through the woods looking for a source of nourishment. If anyone did, they would have already told me, and if they chose not to for some reason, they would have told the council to get them off of my case.

The third possibility was the one that I prayed to not be a reality, or even a partial truth, and I was hoping I was falling victim to one of the real disadvantages of being us.

During one of my first nights out on the deck Jennifer explained why they created activities for the group to do. She and her husband wanted to establish a habit that we would all do for the rest of our... well, forever. A way to occupy our time when we were alone with our thoughts, while the rest of the world was quiet. It would appear, according to her, that vampires have gotten a bad rap throughout history because they have too much idle time on their hands, or really their mind. Thoughts wandered and ideas formed, and while some of these thoughts lead some of the world's greatest works of art or symphonies, she wouldn't tell me which of the great artists were like us, not all thoughts had the same divine inspiration. Before she even continued, I grasped the notion completely. Our immortality and our ability. Those combined could make some believe they are better than mortals, give that belief enough time to bounce around in a bored mind that was tired of living in the shadows, and you have a Jean St. Claire. It seemed I had heard that somewhere before.

This was something I had been thinking about a lot over the last few days. Just one of those disturbing patterns of thought that haunted every moment of my life. I didn't have thoughts of grandeur, or desires to do anything but just blend in. No, it wasn't that. It was the council. This was what they were worried about. That was why they were concerned about whether the Nortons, as they called it, groomed me in any way that might lead to me becoming one of those, a threat to everyone: mortals, witches, vampires, everyone.

It wasn't until Nathan asked what he did that it hit me with the clarity of a crystal bell and a pain deep inside that I had never felt before. Then hours later, another question that I had just blown off came rumbling back with the force of a freight train. We were different, an obvious and unavoidable fact, but what mattered was how Nathan saw me, or if he even considered it, and it was obvious he did. He worried about the fact that I wouldn't age, and he would, he didn't understand the struggles and factors that I had to battle as part of life, and it wasn't until I was heading back up to the coven this morning that the true meaning of his question bit right into me. The past he wanted me to leave behind wasn't all the questions and answers that I was looking for, but it was who and what I was. He wanted me to be just *the me* he met and was with now. The problem, *the me* he liked was *the me* he wanted me to leave behind, and I couldn't change that. That gave me my second cold shiver of the morning. Even thinking about it now gave me another shiver, a third. If I were human, that shiver may have been caused by the freezing water I was standing under. My shower had worn out the hot water, which I didn't realize was possible here.

I got out and got dressed, and then looked at the window down toward the pool area, the normal gathering spot for everyone on the weekends, but not this day. A steady wind driven drizzle created constant ripples in the pool, and an absence of life on the pool deck. A quick duck up though my closet found the roof deck to be a similar scene. The cool mist on my face felt refreshing, and I lingered for a few moments to bathe in it and to allow my mind to harken back to earlier times at the Nortons' where I wouldn't let such weather stop me from walking through the woods behind our house. There was something about these days. They appealed to me more than days full of light.

After a second change of clothes, caused by my standing a little too long on the deck, I headed out to find others, anyone. I didn't want to be alone with my thoughts at the moment. I stepped out of the door to our floor and into a fall-scape wonderland. Leaves of red, yellow, and orange fell down to the floor like a light snowfall. Their origin, unknown, but they were very real. Some passed close enough to the stairs to pile along the edges. I couldn't resist running through them to hear the satisfying crinkle. The normal lanterns that floated in the space giving them life had been replaced by carved jack-o'-lanterns. At first I thought they were just the image of, but that distinctive sweet pumpkin smell told me different. I walked down the stairs, slowly, taking it all in, not wanting to miss a scene. Even something as simple as seeing a leaf fall and slowly slide off one of the floating pumpkins was mesmerizing. This place never ceased to amaze me.

"Happy Halloween!" exclaimed Jack from his landing on the other side of the grand entry.

Was it really already Halloween? Each step down the stairs was an exercise in concentration, even with my level of coordination. There was so much around for me to take in. I took several steps until I saw the spiderwebs complete with red-eyed spiders hanging in the corner beyond one of the floating pumpkins. I was doing fine until something flashed and crossed right in front of me, sending me sprawling backwards, where I plopped down less than gracefully. I watched it float around the room and then right through a wall.

"You okay?" I heard Jack's voice say again. He rushed down his stairs, but I was back up to my feet before he reached the next landing, and proceeded down myself.

"I'm fine," I said trying to sound composed, while I kept my eyes open for any other surprises.

"That is one of Lisa's more well behaved friends, she lets out a few every Halloween to add to the ambiance." Jack stopped at the bottom of the boys set of stairs and looked over at me with a quizzical look. "Your type does celebrate Halloween, don't you?"

"Duh," was the only response I could give. It wasn't like we were from another planet or something.

"Wasn't sure. Especially since a lot of us dress up as you for it." He gave me an odd smirk and almost seemed to brace himself against the railing.

"A lot of us dress up as you for it too," I shot back, wondering if I ever dressed up like a little witch. Jack let go of the rail and laughed.

"Touche."

"This is wild." Above me two more ghosts appeared through the wall and circled through the shower of leaves and maze of pumpkins.

"Every holiday is. You should see Christmas. This whole space is filled with snow and a gigantic tree that reaches up to the top. The first year I saw all this it was overwhelming, but I have to admit, even after seven years it still gets me."

"Things had been so weird around here lately I kind of lost track of what day it was." I had. I knew what days were class days and which days weren't. That was about it.

"I bet, the council and all." Jack walked over to meet me at the bottom of my stairs. He almost looked compassionate. We had come a long way since our first meeting.

"You heard?" I asked, not really surprised. From what I had gathered from the reaction of the others, their arrival was like the arrival of the hottest pop stars to the witch community.

"Gwen has been blabbing of nothing else. You would think she is the one who met with them, and not you."

"I kind of wish it was her and not me," I remarked snidely.

"That bad?" he asked, and then rushed to add, "You don't have to talk about it. I can tell it was hard." He pointed to his head, and I thought back to the emotional energy talk Mrs. Saxon and I had a few weeks ago. I couldn't imagine what kind of energy I was giving off. I was probably the queen of mixed and confusing signals to him. That was how I felt to myself.

"I'd rather not." I stated and then redirected. "This is wild." A third paranormal visitor had joined the other two. While following it around I spotted a group of bats hanging from the far corner. They weren't fake. I could see them move as they breathed.

"Yep, kind of puts to shame those cheap decorations and plastic pumpkins doesn't it."

"I'll say."

The two of us just stood there for a few moments taking it all in. Or I did. In my mind I knew this was all magic, but the rest of me felt it was real. Our grand entrance had been turned into the entry to the creepiest haunted house I had ever seen. Then I remembered what the front door looked like. For once it fit in.

Behind me I heard the familiar sound of heels on the tile. A few steps were muffled by the leaves on the ground. The smell of freshly baked cookies preceded her by several feet. Just knowing she approached caused the tension to melt out of my body. It wasn't the same kind of melting that Nathan caused, with I desperately needed right now, but this would do. Besides, who would turn down a hug from someone they thought of as a grandmother?

"Happy Halloween, Miss Dubois." An arm draped around me from the side, giving me a little squeeze.

"Happy Halloween, Mrs. Tenderschott."

"Happy Halloween, Jack" She moved to him and gave him a similar hug. It was clear she was the grandmother to everyone here, possibly answering a question I had wondered about a long time ago about whether she had any family. It was obvious she had at least one family, us.

"You too, Mrs. Tenderschott," he returned her hug.

"Not too bad is it?" asked Mrs. Tenderschott.

"Not at all," I agreed.

"I was actually coming to find you," she said, now standing in front of me. "I have something new I want to try if you are up for it. If we are going to break through any memory block that is there, I would much rather it be with me than the council."

That was something I couldn't agree with more.

11

"You okay?"

It wasn't until Mrs. Tenderschott asked me if I was okay that I noticed my shoulders were slumped, a completely involuntary action. "There is just a lot going on," I said, and noticed that even my voice sounded deflated.

With all the crap going on, there was one thing that kept me from falling into the depths of the darkness that I felt around me, but that happiness that had helped elevate me on a daily basis was gone. Okay, maybe I was being a tad bit over dramatic. It wasn't gone yet, maybe it was just on hold. That might even be stretching it. The truth was I didn't know where things were, or were going after last night, and that emptiness I felt scared me.

"Oh dear, I know. Let's see what we can do to help that a bit."

I sat there and watched as she did her normal search for ingredients. Her class was the one I was starting to really enjoy most of all, well make that second to Mr. Helms' class. I really enjoyed letting things fly at others, and I think he noticed that, which may be a reason he hadn't let me spar with Gwen too often. The potions class was part science, something physical I could grab hold of. For example, I had realized that there were certain base elements for every potion. To transform someone temporarily into anything you started with zinc. To change someone's appearance, it was a mixture of zinc and salt, although I thought the salt was really just for the taste. I had watched Mrs. Tenderschott mix the type of potion she was mixing enough now to know what the base element was for getting into someone's head, and it more than frightened me a little. A small amount of arsenic. Now, she and I both knew it wouldn't kill me, but what about those who weren't me. A reason to pay attention to her number one rule, be very precise with measurements.

"Okay, so this will be a little bitter." She sat a cup with a small amount of red liquid down in front of me. I reached for it, but she put her hand over the top of it and warned, "Not yet. There are a few more parts to this method. It is a really old one that I have never tried. Edward dug it up in the archives for me. If there is a memory block, this will get past it."

"Mrs. Tenderschott, the Nortons didn't –"

She held up a finger in front of her smiling lips, silencing me. "I know that, and you know that, but we don't know if someone else did before, AND... I believe this might even help you bridge across the block if it was caused by the turning process.

Which, I read something rather interesting that might explain...," her voice trailed off and her normal smile turned upside down. "Never mind."

"What is it?" I asked half-heartedly. I wasn't sure how much more grim news I could take.

"Sorry, I just have a tough time talking about it when you are sitting right here. It's heart-breaking to think about you having to go through something like that."

"Tell me."

She swallowed hard before she spoke. "Some theorize the... the memory loss some vampires experience is because you die as part of the process, and when your body dies so does your brain, causing the gap." She crossed her hands over her chest as she looked upon me with the one look I hated of all, pity. "I just can't bear to sit here looking at you and think that you actually died – "

It was now my time to cut her off, as I had heard enough. "You can stop there. You said there were some other parts to what we are trying today."

She stammered around for a moment before turning back to the door that I knew lead to her private residence. "Wait here." She disappeared into her room.

I waited, and took the opportunity to get a good whiff of the red concoction in the cup in front of me. There were benefits and disadvantages to having senses that were on overload. Yep, the world looked more fantastic than words could describe. Colors clearer, sounds richer, and all that. Things that were great smelling, smelled that much more wonderful, but the opposite was also true, which I regretted at this moment. Mrs. Tenderschott said it would be bitter. She didn't say it was a cup full of only vinegar.

"Here we are," her voice announced as she emerged from her room with two pieces of paper in each hand. She handed both to me when she reached me. I glanced down at both and froze. There in my hands were pictures of my mother, Susan Dubois, and Marie Norton, the only woman I remembered as my mother. Both hands shook as my vision jumped back and forth between the two images. Both were old images, the same I had seen in the documents and journals that Edward had produced from the archives, but they still looked like I remembered, or in the case of my mother, how she looked when I had visited her.

"These will help link you with both women," explained Mrs. Tenderschott. She placed a large silver bowl on the table in front of me. "Put the pictures in there. Your mother first, and then Mrs. Norton. They need to be in the order in which the women came into your life."

I did as I was asked and placed my mother's picture in the bowl. My hand held on to her picture for a moment longer before letting go. Then I placed Mrs. Norton's picture on top.

Mrs. Tenderschott picked up the cup of red liquid and placed it on top of both pictures. "Time over time. Family over Family." The pictures began to smolder under the cup. "Blood over blood. Past. Present. Future. Future. Present. Past." Smoke filled the bowl and Mrs. Tenderschott reached into it and picked up the cup. She held it out for me to take. I did, and as I had done more times than I could remember over the past weeks, I drank the contents, and settled in for another trip to someplace else.

This one didn't take as long as the others before I was in a world of all black. The only difference, this time I was alone, and I was feeling sick. Something in my stomach churned, over and over, and I felt so nauseous I clamped my mouth shut to avoid vomiting all over the place. My mind went to the arsenic that was in the potion, but the next image before my eyes told me it was something else. It was that memory again. The same one that played over and over while Miss Roberts attempted to break through. It had only happened once in real life, but recently I had been forced to relive the moment I turned over and over. Here I was again, lying in my bed. Then something that made me wonder if I was on a drug trip from the potion happened. I sank into the mattress down through the bed, through the floor, through the ground. A pain, sharp and terrifying, radiated through my body. I tried to stay still, not knowing if that would cause any problems, but eventually reflexes took hold and my body writhed in response. The moist trails of tears ran down my face. I fought to hang on, but I felt the sharp punctures, the burning, and the tearing of my flesh. It was too much, and I let out a scream. The scream gurgled as it left my mouth. My hands clawed at the cool damp grass and dug into the dirt beside me. I felt stabbing pains on my arms and legs. Punctures after punctures. Each violation of my skin burned, causing more screams. Each caused me to choke on the liquid that had gathered in my throat. I forced my eyes opened and stared up at the overhanging trees. They towered above me. I felt movement around me and looked. Dark figures were surrounding me, biting me. Their hushed voices were muffled by my own labored breathing. I looked around and down the dirt road I was lying on. My mother lay next to me, her body marred and covered in blood, her hand outstretched toward me, but the life had long left her eyes. That didn't stop me from attempting to reach her grasp. Only another plunge of something sharp into my right leg caused a natural reflex pulling my arm back.

"It's not working," I heard one muffled voice say.

"It has to. It has to," cried another dismayed voice, that I recognized. I tried to sit up to see her, but nothing responded. My legs were useless and even my arms merely twitched in response to the command to push myself up. Inside, a burn spread from organ to organ. I turned my head in the other direction and saw a dark cloaked figured splayed out on the ground several feet away. What appeared to be his head was a few feet further. As much as I tried to tilt my head to see those I heard talking, I couldn't. They stayed outside of my sight, and I turned my head back to look up, hoping maybe they would come up over me so I could see their faces.

The burning consumed my insides like a torch. I knew the darkness would arrive soon, and tried to turn my head again toward my mother, but now it wouldn't move. I was stuck looking up at the trees, as the darkness settled in, with my last memory of the living world would be the sight of my mother's dead eyes, the last thump of my own heart, and hearing Mrs. Marie Norton plead, "Come on. It has to work."

I came to and collapsed with a thud on to the table I sat at. My hands and arms cushioned my head, though the impact wouldn't hurt any more than what I just experienced had. I knew it was all a memory, but my body still felt it all. Each bite stung and burned. Inside I felt my body dying, the organs shutting down, my systems poisoning themselves. I was nothing but a limp rag doll on the table. In the distance, I heard Mrs. Tenderschott calling my name, but my mouth wouldn't move to respond. I couldn't even move an arm or a hand to wave to her for help. I felt the warmth of her hand on my shoulder. She leaned in to check on me, and her breath warmed my cheek as icy tears flowed freely.

Mrs. Tenderschott rushed out of the room, leaving me just a lump with my thoughts. It wasn't long before she returned, and she had help. Two sets of hands pulled me up from the table and then two arms cradled me. It wasn't Nathan's. That much I was sure of. They were different, not strong, and struggled to carry me the short distance they did before they laid me down.

Everything came back at once, and I was more than a little relieved. The sensation of lying there, crying, unable to move would have put me over the edge of what I could handle, if I hadn't already crashed over it. Mrs. Tenderschott sat there next to me when my eyes opened. Neither of us spoke. I just shook my head and reached up to brush away the tears with the back of my hand. Mrs. Tenderschott handed me a tissue to make another attempt at the flood. She backed up and gave me room to sit up. The weight of what I had just experienced forced my head to dangle down from my neck, and I didn't even try to support it, and sat there on the edge of Mrs. Tenderschott's sofa, my arms resting on my legs.

It was after several more dabs and wipes of the tissue before either of us spoke, and this time I went first. "That didn't help," I said, having to force myself not to cry anymore.

"Sorry dear. I was hopeful it would help you break through and recover your lost memories."

Behind a sniffle I said, "It did."

There was a confused silence in the room, and I sat up to try to read her face. I knew what she had tried to do, and she was at least partially successful, probably more. I had to consider one possibility, and that was becoming more and more likely. There was no gap. That was hard enough to fathom with a clear mind, but now I had a flood of memories retaking their rightful place in my mind, and I was drowning.

12

The sofa creaked as I sat back against the cushions, looking for something comforting. I needed something stable, something supportive, and almost asked her to have Nathan join us, but there were enough questions where he was concerned, and I didn't need to add this complication into things. I would need to break it to him later, softly, that I was different now. That was the only way to say it. Before I was a blank slate formed by the Nortons, but now I remembered everything, and I do mean everything. My home. The hot and humid summer days. The cool summer nights sitting out looking at the stars with my father. The cologne he wore that, as I told him often, "made my nose stingy." The sound of my mother's voice when I perfected a spell, and how she sounded when she admonished me for having other things on my mind. It sounded like a familiar problem, though I was six then, and running out through our fields was more appealing than staying in the stuffy house practicing. I remembered it all. Like the time when I was seven and I floated to her a fancy bottle of perfume my father and I got her for her birthday. He was worried I was going to drop it, and I could feel him adding support, which resulted in a few pouted objections of "I got it" from me.

Every moment of my childhood, even my debutante ball. I know everyone said I looked precious in that dress, but I hated it. I wasn't that much of a girlie girl kind of person. Lace and satin weren't for me. They still aren't. It also answered another question. No, Todd Grainger was not my boyfriend. Nor was he someone I even liked. Just friends of our parents. They all thought we made the cutest couple. Even though my mother was well aware that I tortured him often, even once floating him up to the top of a tree where I left him for a few hours, fully aware he hadn't mastered his skills enough to get himself down without climbing, which he could have easily done, but didn't.

Also coming back were spells, tricks, and abilities. I did a lot more than move things and light candles. Potions and spells all rushed back. Each I had to assume would require practice to perfect after so many years of non-use, like the simpler skills, but knowing that I could do them gave me a sense of confidence.

"I remember it all." I said finally, causing a startled look from Mrs. Tenderschott. "I remember my parents, my childhood, everything. I even remember the day they came to take my father." I settled back further on the sofa and looked up at the ceiling to try to clear everything else from my head. I wanted to be clear with the details, or what I remembered of them. They made little sense to me, but maybe they would to her. "Three dark cloaked individuals came for him just after the twilight. They came right to our home and broke down the doors, forcing their way in. They had my father before we even knew they were there. He fought, but was quickly knocked unconscious right there in our own parlor. It was me and my mother that gave them the biggest fight. Each of us shooting fireballs at them, being careful not to hit my father. They ran for the door, and I pulled the wooden floor planks up into a wall in front of them, but they broke through it and made it out the front door. I followed them, but they were fast, Mrs. Tenderschott. Really fast. They were halfway down the main drive before I reached the door. I was still able to grab them all and yank them back to the porch. Looking back on it now, that was a mistake. Now we had three angry vampires in close confines with my mother and me." I stopped and leaned forward to explain. "See, my mother and father had told me about them, and about Jean St. Claire, who was rather prominent in the area, but I had never been around any before then, and completely underestimated their speed and strength. My mother was bitten before I knew it. It was when I turned to help her that they took off again with my father. We both gave chase down the drive, but at the time I didn't know how bad my mother was wounded. Her dress hid the amounts of blood that was gushing out of the gash. I tried again to stop them, this time one of them returned on his own, avoiding my attempt to grab him. He was nothing but a blur when he picked up my mother and threw her to the ground. He slowed down as he bit a chunk out of her throat, stifling her last scream, and then spat it in my direction. I ran to her, but... and I remember his cold icy touch when he grabbed me and did the same to me. I never saw his face, but I remember the sound of his scream as he tried to get away. I grabbed him, and with a quick spread of my fingers dismembered him right there on the driveway. This is where it gets confusing. I was in and out of consciousness a few times, and I don't remember when the Nortons arrived. I could hear their voices as they were biting all over my legs, and I know they weren't the other two that carried my father off. Those were men, and they were large. One almost reminded me of Reginald Von Bell."

She sat there in silence staring at me. I couldn't tell if it was from shock or sadness, but which ever it was, it melted away her normally pleasant demeanor and left behind just a shell of herself, distraught. I was there with her, just a hundred times or more so. These were events that I lived, and had forgotten about for decades that now came rushing back after I was forced to relive that moment.

"I still remember nothing between then and my life with the Nortons, but I am wondering if there is a logical explanation for that."

Mrs. Tenderschott leaned forward and placed her hand on my knee. "What is it dear?" she asked compassionately.

"Time moves so slowly for us, maybe what I thought was just years was really decades." There was that stunned silence again, and I wondered if she would even understand. "Anyway, I know who I am now, so that helps," I said, attempting to sound happy and upbeat, but there was a downside that I couldn't ignore. "But I now know for sure that the Nortons were who turned me, and I am no closer to understanding why."

"You said you heard their voices," she got up from her chair and headed to her kitchen. "What did they say?" she asked just before she reached the door. Her feet shuffled, not her normal smooth stride. Her speech matched her walk when she stopped and stammered, "Do you want some coffee or tea? I need some." Her hands gripped nervously at her periwinkle blue dress.

"Well, I heard him complaining it wasn't working, and she answered repeating it has to, over and over. That was all I could make out." I sat there and thought about what they said and searched for any meaning other than the obvious one. There wasn't one, much to my disappointment. "I think they were talking about the process. They were biting me on my leg when they said it."

"What part of the leg?" she asked from beyond the door.

"Well..." I thought about where I felt the pain. "My thighs."

"That makes sense, they were probably going for the femoral artery. Better blood flow."

It made sense, but I was rather startled at how plainly she said it. Nonchalant, casual. Her voice held more emotions each time I complained to her about what Gwen had done to me today. "It still doesn't answer *the* question. Why?"

"Well, you now know who," she said coming back into the room.

"Yep," I agreed. "But not why. It still leaves two reasons." One was good, the other was the worst possible outcome.

Mrs. Tenderschott sat down, not in the chair that was positioned right in front of me, but in her easy chair across the room, next to the table with the doilies under the lamp. She sat back and looked upon me in a grandmotherly way. "Larissa, I will not ask you if it really matters. I know it does. My question to you though, what if you never find out? That is a very real possibility."

"It is." I tried not to show my disappointment outwardly. Steady and calm were my thoughts. I couldn't let her know it was a possibility I wasn't able to accept. I wasn't sure if it was a desire to avoid the topic or not, but I leaned forward and stood up to my feet. There was none of the wooziness that I had expected. "Thank you for helping me recover all my old memories. You have given me my life back."

"Oh dear, I am just sorry it took so long." She rose and walked across the room and gave me a hug, that I returned whole heartedly. "So, what are you going to do the rest of the day?"

"Not sure," I said, as I thought about the options. "I want to see Nathan, and tell him about my memories." I did and also wanted to talk about what happened last night. The normal warm smile returned to Mrs. Tenderschott's face at hearing that. "Then I am not sure. Normally on Halloween I would be reading something scary or watching scary movies with my mother... Marie Norton." Another memory from my childhood popped into my head. "When I was younger, the parents threw huge costume parties, but I was too young to attend, so I mostly stood at the top of the stairs and watched."

"Well, as you see, we don't exactly ignore the holiday here. There will be more later on in the day. How about this?" Her voice bounced with glee. "Why not get young Amy and bring her by later for some trick or treating. I have some goodies for her. I could cook some fresh cookies."

"That sounds like a great idea. Let me go see if I can find her."

"You do that," she giggled, and I sprinted out of her room and down the hall.

I was sprinting across the entry, and toward Mrs. Saxon's room, planning on seeing Nathan first and then coming back for Amy, priorities, and such, when I heard his voice call me. How he saw me? I wasn't sure. I was moving at my full speed. Maybe he just saw a blur and assumed. I slammed to a stop on the tiles. The soles of my shoes screeched on the tile.

"Hi." I said and waved. Then I folded my hands behind me. Nervous energy kept me from standing still as he walked down toward me. I twisted back and forth, looking up at him from time to time.

"I just came looking for you," he said.

"For little old me?" I asked coyly as the abundance of energy I felt inside attempted to bubble out. When he finally reached me, I put my hand out, and he stood and stared at it curiously. To get his attention, I wiggled it a little, and he eventually reached out and took it. "Hi, Larissa Dubois," I said in my worst southern accent I could muster. Scarlett O'Hara had to be rolling in her grave somewhere. Now my love for that movie made sense.

Nathan worked to keep a straight face as he introduced himself back, "Nathan Saxon, nice to meet you."

I couldn't contain it anymore, "I know who I am. I know all of it. Mrs. Tenderschott did this thing with two photos, and I remember it all –"

"Whoa... slow down. What happened?" He asked.

What I had just told him must have been nothing but a blur to him. It wasn't much more than that to myself, so I forced myself to slow down. An excruciating exercise at that. "Mrs. Tenderschott broke through and I remember my childhood." I said rather slowly, and I probably should have used the same speed when my hands grabbed his cheeks, with a light slap. "I remember my parents. My real parents Nathan. I remember it all." I spied one of the jack-o'-lanterns floating in the corner of my eyes and felt my lips curl up. "Watch this." I pointed up to the jack-o'-lantern, who then said, "Hello Nathan," and started singing the song 'One-eyed-one-horned-flying-purple-people-eater.'

"Holy crap!" Nathan started laughing as the orange orb with a toothy grin carved into it started a second chorus.

We were no longer alone. Pam stood on the stairs dancing to the concert, and Martin and Dan were descending the stairs on the boy's side.

"That's new," Dan said.

"That's all Larissa," Nathan proudly said, and hearing him brag made me beam inside.

"Way to go there Larissa." Rob slapped me on the shoulder as they walked around us toward the door.

"It's raining," Nathan reminded him.

"Yep, but we still need to stretch our legs," remarked Robert, and out the door they went.

Now Apryl and Maria had joined Pam's dance party. "Hey Larissa, what other songs does it know?" Apryl called down.

I gave a flick of the wrist shutting off our orange jukebox. "I got a few more tricks up my sleeves, but I will save those for later." I grabbed Nathan and pulled him into a tight embrace. Something I had needed since the night before, but that was not the only reason. I whispered into his ear, "I remember everything. All my abilities. Everything my mother and father showed me. What I learned in the coven there. Everything. Is there someplace we can go talk?"

His next move was an instinctual grab of my hand and yanked me up the stairs. There was only one destination in that direction, and I felt silly for not thinking about it first. In my mind I had thought about the pool deck or a walk in the woods with him, but whereas I didn't mind the rain, he probably would have. Though I would have to say seeing that black t-shirt soaked and hugging against him wouldn't be a bad look.

"So, I guess we couldn't use your room?" I asked as he closed the door on mine.

"You remember things?"

"Not just things," I said as I danced around him. A few little twists of my wrists had the pillow and sheet from my bed dancing with me, like a cotton conga line. At least they had purpose now, I never slept. "I remember everything." My arms wrapped around his neck as I swung around him. His left arm wrapped around me and pulled me close. "I remember everything," my lips whispered just a hair's width from his, then they touched. I kissed him like I have never kissed anyone before, and this was something I was sure of now since I could remember that I hadn't ever kissed anyone before Nathan. I didn't hold back, and let every inch of relief and happiness that had built up inside of me explode out to him. A weight had been lifted and feeling how he kissed me back took away another weight. We were good now.

I finally let him go, and resumed my dance around him. He settled back on the bed, stunned, which I hoped was from the kiss. "I remember it all. My parents and my childhood. Every moment, memories are running back to me, like the smell of our lavender fields on late summer nights. Oh... oh...," I rushed over and jumped on the bed next to him, losing my concentration causing the dancing bed-man to fall to the floor. "Lying in the fields with my mother, looking up at the stars, as we each tried to quiz the other on quick spells. I was still learning at that time, but she could cause the air to sparkle around her fingers, like fireflies. My favorite was causing a small breeze to pick up some of the purple flowers and dance above us, which I completely controlled. My own purple ballet. Oh... did you know I used to take ballet? My mother had a teacher come out three times a week to teach me, her name was... Mrs. Banks, yep, that was her name. Tuesdays, Wednesdays, and Fridays. We would use the parlor to practice in," I rattled on and could see Nathan's expression as he tried to keep up. "Sorry, I am talking too fast, it's just everything is rushing back at me so fast now," I realized I just did it again, and took a beat before trying to explain again. Slowly I said, "I feel like I am me again."

He grabbed me with both hands and pulled me in, wrapping his arms the rest of the way around me. "This is great. I haven't seen you so happy before."

So that was what this feeling was. It had been so long. "I really am," I whispered back. "I have so much to tell you about, well... me."

"That is great. I can't wait to hear about it. I just have one question."

"What?" I asked in great anticipation.

"Do does the old you still like me?" He asked with an uneven smile, and I hoped my mind wasn't playing tricks on me, but I noticed a small tad of concern. Wanting to stretch this out a bit more, just for fun, I sat back on the bed next to him and just looked at him as stoic as I could. Those few seconds seemed like a lifetime, and I felt I showed a lot of self-control just sitting there. I let my hands sit in my lap and twiddled my fingers together nervously. That part wasn't an act. Anticipation of what was next was killing me, and I needed to let my nervous energy out somehow. I just wasn't sure who would break first. Would it be me that couldn't hold it in any longer, or would he give up? Not that I wanted him to, I just thought my next action would be better, more like one of those perfect moments, if he almost did before he was saved. Inside I was screaming, *"Dang Man! Come On!"*

When I was about to give up I saw it. His shoulders slumped and with him his hopes. That was when I sprung my trap and leaped on top of him, sending him crashing down on my bed, with me straddling him, my hands held his above his head. "What do you think big boy?" I asked, and then leaned down and kissed him again. I felt his answer on the inside of my thigh, and sensation that stirred deep inside of me. I let the rest of my body rest on him, and gave him back his hands, which quickly found the small of my back.

We laid there and kissed our problems away, while Nathan's hands made a few cautious explorations to reinforce the feeling of our future together. I was glad he was being as gentle as he was. There were feelings inside that surprised me, and required some effort to resist. The more he explored the more intense those feelings were, and the tougher to ignore.

"So, I guess that means you found all the answers you needed." He whispered.

The shove back from Nathan must have been some kind of instinctual reaction. I hadn't thought about doing that, nor had I thought about holding him there at arm's length, and he appeared to be as confused as I was. "Not really, there are still a few questions." I got off of him and sat at the foot of my bed while he sat up.

"But you said, you remembered everything?" Nathan sounded as confused as he looked.

"Well, almost everything," I corrected. He was right, I had said that, and a heavy dread settled in, joining my quickly deflated mood as I remembered the one last question, and what the topic caused the last time it came up. There was no keeping it from him, not this time. I had already made that mistake once. "There are still questions."

The look in his eyes was my kryptonite. "What questions?," he asked. His tone slicing through what little remained of the party atmosphere that had filled the room.

"About the Nortons." I bit my lower lip and looked away not wanting to see the reaction I knew was coming. The fall from the top was always worse than the fall from the middle or the bottom, and for the first time in a while I felt like I was at the top. Now I was free falling back to that place I was last night, needing someone to save me because all I ever did was dig the hole deeper. One of my many talents. The problem was, based on the frown on Nathan's face and his stern eyes, he didn't appear to be ready to throw me a life vest or a rope. So, all I could do was put my talent to work. "All I know is they were the ones that turned me, but I don't know why –"

Nathan exploded off the bed, "Isn't that enough. They did it. That should tell you all you need to know."

"But the why is what the council is worried about," I interrupted him, talking over him, attempting to be heard over his rather loud protest. When he stopped and turned around. "I need to know why, for them, and for me."

"To hell with the council!" He stormed to the door. "Why can't you just leave things alone and move forward. Life is in front of us, but you stay so focused on the past, you are ignoring the future."

I got up off the bed and walked over to where he stood at the door with his back to me. When I reached him, I let my hand trace down the ripples of his back. He didn't move or recoil away from my touch, which was a good thing. "I am focused on the future Nathan, I am. I just need to clear up some details first, then everything will be perfect."

"Yea, sure," he said unconvincingly. I felt the muscles in his back and arm flex as he reached for the door handle. When I heard it click, my hopes fell off the cliff. "I have a few things to do today."

"Okay," I said breathlessly. I wanted him to stay, but couldn't think of a way to make him besides physically restraining him, and I wasn't ruling that out. If he wouldn't stay, I would need to see him later, not seeing him again today was unacceptable. I thought hard for an excuse, then it came to me. "Mrs. Tenderschott asked me to bring Amy by to trick-or-treat later, why don't you come with me?" I didn't ask, I suggested, and hoped he would take it.

"Sure," he remarked with a lack of enthusiasm and opened the door. At least I got a "see you then," before he closed the door.

The rest of the day disproved the theory that I always had that time moved quickly for those like myself. When you could live forever, what were a few hours? Well, I found out that not all hours were equal. Yes, they were all sixty minutes, but the minutes of these few hours clicked by slower, and no it wasn't because I remembered a time control spell, though I had one. I also had one that made it go faster, but I can't use it on myself. Just the anticipation of seeing Nathan again, and the worry about what was going through his mind, was the secret to make the afternoon drag.

I completed all my homework, even a history paper that wasn't due for several days, and then did a little inventory of all the things that had changed in my room since I had returned. My favorite lamp was still there, but the bed was a little different style. No longer a sleigh bed, but a four post bed, like the one I had in New Orleans. Even the clothes in the closet had changed, slightly. My jeans and t-shirts were still there, but there were a few longer skirts hanging there, thankfully nothing like what Gwen would wear. I was still undecided about their presence. They were what I used to wear. The cotton grey one was one of my favorites, but that was then, and that then was a long time ago. The coven picked them for a reason, so there had to be some interest in them still in me.

The books on the floor still lay there stacked, taunting me. The way to the answer I needed was inside, I now knew enough to know that for sure. I also knew enough to know Edward was absolutely right about his warnings. This was way too advanced for me, or really anyone I had ever known, and I knew some powerful witches back in my day.

Rain pattered against my window harder than it had earlier. Not that it would have deterred me from heading outside. I quite enjoyed the rain, but I was tired of bouncing around the walls of my room and my own thoughts, even though much of those thoughts were wonderful memories that brought smiles to my face, there was still the heartbreak that overshadowed it all. I wanted something to do, so I made my way out and down the stairs, on a mission. I just needed to find a way past the barricade to that mission.

Knocking loudly didn't seem to work. Even banging brought no one. An attempt that I was rather scared to do, not wanting to attract the attention of Mrs. Parrish who might put the damper on my plans. Waiting for someone to come out was fruitless. There were only three of them in there, and who knew when anyone would. Then I remembered a trick, a way my mother and I used to talk to each other from different rooms. Remembering that Amy once talked about seeing the pool out of her window, I knew what side of the hall she was on, and then spoke the words while thinking of her, "hear me."

My voice was just a whisper, but it echoed in the entry. I knew from experience that no one else would hear anything except who I was talking to. "Hey girl, come out to the door. There is something we need to do."

It wasn't long until a very confused Amy opened the door. She looked out, just sticking her head out of the crack of the door, obviously not sure what to expect. I bent down to her eye level so she would see my smiling face.

"How... how did you do that?" she asked.

"It's a witch thing," I said and winked.

"Wow." She opened the door the rest of the way and stepped out on the landing.

"Why don't we go find you a costume for Halloween?" She stood there wide eyed, and I wondered if she even knew what Halloween was, so I asked. "You do know what that is, right?"

"Yes," Amy said wearily, and it wasn't more than a few moments before I knew why. "Where can we find one?"

Now that was a good question. I had thought getting her out was going to be the biggest obstacle. Now that she was here, she couldn't take me to her room, and I couldn't take her to mine. I had bothered Mrs. Tenderschott enough today, plus I wanted Amy's costume to be a surprise when we stopped by later. There were tons of doors to choose from up and down the halls, but this wasn't the right time to go exploring. An idea percolated up the top, and it came with a benefit that nothing else would. "I know a place. Follow me."

We walked down the stairs and were about to head down the hall when I heard Tera call my name. I turned around to see her and Lisa coming out of the door of the witches hall.

"Where you two going?," she asked.

"We have to get Amy a costume for Halloween."

Right then, Tera waved her hand over her head and turned into a traditional pop-culture view of a witch. Dark dress, hat, broom, and green skin. "Like my costume little girl," she cackled.

Amy grabbed my leg, and I felt the little girl shake her head no. Tera had to have seen Amy's reaction. She quickly switched back to her normal appearance of jeans and a dark blue sweater. "Sorry about that Amy."

I reached and rubbed Amy's back to comfort her, and felt her grip tighten on me.

"Anyway, why don't you join us for our own version of a Halloween party at ten tonight. In the ritual room."

"A party?" I asked, not knowing what to expect around here. I knew what I had seen in movies and television, but somehow I didn't think she meant bobbing for apples or anything like that.

"Yep, Lisa will use a Ouija board to summon some of her friends. She has done it the last four years, it's great."

"You really should come by," added Tera.

"Okay, I might do that," I agreed, not being completely committal. I didn't know what the day held, but had some hopes that I would spend time with Nathan working whatever this was out. "Well, we have a costume to find." I reached down and grabbed Amy's hand and continued down the hall. She held on with a death grip, and hearing Tera cackle behind us, "I will get you my pretty, and your little dog too," didn't help.

At Mrs. Saxon's door I was unsure who would answer, and how I was going to even ask what I needed to. There was a bit of relief when she answered instead of Nathan. Not that I didn't want to see him, but I wasn't ready to deal with that yet, especially not with Amy here. "Sorry to disturb you Mrs. Saxon, but it is Halloween, and this little girl doesn't have a costume, and..." Mrs. Saxon seemed more than a little perplexed at my long-winded request. "Seeing that she is a shapeshifter, and I am what I am, there really isn't anywhere we can go to look for one that I know for sure we are both able to enter except, well, here. Could we use the room upstairs?"

The perplexed look disappeared, and a motherly smile replaced it. She backed away from the door to let us in. "But of course. I do seem to remember a bunch of costumes up there the last time I was in it. By all means." When we walked in, she approached and gave me a quick hug. A shocking display of affection that she had never done before. While she embraced me she whispered into my ear. "I heard. Congratulations."

News traveled fast in this place.

Amy and I walked up the marble steps and stopped at the familiar door. She looked up at me, again looking confused and concerned. "What's wrong?"

"I don't remember any costumes in there Larissa." She shook her head as she spoke, and she was correct. There weren't any when I was there either, but at the time neither of us needed one.

"That's okay. I have a feeling they are in there now. You just need to think about what you want to be. Can you do that?" She nodded eagerly with her gapped smile on full display.

I kept the thought of costumes for a little girl in my mind when I turned the handle opening the door. The room, just like the rest of the coven, didn't disappoint. The room was no longer a bedroom. It was the largest closet I had ever seen, and everything was a costume of some sort. Amy ran in, letting go of my hand screaming "Wow." I had to agree.

Over the next couple of hours Amy tried on everything from a 20s flapper dress, something that I had seen firsthand several times, to a full body bear costume, which was so full of stuffing Amy found it fun to run and jump on me with it, sending us both to the floor laughing. It felt good to laugh.

I let her pick all on her own, even though I tried to sway her to the ballet tutu and slippers that reminded me of my own from when I was her age. It felt great to have those memories again.

"I can just turn into something," Amy said, as she ripped through another rack of costumes.

"I know you can, but isn't this more fun?"

"Yea," she said, scarves and hats flew in the air from the box she plundered through. When she stood up, she looked around the room and stopped. That was when I saw the look. The look that told me she had found exactly what she wanted to be. Slowly she walked toward it, and I finally saw the focus of her attention. A pink dress with fairy wings on the back, complete with a gold crown and wand, of course. There was no hesitation when she grabbed it and ran behind the screen to change. She squealed twice, and I recognized that squeal. It was pure joy. Just like the joy I saw when she emerged spinning around. It was perfect, well almost.

"Come here," I said, and grabbed her hand, guiding her dance to bring her in front of me, and more importantly in front of a mirror. That brought on more dancing and admiring of herself in the reflection. She reached down and pulled the skirt out as she spun. I grabbed her shoulders and held her still for just a moment. "You look like the perfect fairy princess, but there is something else you need that would complete this." I removed the crown from her head and then used my hands to try different hair styles on her. This was something I wasn't good at. I mean, I knew what looked good, but had no clue how to get it there. My hair had some natural body to it, which allowed me to get away with not doing anything to it. "Here, let me try this."

I waved my hand over her head, allowing my fingers to run through her hair in a circle, while I thought about how I wanted it to look. Slowly the strands followed the picture in my mind and curls formed along the lengths of her hair. Her blonde locks fell down, wavy, along her shoulders. It was perfect, and I put the tiara back on top. Princess Amy squealed again as she leapt at the mirror to get a closer look.

"So, what is going on in here?" We both turned to see Nathan standing in the doorway, black jeans and black t-shirt, and the rest of him an image of perfection. Amy ran to him. Then Nathan knelt down and bowed his head. "Princess Amy."

She wrapped her arms around his neck, and he picked her up with ease. "Your chariot, your majesty." He carried her back into the room.

"It's Halloween, she needed a costume," I said.

"But of course." He leaned in and gave me a quick kiss, causing a "Ooooo" from Amy. I stuck my tongue out at her childishly, and she returned the gesture. Maybe they were right, she was my mini-me. I could deal with that.

"Mrs. Tenderschott has invited us to trick-or-treat, why don't you join us?"

Amy didn't give Nathan a chance to decline before she buried her head into the side of his neck and begged, "Please Nathan. Please come with me."

I added my own beg with pouty lips to it, "Please Nathan."

"All right," Nathan agreed, much to the pleasure of Amy who hugged him around his neck and screamed. "On one condition." I didn't see this coming, and I was afraid of what that condition was. Even though his pause lasted only a second it gave me enough time to imagine him asking me to drop my search into the past. There were no doubts circling in me that was it. What else could it be? Then he surprised me. "You go with me to Lisa's Halloween spectacle."

"Oh. Sure, I was planning to go anyway," I said casually, almost like it was an afterthought and not letting on at all how relieved I felt. His smile added to my relief. He then turned and headed to the door with the pink clad princess Amy in his arms. I trailed behind by a few feet. The only thing missing from this almost perfect family photo was a bag or one of those crappy plastic pumpkins in Amy's hand ready for the loot she would collect throughout the night. Back when I was her age, it was mostly just parties at our home, or the home of our parents with tons of food and homemade decadence. I imagined that was what Amy might experience tonight. I doubted Mrs. Tenderschott had a bowl of candy. She had mentioned cookies, but if I learned one thing around this place, never expect anything, just go with it.

"Can I go with you to that thing?" I heard Amy ask Nathan.

"What thing was that?" he asked as we exited the door. Nathan didn't even acknowledge his mother, sitting on the couch, but I noticed. It was like an odd glimpse into the future. One which I wasn't sure she would truly accept, until now, or I hoped I was reading that right.

"The Lisa thing," Amy said.

"Oh, Larissa?" Called Mrs. Saxon before I had stepped out into the hall. I turned, back to her now thinking I was wrong. "The last of the council are leaving tomorrow, but they would like another few minutes with you, say 10 o'clock?"

"Okay," I agreed. It wasn't like I had a choice.

"Have fun tonight." She waved, and I joined Nathan and Amy out in the hallway.

"Oh no. That is too scary for you. I almost wet my pants last year," replied Nathan.

Amy looked back over his shoulder at me, and asked, "Please?"

"You heard him. If it's too scary for him, it's probably too scary for me too. So, I don't think it's a good idea."

Disappointed she turned back around just as Nathan put her down on the ground. "Time for you to walk squirt." She grabbed his hand and then reached back for mine. Other than the first time, she never winced at my cold touch.

13

Mrs. Tenderschott didn't disappoint. Not that I expected her to. She never had, and I doubt she ever would. She had fresh cookies and milk out and ready for Amy when we arrived. Enough to give the girl a stomachache, though I doubt she would let that happen before she walked her back to her room.

Nathan and I left to head to what Nathan had called Lisa's Halloween Spectacle. He had refused to tell me what it was. Only saying, last year he about wet his pants. We arrived at the room, which I would be lying if I said I wasn't a little hesitant to enter. The two times before hadn't been that pleasant. Even Nathan paused at the door and let his thumb rub against the top of my hand. I guess I had squeezed it a little. He opened it, and we passed through the black curtain that always hung just inside the door. A cool breeze blasted at us as he pushed through. The room itself had a layer of fog above the floor, but the skylight was clear, allowing the moon to cast shadows everywhere. Those stupid cherubs up on the walls still appeared to taunt me. Now I could set them ablaze, or yank them from the wall, but I decided better of it, for now. That may change, and I gave them a look to make that clear.

A dark cloaked figure approached us from out of the fog. Its presence sent us both stepping back. Under the cloak was the hideous face of a green ghoul. I was pulling Nathan behind me and readying myself to step up to the threat when I heard Marcia's voice ask, "What? No costumes?" She reached and pulled her mask off, and I dropped my hands down. I am not sure if she knew just how close she was to being thrown across the room. With my reactions, she would have never seen it coming.

"Costumes? You didn't say we needed costumes." I pulled Nathan forward and looked at him.

"I forgot," he said sheepishly.

"No worries." I thought for a second, and then remembered the costume I saw earlier. That gave me exactly what I needed to be, and what he needed to be as well. I grabbed Nathan's arms and pressed them firmly down against his side. "Stand still."

"Okay," he nervously agreed.

I put my hand over his head and slowly drew it down his front. Inch by inch, his clothes changed. The t-shirt and jeans were replaced by a beige cotton suit, white shirt, and wide striped tie. His sneakers were now leather laced up loafers. When I was done with him, I turned it on myself, which was much quicker. A silver flapper dress, my size, with a pillhat, and black heels. Nathan pulled at his sleeves, somewhat admiring his new threads. I grabbed his arm, and looped mine through it, and introduced ourselves to Marcia. "Jay Gatsby and Daisy Buchanan, it's nice to meet you."

She laughed, and Nathan leaned down to me and asked, "From the movie?"

Now he had me laughing. "No silly, the book. It was one of my favorites. Plus, this is the timeframe I grew up in." I expected a reaction at hearing that, but he reached over and placed his hand on top of the hand that was looped through his arm, and led me in through the fog. Other figures appeared in the fog as we moved in closer to the center. One dressed in a teenage sized princess costume, much like Amy was wearing, moved to the other side of the room from Nathan and myself. She didn't have to take the white mask off her face for me to know that was Gwen.

"Let's have a seat, like the others," instructed Nathan. This forced us to descend into the fog, or so I thought. Once we were seated, we were below it, and I saw Marcia, Tera, and Lynn seated in a circle, with Lisa in the center. An eerie déjà vu moment, but this time Lisa had something with her. A Ouija board. Not that I believe she needed it. Her hands already positioned on the planchette.

She looked up, and made eye contact with each of us, before tossing the black hood she wore off of her head. "Okay, I need everyone to remain completely quiet while I try to make contact." Her hands left the planchette, and were crossed on her lap while she sat up straight.

"Are there spirits here with us now?" Her voice echoed up to the skylight, and her hands never moved from her lap, but the planchette shook ever so slightly. Now knowing the capability in the room, I had to be a little of a skeptic, but I wasn't going to be the one to spoil the fun.

"If you are here. Give us a sign." The white planchette flew across the black board from one side to the other. Lisa waited for a few seconds to let it settle down before she asked, "Was that you?" Right on cue, it moved to the yes on the top corner of the board. A chill fell over the room, and a breeze tossed my hair and pillbox hat. After it moved on, I felt my hat still moving, and reached up to secure it. It was then that I noticed a pair of eyes peering at me from behind her white mask. Even as I grabbed the hat, I felt a force pushing at it. *Two can play at that game.* A clang echoed in the room when Gwen's tiara fell of her head to the floor.

Lisa smirked, and warned us, "Okay you two." Everyone's eyes shifted between Gwen and me. Lisa focused back on the board, and asked another question. "How about showing yourself to us?"

Vapors formed around us and swirled. They had forms to themselves, but not like people. Just shapes that moved around us and in and out of each of us. There were dozens of them dancing around us. As each passed, so did a cold spot, sending shivers through Nathan.

"Would one of you like to speak to us?," she asked, but nothing moved on the board, and Lisa explained, "Sometimes they are a little shy about talking to us, or don't even know how they can." Then she asked, "How about one of you just telling us your name?"

This appeared to be a question this spirit had no problem in answering. The planchette moved from letter to letter, with each of us calling each one it paused over. "J." "A." "M." "E." "S."

"Okay, James. Nice to meet you. Do you live here in the coven?"

In what would have been the perfectly creepy dramatic moment in a movie, the planchette sped to the "YES," sending a few gasps in the group of girls. I even thought I heard Nathan gasp. I was still skeptical about this.

"I always had suspicions that this coven was haunted," remarked Lisa.

"Ask if he is cute," requested Tera with a giggle.

"There you go, you got a boyfriend," commented Marcia, with an elbow to the side of her friend sitting next to her.

There was no slap back or denial from Tera, just a snarky shot at one of their own, "Only if Gwen doesn't take him first." This drew a stare and a head tilt from their pink queen.

I was about to add my own when I felt Nathan's warm breath on my cheek. "Let it go." I did just that.

"All right, James. It appears you are talking to us, even though you said you wouldn't. Why don't you show yourself? Since we all live here together, let us see you."

The planchette shook on the board, almost as if whoever were controlling it was uncertain of what to answer.

"We won't hurt you. You are safe with us," Lisa said, directing her voice up toward the rafters of the room, but the planchette still shook in the center of the board. "If you live here in the coven, perhaps you were a witch like us. Were you?"

The uncertainty disappeared and the white triangle shot to the "YES."

"Then you are safe with us. We are just like you. I am one who can interact with your world. If you want, you can use me as your vessel."

"This is where it gets good," Nathan whispered into my ear. I felt his arm hooking me around my waist, and I leaned into his warmth.

A white vapor appeared in front of us and crept toward Lisa. When it touched her, her eyes shut, and her body shook. When Lisa opened her eyes again, there was nothing but the whites showing, and her long dark hair flowed behind her. Her blank eyes looked around at each of us. "So, you are all witches?" asked an unfamiliar male voice.

"Yes," Marcia answered.

Lisa's blank eyes focused on Nathan, and I felt him swallow hard. "He's not. He's human," said Marcia. Then the blank orbs focused on me for a moment before moving on.

"James, when did you live in this coven?" asked Tera.

"Many many years ago. I first came to this coven in 1883," the voice said. It had an eerie edge to it that echoed in the room.

"Someone older than you," whispered Nathan. A comment he would pay for later. I wasn't sure if James could hear Nathan or not, but Lisa's freaky glare returned to me.

"Were you an orphan, like us?" asked Marcia.

"Yes, I was. My parents were killed by the Council of Mages for violating our laws. They spared me and allowed me to attend this coven to learn the proper ways."

That was an answer I really didn't need to hear. His continued focus, which only moved slightly when answering someone's question, was already making me feel uncomfortable.

"Was Mrs. Tenderschott an instructor here?" Tera asked, half laughing.

"I don't remember that name. Master Lewis was in charge of the coven when I was here. He taught English and defensive spells and responses to threats. Master Reynolds taught science and potions. Master Tyson handled math, and our combat training."

There was a slight murmur amongst us all at hearing his response. Even I muttered, "combat" under my breath. We had nothing like that now. James, I mean, Lisa appeared to tense up, and again stared straight through me. It was intense and uncomfortable, and I leaned into Nathan harder than before. Not for protection, but to convey a vulnerable and non-threatening image, but it didn't work. If anything, it brought more attention.

"Was Edward the librarian?" Nathan asked.

"Yes, he was. Is it still so?"

"Oh yes. Edward is still here–," Marcia started.

"You are different," James interrupted. Lisa's body now leaning forward in my direction.

"Lisa, I think it is time for your friend to go," Marcia said, sounding a bit frightened. The others were no longer sitting relaxed in the circle. Each tense, looking ready to pounce.

There was no response from Lisa. Her body sat there leaning in my direction with those empty white eyes burning a hole right through me. I swung my legs behind me ready to leap, and Nathan knew it. He removed his arm from around me. The vapor exited Lisa and was on top of me before I knew it. I felt its cold presence, and lost sight of the room, only hearing the voices of my fellow witches exclaim, "Lisa!"

"You are different," stated James. "Vampire!" His voice exclaimed, as he reached toward me. Right then, everything else went black, and I heard another voice.

"Happy Halloween Larissa." Images of that alley way and Reginald killing Mr. Norton flashed in my head. Then a dirty cobble stone street, still wet from the afternoon rain. The flicking of the gas lamps chased away the darkness with each dance back and forth. His voice, called from behind us. "I see you." My mother's arm wrapping around me as we kept walking. Jean St. Claire's pale face glistened in the darkness across from us. My father's voice said, "No you don't," just as a streetcar clattered by, its bell sounding as it went by.

When it passed, Jean was left on the sidewalk, continuing to look in our direction, but unable to see us thanks to a spell from my father. "You hid then, but you can't hide now," he cackled, and a shriveled hand reached out of the darkness toward me, with that same red ring that I had seen many times in his little visits. It got closer, and I had to force myself to remember I was in mixed company, and couldn't respond. I hoped my lack of participation would frustrate him.

There was no way to know for sure, but I was quickly released, back into the room. The white vapor still in front of me, but now being held back by two other vapors, with Lisa standing behind it. She was attempting to put the genie back in the bottle.

"Sorry about that Larissa," Lisa said, and she pulled back with both hands sending the vapors up toward the ceiling where they disappeared.

"No worries. Everyone deserves one good scare on Halloween," I remarked with a crooked smile, and stood up, almost laughing. No one knew what had really happened, and I wanted to keep it that way.

"Last year was Tera's turn. I let James mess with her, and even possess her for a few moments."

"Yea, no thank you on a repeat visit there Lisa. That was horrifying." I didn't doubt it was based on the expression on Tera's face.

"So, it was the same spirit?," I asked, still trying to recover from my own haunting visit.

"James is one I met the first night I was here. He is harmless and to be honest enjoys doing this kind of stuff. He was a necromancer like me."

14

To say I trudged down to my morning meeting with the council would do a disservice to anyone who had ever trudged anywhere before. I am sure they languished their trip as much as I did, but I literally had to drag myself down the stairs. The enthusiasm that Gwen had about the council's presence here in our coven was not something I shared. Not that we shared a lot between us. I assumed it was in the same room as my previous meetings, and also the scene of the last night's entertainment, which Jean interfered with, leaving me with a bad taste in my mouth.

The room looked much the same as it did last night sans the layer of fog that hung just above the floor. Without anyone telling me to do so, not that there was anyone else there, I moved to the center of the room and waited, expecting the council members to appear from the shadows as they did before. The wait gave me a moment to put my plan together to get those cherubs, and I think they knew it. Two of them appeared horrified while the other one appeared to give me the middle-finger. A gesture I was more than happy to return. Though I should have checked my surroundings first. That wasn't one of my finest moments with an audience behind me.

Mrs. Wintercrest coughed behind me, and I turned around more than a little embarrassed. She was not pleased. Neither was Miss Roberts or Mr. Signorn, or the blonde standing behind them, Mrs. Stephanie Morrison. A frail and pale thing that looked like she belonged more with my other group than the witches.

"I hope we aren't interrupting anything." Even though she was shorter, she still managed to look down her nose at me when she spoke.

"No. Not at all."

"Good, before we departed, we wanted to check to see if you had remembered anything of interest recently." She strode around me, dragging her black cape behind her. "I understand you had a little breakthrough."

"Yes ma'am. I did."

She stopped and turned on her heel right in front of me. "Well then child, tell us what you recall about the Nortons and what they were preparing you for." Her icy blue eyes could have cut steel.

"They prepared me for many things, but not in the way you are thinking. It was a loving family environment, and they taught me about the world and how to live in it. Much in the same way I am being taught here, and..." I raised my voice, which caused her brow to respond in kind. "The same way Mrs. Paulette and Mr. French and Mr. Alva taught me in the Orleans' Coven. You might say, they were grooming me to be the best witch I could be, maybe even a powerful one." I opened my eyes wide so she could see the full black orbs glaring back at her.

She was not amused. "Tsk. Tsk," she moved around me again. "I see you have a bit of a rebellious streak in you, and it is not an attractive feature," she sniped from behind me. "You are to let Miss Roberts into your mind once again, so we can find the truth."

My body jerked around before my mind could think my actions through. It was not a controlled movement either. This was a vampire movement, just a flash in their eyes that caught all of them off guard. Hands were raised up, not quite ready to attack, but undecided on what to do next. "And if I refuse?"

"That would be unwise," Mrs. Wintercrest said. Her eyes slowly raised to meet mine.

"And disrespectful," Mr. Signorn added, weakly, from several feet behind her. "She is your Council Supreme, you must respect and obey her."

I didn't look back at him. Instead, my glare stayed on Mrs. Wintercrest, and what I could see of Miss Roberts behind her. She didn't seem eager to step forward. Unfortunately for her, her Council Supreme had other plans. "Sarah, would you do the honors?"

She hesitated, before she was asked again, "Sarah." This time sternly.

Miss Roberts' movements didn't match the stern order she received. Mine didn't either, but I let a hint of my fangs show as she moved toward me tentatively, with her hands up.

"How do you want to do this?" I asked, maybe a little gruffer than I should have. I was also taking more enjoyment in her reaction than I should have.

"Don't even try it," She warned, with a shake in her voice that appeared to extend to her hands.

Calmly I said, "I mean, how do you want to check my memories? Is there a potion you want me to drink, or maybe a spell you want to try?"

She didn't respond but stepped closer another slow step. Her hands reached up for my face. Their movement was timid and tentative, and jerked back when I remarked, "It's okay, I don't bite." I thought I heard a snicker from further back in the room, but didn't recognize the voice. It wasn't Miss Roberts. There was no mistaking that. She had a complete deer caught in the headlights look in her eyes. I apologized, "Sorry." It still had a little sarcastic edge. Her hands moved forward again, and I braced myself for what I knew was coming. I had never performed this, or experienced it, but I had seen it a few times. At least that was the memory that was coming back.

Like I saw my father do twice, Miss Roberts pressed her hands on either side of my head. Her figures trembled as they searched for the spot. When she finally found it, I instantly felt her presence in my head. Unlike before, the room around us didn't fade away. I just felt memories coming back, and I let them flow. Even the ones I hadn't seen yet myself. There was no way I was going to give them any reason to believe I was holding anything back. She had to feel I wasn't. What I knew from our shared state was she felt overwhelmed by the flood of memories, and I didn't slow anything down for her. Why should I be the only one like that?

The slideshow of my past ran in fast forward until the day of my attack. It was only then that it slowed down. Not for her benefit. I could not have cared less if she needed me to or not. I needed it to. More details of that moment were filling in that I needed to see. That also meant I would experience them again, and she would too. Every hit. Every slash. Every bite. I wanted to see if I could see the faces of those attacking me, just to see if either of the Nortons were involved, but I struggled to maintain concentration on the details. My joined condition with Miss Roberts made sure I felt what she felt, and she was going through this attack for the first time. Every bite tore her to the core. If I was having trouble focusing on the images that flowed by, she found it impossible. Her own pain blocked any kind of comprehension.

When the images passed on, I felt her relief. The show quickly moved from hearing the Norton's voices to the day I woke up in their house, and then through the mundane day after day routine. The detail and familiarity of each of those brought a tear to my eye. How I would love to return to those days.

Miss Roberts released her grip, and she backed away, staring at the floor with each step. Mrs. Wintercrest looked on eagerly beside them. Her mouth agape, appearing to ask a question without a sound.

"She remembers it all, and just like we thought, the Nortons were the ones that turned her," she looked up and leered in my direction, but avoided eye contact as she moved back to her spot behind Mrs. Wintercrest.

"Then, our fears are true," Mrs. Wintercrest said. She looked around at everyone in the room.

I erupted, "No, they are not." There was a primal edge to my voice that startled everyone, including myself. I pulled it together before I spoke again. "All we know for sure is they were the ones who turned me, which I kind of already figured out. Nothing in my memory tells you why, and YOU..." I felt my tenuous grip on my emotions slipping. It slipped further when a finger jerked up to point at Miss Sarah Roberts. "YOU saw my life with them, so YOU know what it was like."

She shied away from looking at me, and instead looked pasr me into an empty, less threatening, corner of the room. "I saw nothing that told me why they turned you, so one can only assume..."

That word caused my body to twitch, and in an instant I was right in front of her. Miss Roberts gulped, and small beads of sweat developed on her face. The primal thumping that gave her and everyone else in the room life were now a drumroll. Well not all, there was one in the room who was still calm, and I didn't know who or where they were yet.

"I... I...," she tried to answer, but a dry mouth robbed her of the ability to talk. She swallowed hard, tried again. "I saw them turn her, but saw nothing that said why."

Hearing the truth come from her mouth backed me down a few levels, but the revelation was met with a rather perturbed reaction by Mrs. Wintercrest, who turned away from her fellow council member. "Well, that proves nothing Miss Norton. We will be in contact with you." With that, she led the others out, leaving me standing there in the room. They left through the curtains and for a second I thought I was alone, but I still felt the regular thumping of a heart. The one that stayed level and steady the whole time. Its source approached from behind me, and I readied myself for its arrival.

"It was nice to see someone standup to them." I recognized the voice from my earlier meeting with the council as Master Benjamin Thomas. I relaxed and turned in his direction. He emerged out of the shadows of the far corner, black eye makeup, nail polish, and all. "They spend so much time on top of that pedestal, I am sure that fall more than bruised them, but they had it coming." He kept walking past me and toward the door. "I will watch your future with great interest Miss Dubois. Great interest. Enjoy learning about your past." With that, he was gone through the curtain.

15

Time marched on with what appeared to be some level of normalcy for the next few weeks. Of course, around here normal was relative. It was basically classes, classes, and more classes, but now I really enjoyed them. The witches only classes that is. My normal schoolwork was still the same, and history was still a boring struggle for me. The recent unlocking of my memory opened the flood gate that held back my magical abilities. Most of what Mrs. Saxon, Mr. Helms, and Mrs. Tenderschott were teaching me now was mostly a refresher and I had it mastered on either the first or second attempt. Much to the displeasure of Gwen who didn't like my sudden improvement in capabilities. Her attempts to mess with me ramped up proportionately with my own strength. I guess our truce was now officially over.

Jack tried to explain she was just jealous, which I could understand, and had to accept as the truth. He would know best. What he explained took a direction I wasn't expecting. It had nothing to do with what I could do as a witch and more to do with the other thing I was. "Just think about it," he said. "Why wouldn't she be jealous? When she is sixty years old, she will be all saggy and all, and you will still look like a sixteen-year-old."

It took all I had to hold back my laughter. Later at our nightly study session, Nathan wasn't as successful and spit his drink across the table when I told him about what Jack had said. Time had even healed our wounds. I hadn't dropped my desire to find out what I could about the Nortons, Marie to be more precise. I just hadn't mentioned it in his company, and he hadn't brought it up. Not that the issue had been solved, just avoided. That was good enough for now, and it allowed us to settle into a sort of rhythm. Walks to class, nightly story time with Amy, and study sessions, which was usually light on the studying. It was us, listening to music, talking, walking through the woods and out to the cove which had kind of become our place. Sunsets, and even a few sunrises that Mrs. Saxon didn't know about, or I hoped she didn't. There wasn't much else to do in this place, not that there wasn't anything we could think of doing that the building didn't provide. One night we even invited the dog pack to go bowling, and of course, poof, the room we walked into was a bowling alley, complete with neon and strobe lights.

Nathan also hadn't brought up the other touchy subject since that one time on the beach. There was no solving that.

"All right squirt. That is it for the stories tonight."

Amy put up the same protest as always. The little pout, followed by her hopping down from whose lap she was sitting in, mine this time, before giving us each hugs and heading back inside to get to bed. Mrs. Parrish had stopped coming to retrieve her each night. I took it as a show of trust, but just wasn't sure which of the three she was trusting. Part of me thought it was probably Amy, who seemed rather mature for her age. Mrs. Saxon never gave me any more details about all she had been through before Mrs. Parrish found her, just that she was kept in a cage and forced to perform like a circus animal. How that little girl remained sane through all that I hadn't a clue. I knew what I was going through and hoped on the inside she wasn't in the same shape.

"Okay, history report," Nathan said, opening his folder.

"Done." I sat back in the chair rather smugly, and enjoyed the surprise on his face.

"Really?" he asked, unconvinced.

"Yep, I wasn't into disco night, so I sat down and did it last night. I even typed it up and all. Want to see?" I didn't wait for an answer. My folder opened and three stapled pages slid across the table to him.

"Impressive."

"Which? The trick or the paper?" I asked to clarify.

"The fact you already have it done."

"Some new habits I am trying. I have a few questions about the trigonometry, though, and," I leaned forward and gave him a cautionary wag of a finger, "if you make a modern math comment, I will give you the ears of a donkey, and not even your mother would be able to remove them."

"I promise, I won't. What problems?"

"The theorems. It's too theoretical, nothing absolute. You know what I mean. I can't just add two and two together and get four. It just doesn't make sense."

I pulled out my paper and pencil the old fashioned way and was about to show him the problem that still perplexed me when Nathan gave me another problem. "Speaking of things that don't make sense. Mom wanted me to tell you a few members of the council will stop by tomorrow to check in."

The pencil fell to the table, bouncing off the eraser end and down to the concrete pool deck. While it was in the air, I fell back in my chair. It had only been three weeks since the last of them left, and I had gotten used to them not being around. "What do they want?" I asked, but before Nathan could answer I added on another, and more curious question. "And why is she having you deliver that message?"

"Well, um, I don't have a clue what they want. I am not a witch. And second, she said you act disappointed and scared when she delivers news like that. She thought you might take it better if I gave it." He added on one of his Hollywood smiles, but this one was a bit overcooked with extra cheese.

"Does it look like I took it better?" I gestured to how I was sitting, slumped back in the chair.

"No."

"Did she say when they will be here?" With a flick of the wrist, I retrieved my pencil from where it rolled.

"Before class she said."

"Great. Great. I thought I was done with all this, but I guess not." I let out an airless sigh. "Come on help me with this problem so you can take me for a walk. I need to unwind now."

Nathan helped me, or so I led him to believe. After his third explanation, I gave up and made it seem like I got it, but I didn't. I still saw two different theorems that could have applied to this problem, but I seriously doubted I would even need this stuff in the real world. If I did, hopefully Nathan would be there to help then too.

With that problem done, and another weighing on me, we went for a walk through the woods. The threatening weather overhead kept us from heading out to the cove. Nathan was still funny about getting wet, and he didn't appreciate my jokes about him being so sweet he would melt. I couldn't care less either way, and enjoyed the rain. To walk hand in hand like we were, but during a rain shower sounded like my perfect form of heaven, but I settled for what I had. It wasn't that bad of a tradeoff.

Out here with him, nothing else mattered. Even the old questions and problems that haunted me all the time had faded to where they didn't exist when he was around. Moments we shared like this were my perfect therapy and gave me hope for something that would feel like a normal life. I wasn't ready to admit to Nathan yet that I felt that even stronger when it was us and Amy. That might send him running. Not that he would be able to get far before I could catch him.

We were heading back when I heard the snap of a branch behind us. It was loud enough for even Nathan to hear. I felt him twitch and start to turn, but set him at ease.

"Hi Rob." A few seconds later I heard the hollow echoes of the breath moving in and out of the chest of a large beast. One that smelled like a dog. Each of them had a distinctive smell and I could pick them out from one another from several football fields away. A challenge they put me up to once. The large grey wolf came on my side and joined us in our walk. His muzzle nudged my hand, and I reached up and gave it a pet. "Looks like we have a dog now."

There was a little growl from the wolf, and a laugh from Nathan.

"Good thing he is house broken." Nathan's jab appeared to be enough to cause Rob to phase right back to his normal form.

"You two would be lucky to have a dog as cool as me."

"Yea, yea." Nathan reached down and grabbed a stick and threw it out in front of us. "Fetch."

Rob laughed, and took off running, phasing mid trot. When he reached the stick, he picked it up with his mouth and ran back. He didn't lay it at our feet like a dog might. This wolf phased back into a human and removed the stick from his mouth on his own before handing it back to Nathan. Who offered it to me, and I refused, "Witches are more into cats."

Rob whimpered at first, then said, "That is rather stereotypical of you, don't you think?"

I didn't respond and kept walking.

"Okay, Larissa, what's wrong?" Rob asked, he joined us walking at my side.

"Not a thing," I responded sternly, then noticed my tone. I wouldn't have believed myself.

"You don't normally have this mad at the world look on your face. Let me guess, more visions of your friend?"

I shook off his suggestion. "I've kind of gotten used to them."

"The council is coming again," announced Nathan.

"Oh, but why? Didn't they learn everything they needed last time?"

"They want to keep tabs on me," I responded. That was all I wanted to go into. My being considered a threat was something I wanted to keep below public knowledge.

"Want me to shoo them away?" asked Rob, with a little growl.

"Nah, this is my problem." It was one of many, but it was the one that most consumed me at the time.

"So, I was thinking," Rob started, and left a door wide open that both Nathan and I jumped through.

"That is odd for you," I quipped, but I had to admit Nathan's shot was better.

"And they say you can't teach an old dog new tricks."

Even Rob had to smile at that one. He was a good-natured person, and always ready to take a little ribbing, especially if it was funny. Nathan warned me early on though, he could give as good as he took, and he was right. His quick-wit caught me off guard several times. Martin was the same way, but you had to watch Dan. He had his limits before things would boil over inside of him. "Mini golf, and maybe invite the others."

Nathan and I looked at each other. I could see the wheels turning in his head. I knew they were turning in mine. Thinking of a bowling alley or movie theatre were pretty generic ideas that the coven could easily construct. Would we need to think of each and every hole for this? That sounded like a challenge to me, and I had a feeling Amy would love that. We both nodded our agreement as we stepped up on the pool deck.

Back inside Nathan looked up at the leaves that were still falling from the ceiling creating just the perfect amount of foliage cover on the ground and remarked, "Another week and it will be snow."

I must have looked at him inquisitively because he went on further to explain. "On Thanksgiving it changes from leaves to snow until mid-February. A tree sprouts up in the entry for Christmas."

"And then your mom's tree decorating party," added Rob.

"Yep." Nathan leaned in closer to me. "That is a big deal, and you are invited. Everyone is, but you can't say no." He gave my hand a little squeeze.

We stopped there in the center of the entry, like we always did. There were a few nervous moments while we waited for Rob to head up stairs. He lingered longer than he needed on each step, and each look back at us was obvious. He wanted to catch us. Not that we were keeping anything a secret. We still tried to avoid any big public displays. I let, or caused, a few of them to happen, but I had good reason. Once he disappeared behind his door, I became the aggressor. If I had waited for Nathan, the seconds would continue to tick. He often said he liked to look down into my eyes for a while. I didn't buy it, but that was my own issue. I bought what he was doing now, which was welcoming my kiss, a mixture of hot and cold that created electricity between us. His hands caressed up and down my back. One ventured a little lower, testing uncharted territory for only a moment. I didn't put up a fight. I may have instigated this kiss, but I that didn't mean I stayed in control. Once in his grasp I gave into him every time.

16

The next morning, I sat in my room waiting for Mrs. Saxon, or anyone, to come get me for our meeting with the council members. When no one arrived when it was time to go to class, I headed on down, a little after all the others, so they didn't wait for me. I didn't want to face a ton of questioning about what the council wanted, and just told everyone that Mrs. Tenderschott and I had something to do. A little lie that didn't amount to many questions. I hadn't planned for them being late. Now I had to face my little lie head on.

My friends looked at me curiously when I entered Mrs. Saxon's class. Instead of going to my seat, I pivoted back to the center path to the front and walked up to the table where she was still finishing her notes. This now got everyone's attention.

"Where are they?" I whispered.

"Your guess is as good as mine," she said as she looked up.

I turned and headed back to my table. Gwen's hand grabbed mine when I passed her table. I looked down, startled by her move. Her gaze met mine and lacked the normal vinegar bitterness.

"Is it the council? Are they coming to talk to you?" She asked with an eagerness in her voice. I had almost forgotten about her fandom obsession regarding them.

I didn't answer, and just walked to my seat next to Apryl, hoping my lack of response wouldn't start any frenzied uproar, but I was wrong. The murmur started as soon as I took the first step away from Gwen. It came from the side of the room where all the witches sat. Gwen's voice was leading the charge. She even asked Mrs. Saxon, "Are they coming here again?" If she were any giddier, she would have giggled.

I sat down next to Apryl, and got a quick, "So that is what you had to do?"

"I didn't want to talk about it all night," I replied, and that was that. Apryl nor anyone else on my side said another word. The murmur among the witches settled after another few seconds and Mrs. Saxon began her lecture.

We were getting our homework assignment when the door opened behind us. That was when Mrs. Saxon lost control of the witches again. It wasn't Mrs. Tenderschott or anyone that would have seemed normal to interrupt the class. This was the fully robed Mrs. Wintercrest, standing in the opening to make the formal announcement, "We are here." Then the door closed. A hush fell over the room.

The vampires, shapeshifters, and werewolves all looked around at each other confused. The witches all looked as if God himself had walked in. They were awe struck. Their eyes and mouths were wide opened staring back at the door. Mrs. Saxon motioned for me to join her as she started walking out. At the door, she announced, "Go on to your next class. I will see you all in the morning."

I got up and followed. When I passed by Laura, she asked, "Who was that?"

"Head witch," I remarked and followed Mrs. Saxon out and into the hall.

I followed Mrs. Saxon who seemed to know exactly where she was going. After a few doors I figured it out too and wasn't surprised when she opened the door to our ritual chamber. I also wasn't surprised to see the four of them up on those same pedestals, as they were the first time. In attendance were Mrs. Wintercrest, Master Thomas, and Elizabeth Mauro, who was a quiet observer during their last visit, and of course sitting right next to Mrs. Wintercrest was the head of my fan club, Miss Sarah Julia Roberts.

"Good morning Miss Dubois, Mrs. Saxon," greeted Master Thomas, he was the only member of the party that didn't share a grim expression.

"Morning Master Thomas," I said.

"No Master. Just plain Benjamin is fine." The flamboyant man appeared to be the only one on the panel that wanted to be here.

"Miss Norton," started Mrs. Wintercrest. She leaned forward across the black pedestal. "We are here to check in to see how you are acclimating here in this coven. Now, I am sure Mrs. Saxon will give you a glowing report." She cast a disapproving look down at Mrs. Saxon who stood at my side. I could feel the discomfort radiating from her. It was strong, and I wondered if Jack could feel it as well. "We have collected what we need from the building, but wanted to give you a chance to tell us your side."

"My side?" I asked, confused as hell to what she was referring to.

"Yes, your side of how things are going for you." She sat back and crossed her hands on the top of the podium in front of her with a smug look on her face. That same look was shared by Miss Sarah Roberts, who leaned forward.

"I am not sure what you mean. What exactly do you want to know?" Still as confused as I had ever felt since I arrived at the coven, and that was saying something.

"Miss Norton," she leaned forward and exploded. "We don't have time for games here. You can either explain yourself right now, or leave us to draw our own conclusions."

Just then, Master Thomas leaned forward. A calming hand, black nail polish and all, reached in front of Mrs. Wintercrest and appeared to restrain her without even touching her. "Larissa, we just want to hear how you are doing? Your classes? Your training? How you are getting along with others?"

I suddenly felt like a child having to survive through the monthly protective services visit while in foster care. The coven gave them the report teachers and my foster parents would normally have provided. Now it was my time to tell them I had been a good girl and was doing all my homework and eating my vegetables.

"Larissa?" he asked again.

"My classes are going well, and I assume by training you mean my craft, spells?"

"Yes."

"That is going much better than before. Every day I remember more about my life before, and that includes spells and my capabilities. Some I still have to hone, but I feel that is from lack of use."

"She is an exemplary student –," Mrs. Saxon started, but a quick slash of Mrs. Wintercrest's hand cut her off. She kept her hand outstretched and pointed a single finger on it in my direction.

"Most of what I am being taught are things I already know, or knew. Now I just need to practice perfecting it."

"So, you are remembering more of your life in the Orleans' Coven?" Master Thomas asked.

"Every day. Sometimes just a sound or a smell triggers it, but mostly it happens during training. A feeling of familiarity will come over me when I am trying to learn something, and then all these memories of when I first learned it, or even a time I used it, come back. Then it is like bang, I suddenly know exactly what to do, and how. It just needs to be perfected, but like they say, practice makes perfect."

"Yes it does," he agreed with a smile. "Do you find focus to still be a problem?"

"Some," I said, not letting on about how much. Things had become easier, thanks to my memory coming back. That just meant my abilities were stronger, not that my focus had greatly improved. Though my mother had provided some help there. Her method to clear my mind and capture small momentary spots, what she called bubbles, of focus seemed to be a key to push the chaos from my thoughts.

"Very good. That is wonderful news."

"How are you getting along with others here?" Miss Sarah Roberts jumped in, stepping on Master Thomas mid-compliment, and I instantly hated her for robbing me of that moment.

I turned in her direction, ignoring the others. I knew from the first visit this girl was going to be a thorn in my side. Something I even expressed to Mrs. Tenderschott. Her advice: turn the other cheek, and kill her with kindness. That appeared to be her tact when it came to the council. Making enemies out of any of them would only cause problems. Which I understood. It was a point she had made several times to me. What really got through to me though was when she mentioned if I didn't respond it might frustrate them, and that sounded like a great idea to me.

"I believe I am getting along with everyone here fine. I have made some great friends here, no matter who or what they are; vampires, witches, shifters, and werewolves." I sure hoped they didn't ask about Gwen.

"She is a model member of the coven," Mrs. Saxon added, and paused to make sure no one was going to cut her off this time. "She is different from many of our members, being quite a bit older and more mature. I believe this is why she has been so great with helping with a young shifter who just joined us a few weeks back. The young girl and Larissa have really bonded."

"And you approve of that?" Mrs. Wintercrest asked, alarmed. Her attention now aimed at Mrs. Saxon, but I didn't feel any less weight on my shoulders on this. It was still about me.

"Whole heartedly," she replied confidently, with a glance in my direction.

"I see, another example of your poor judgement, but we will get to that later," Mrs. Wintercrest admonished with a wag of her finger. "What about those outside of the coven?"

I was back in the middle of her crosshairs, but no less confused by her line of questioning. I hadn't left the coven. Looking up at the panel I noticed Master Thomas, mouth open, and a finger held in the air, as if he were about to speak, but he hadn't said a word yet. Instead, his eyes were focused on me. I waited another minute, he remained frozen in that pose. Like a stone statue. I went ahead and said the obvious, "I'm not sure what you mean."

That must have been the trigger that released Master Benjamin Thomas. His finger rotated around from toward me to down the line of his fellow council members. The mouth that was frozen open, now moved. His very southern voice filled the room. "Now Mrs. Wintercrest. We," he motioned with his finger back to himself and her, "have already discussed this. She is not responsible for any of that. I am sure if she were given a choice, she would rather none of it happen. Am I right Larissa?"

I was about to tell him I didn't have a bloody clue what he was talking about, but Mrs. Wintercrest butted in, "That is your opinion. What matters is that it happens, and we don't know what they talk about." The witch Council Supreme turned her face toward me, and looked down upon me, her head tilting back and forth. Like a predator playing with its prey, just before the violent pounce. "It's all a secret, isn't that correct Miss Norton?"

"I... I," I stuttered not knowing how to answer, not that I had a chance. Master Thomas slammed shut the door on that opportunity.

"You can't be serious," he exploded, exacerbated, falling back into his seat.

"Mistresses and Masters, to what are you referring to?" Mrs. Saxon asked. She emerged from the corner she had stayed in and appeared to have recovered from the slap she took just moments ago. "Larissa hasn't left the coven grounds since she arrived."

"Mrs. Saxon, I am surprised that you are thinking so linearly, so human. You of all people know there are many ways to communicate, and your young student here—many decades your senior—is communing with the likes of Jean St. Claire. And, right under your nose."

"Larissa, is it true?" she stormed over and stood in front of me. The sounds of her footsteps led me to believe she would be fuming when she reached me, she wasn't. She appeared concerned as her arms reached out and grabbed my shoulders, not to shake me, but to caress, and hold me. "Has he contacted you?"

"Yes... no... I mean, there have been visions. Like the ones that Reginald used," I said, looking right into her eyes. The council had all but disappeared to me.

"How often?"

"Every couple of days. They only last a minute or so. Mrs. Tenderschott believes he is using voodoo or some other type of black magic to use the link that was there with Reginald."

"Probably so," she agreed. Her hands rubbing my shoulders, but appearing surprised, and disappointed at the same time. Just like before when I had the visions that involved Reginald Von Bell, Mrs. Tenderschott and I had either forgotten, or neglected, to tell her about this. It never even crossed my mind. I just treated them like bad dreams, and I seriously doubted Gwen told Mrs. Saxon about every bad dream she had where she walked to class naked or had a single hair out of place on her head.

"Conspiring, right under your own nose," Miss Roberts sniped from her perch next to Mrs. Wintercrest. "And to think you allowed this girl to associate with your own son."

Now it was Mrs. Saxon's turn to be at a loss for words. She turned to face them, but the knife I had firmly stuck in her back by not telling her was clearly present in her body language and lack of response. As much as I tried to heed Mrs. Tenderschott's advice about being pleasant this was no time to hold back or play games. I stepped forward in front of Mrs. Saxon. My movement may have been a little too quick for the council's liking, but I didn't care. I am sure my tone would be harsher than they liked too. "There is no conspiring, just him threatening and terrifying me with every visit! Is that what you call conspiring?"

"Well then, you have nothing to hide," Mrs. Wintercrest started.

"No ma'am, I! Do! Not!" I leaned forward, to make sure it was crystal clear to all of them. I even stepped forward toward their platform. Inside I wanted to climb up to the top and stand there looking down at them, but I felt that might have been a little over the top.

Others appeared to sense where this was heading too. Master Benjamin Thomas left his seat and joined Mrs. Saxon and me down on the floor. He appeared beyond frustrated as he rounded the platform. The tails of his long black duster trailed behind him as he rushed to our side. "That is enough!"

"Not quite, Master Thomas," Mrs. Wintercrest shot back. "We have a truth to uncover, and that is why I asked Mrs. Mauro to join us today. She has a way of getting to the heart of a matter, as you more than well know."

Without another word, a black cloud rolled from the fingertips of the silent member of the council, surrounding myself, Mrs. Saxon, and Master Thomas. It was heavy, and thick, with the putrid smell of spoiled meat, which reminded me of the downside of my enhanced senses. It coiled around us like a snake, and on the first squeeze, it burned. The pain shot through me, and I screamed, and attempted to muster everything I could to push it away. Nothing happened. The cloud didn't move as I pushed air at it with the force of a category five hurricane.

"Larissa, do you trust me?" Master Thomas asked. He stood calm amidst the coils.

I nodded. There was no reason not to trust him. At the moment he and Mrs. Saxon appeared to be the only ones on my side, and I had just betrayed Mrs. Saxon, so I couldn't be too sure about her.

"Then just relax and let it take you. If you fight it, it will hurt."

Another brush against my right arm gave me a firm reminder of that, and I grimaced against the pain.

"Just let go," he reminded.

I let my arms fall and tried the best I could to relax. Not an easy feat with the events of the last several minutes running through my head and deep frying every essence of who I was. I looked around, and everyone else, including Mrs. Wintercrest and Miss Roberts was doing the same. The cloud didn't seem to discriminate against who was in the room.

My nerves balled and prepared for another shot of pain as I watched the cloud close in on my left shoulder. My body had already winced before it made contact. The pain was still there, but it wasn't that bad. Like a light abrasion, or skinned knee. It continued around me until it looped up and over my head blocking out all the light from the room, depositing me in a cone of darkness. A familiar darkness, with a familiar dank space that smelled of death. I knew where I was. That spot where I always saw him, but there was something else to this place as well. I had been here before, a long time ago. Where and for what, I couldn't put my finger on.

"She is hiding it," Miss Roberts exclaimed. I didn't see her, but I heard her loud and clear.

"Give it time," responded an unfamiliar voice. I had to assume that was Elizabeth Mauro.

The next voice I heard sent a chill down my already cold spine. Then the horror marathon began. Not just the highlights but full length reviews of each one of the visits Jean St. Claire paid me. Sights, sounds, smells, and feelings, taking me on a tour of Jean's greatest hits. All eerily familiar, and even though I had already experienced those moments the first time, they were no less filled with terror the second time around stoking a burning fear deep inside. The only solace I had, or hope I had, was at least the council members would see I wasn't hiding anything.

When the show was over, the darkness lifted like someone pulled up the shade on a window, and there we all were, right where we were before. I pulled my self together and wanted to proclaim my innocence with a nice defiant, "see," but again Master Thomas beat me to it.

"As you can see, she is not colluding or planning anything with Jean St. Claire. It is quite the opposite, just like she told you. Now, I think we have seen enough."

Mrs. Wintercrest sat up straight in her chair and again looked down her nose at me. Which wasn't the reaction I had hoped for, or the one I expected. Her face contorted, and angry as she slowly leaned forward, looking over the edge of the podium in front of her, and down at those of us standing on the floor in front of her. "It's worse. It proves nothing about our initial concerns, and shows us the danger she has placed this coven in is far graver than we first imagined."

"That is why she needs our help," interjected Master Thomas.

It appeared Mrs. Wintercrest was having none of it. Her head was tilted back as she shook it. Mrs. Mauro sat silent, as always. I couldn't help but notice Miss Roberts appeared to be taking some immense pleasure in this.

Mrs. Saxon stepped forward to speak, but a gently placed hand with black fingernail polish stopped her. Instead, he stepped forward, and then rose off the floor to eye level with Mrs. WIntercrest. The ease at which he pulled off such a feat amazed me. There was no spell, no hand movement. He flew forward as close as he could without bumping the podium. "She is one of us. Do I need to remind you of our purpose?" The friendly tone his voice always possessed had disappeared. He was now delivering a lecture, but Mrs. Wintercrest appeared to be unaffected.

"No, you do not. I am more than aware of it, and I will point out a fact. She is not one of us, so that doesn't apply to her. Evidence of the danger she poses is all around us. Just look at the first attack. Jean St. Claire's continued attempts to reach out to her just shows that there will be others."

"Exactly!" Master Thomas exclaimed.

A hand rose from his Council Supreme to cut him off before he could continue with any more of his opinion. It had become clear to me she wasn't interested in hearing any of it from anyone, and an uncomfortable, and unsettled, feeling had settled in. Again, they were considering me a threat, make that a significant and profoundly serious threat, even a danger, which was the word Mrs. Wintercrest used often. Before it was me that was the threat, and while whatever Mrs. Mauro did showed them I wasn't colluding with Jean St. Claire, it gave them a new angle to hate me for.

"Not exactly Master Thomas. Her presence here puts everyone here at risk. It is only sheer luck that no one was seriously injured, or even killed, during the last intrusion. We may not be so lucky the next time." The uptight and lecturing Mrs. Wintercrest stood up from her seat, and the others joined her. "Mrs. Saxon, I shouldn't have to remind you of the risk. You almost lost your son in the first attack, but yet you continue to take risks and allow him to engage in a relationship with this abomination. This brings into question your ability to lead this coven."

"Now wait a minute there," Mrs. Saxon started, but again, Master Thomas grabbed her arm before she could approach the platform. She made one, and only one attempt to pull free.

"Mrs. Wintercrest, while it is your position to oversee all covens, you cannot unilaterally decide to change coven leadership. You need the entire council's support to do so. While I will not attempt to speak for you, or any other member, I can only speak for myself. I trust Mrs. Saxon's leadership here, and believe Larissa Dubois, whose family was a distinguished family in our ranks, is a valuable member of this coven and should remain. As a witch we owe her our guidance and support, and she has done nothing to prove she doesn't deserve any of that."

"Well, I do not."

"Neither do I," added Miss Roberts. Mrs. Mauro remained as silent as always, but there was a shared nod between her and Master Thomas. One that appeared to be accompanied by a smile. An expression that seemed to be rare among the council members.

Master Thomas, who appeared to me to be the best orator since Abraham Lincoln, stepped forward, and hooked his hands on the lapels of the duster he wore and strode the length of platform. I half expected him to start his next statement with, "Ladies and Gentlemen of the court." Instead, he became a moderator, "Then ladies, we find ourselves at an impasse here. Two to two, and any such decision has to be unanimous, not just a majority, which you don't have either. There must be some middle ground we can reach in all this to end the hostilities that have emerged." He stopped right where he was and turned toward the other three members of the council in attendance, hands spread out waiting for their reply.

There were several shared looks between Mrs. Wintercrest and Miss Roberts. Not a one of them was pleasant, which made me squirm even more. My head had already played her voice giving the response that I expected. A stiff and stern no, and that I must leave, or something even worse. If worse was possible. No one had yet truly explained the extent of what this council could do. The story of what James said happened to his family was never far from my thoughts when my imagination explored this topic. Being burned at a stake was another popular conclusion.

To say I felt helpless here would be an understatement. No matter what I said, they didn't listen, and even then, there wasn't much to refute about their latest concern. There was an attack, because of me. There probably would be another one day. I didn't have any doubts on that. Maybe it wouldn't be a full on attack against the coven itself like the last one. Maybe he would be, or was, lying in wait in the woods to catch me alone. Maybe he wouldn't care if I were alone, and come after me while I was out there with Nathan one day, or one Friday night out there with Apryl, Laura, or one of my other friends. Then the most terrifying thought hit me. What about Amy?

A theme that was made clear around here was the threat the outside world was to each of us. Learning how to protect ourselves and live among the outside world was the main topic of the curriculum. By me being here, I have put everyone in greater risk. Your enemy is everyone and everywhere. This time it was me.

"Not without protest," Mrs. Wintercrest conceded.

"Your protest is very clear and noted."

"Miss Norton is to remain in this coven under strict supervision, and mustn't leave for any reason. Not until a final determination can be made regarding her place in our community."

"Done!" Master Thomas agreed, without consulting either me or Mrs. Saxon. Not that I would have said anything different. I didn't feel I had any counter argument or chips to play in this negotiation.

"That is not all," Mrs. Wintercrest announced.

"Of course not," remarked Master Thomas. This drew a little of Mrs. Wintercrest's ire to his direction.

"Mrs. Saxon will be held fully responsible for anything that happens, and, if there are any incidents, she will be rightfully removed and dealt with."

This time Master Thomas did pause before responding and looked at Mrs. Saxon who quickly agreed. Then the speaker of the moment gave the reply, "Done! Is that all?"

"Yes it is." Mrs. Wintercrest stepped to the side away from her chair and then disappeared into the darkness behind her. Mrs. Mauro followed. Miss Roberts lingered for a moment. She appeared to revel in looking down on me with that smug look on her face and gave one last look back before she disappeared as well. I still didn't know why she hated me so much from our very first meeting. She was just one more name on a lengthy list of people who didn't really care for, let me correct that, hated me.

"Ignore them," said Master Thomas, without looking at either myself or Mrs. Saxon. "They are just all blowhards."

"Am I really a threat?" I had to ask. I had to know. Gwen's description of Master Thomas was that of a smitten schoolgirl, but what she missed was his fair nature, and eloquent tact. He truly appeared to be advocating on my behalf. Why? I didn't know. He owed me nothing, and didn't really know me, but one thing was certain. I valued and wanted to know his opinion.

"No more than anyone else is. Many covens have individuals that are under threat, or being protected from something. Your... I guess condition maybe unique, but your situation isn't."

"Then Master Thomas, why all this?" Mrs. Saxon motioned around the room with her hands.

He turned and leaned back against the podiums that stood atop the platform, and crossed one ankle over the other. Then with folded arms, he held out a single hand and pointed right at me. With how I felt, it could have been a gun that had just discharged a round right through me. "Between the last visit and now they were able to research your family. They know exactly who and what they were. Your family was one of the most prominent families back then, and not just in their coven. I am sure you already know that."

I nodded.

"Good, you need to know who your family is. Honor them, and continue their line." He leaned forward and off of the podium and stepped forward. "Because of the prominence of who your family was, and who you are now, I think they see you as a threat, but not," he rushed to clarify, "in the way you are thinking. They may talk about you being dangerous and all, but the danger you pose to them is... how is the best way to explain it?" He appeared to ask himself, as he paced a few more steps toward where me and Mrs. Saxon were standing.

"There really isn't a better way to say it than to say you are a danger to them and the powers of position they hold so dear. With who your family was, how powerful you could be if you mastered your ability, and your new attributes, you would be an obvious choice to join the council and continue your family line, and even be considered for the Council Supreme."

"But I don't want to be Council Supreme or anything like that. How many times do I have to tell them that, or try to explain that the Nortons didn't train me or groom me for anything of the such?" I was at the point where I believe even a signed letter, or Marie Norton herself sitting here telling them so wouldn't make a difference.

"You don't have to convince me Larissa, and don't completely dismiss what the future for you may hold. I am just telling you how they see things. I would expect continued inquisitions like this for the time being. One day, they will get bored with it," his smiled skewed, "I hope."

"Oh boy, I can't wait."

17

Outside Master Benjamin Thompson stood next to Mrs. Saxon. The two were whispering intensely back and forth until I came through the door, then it all stopped, and the stares began. Each watched as I walked by. Neither made any attempt to talk to, or even acknowledge me. Probably official business, but seeing them wait for me to leave before they began talking added a little extra sting to my ostracized mindset. My mind was a tempest of questions, which one might think I would be used to by now. Though the normal tempest were all questions I searched for answers to. The questions added to the mix now were questions that in their own way were more disturbing. Their answers were chilling.

My head needed to be clear, or clearer, before I headed back to class. It wasn't a question of being able to pay attention, it was a question of being able to hold myself together. While most wouldn't know what I was feeling unless I had a true physical outburst, I had to remember Jack would know what was going on inside, and while I knew, and now trusted, that he wouldn't tell anyone. I didn't even want him knowing what was going on in my mind. Perhaps a quick walk outside would help. It always had in the past. Well, most of the time. My trusted method had failed to work completely the last few weeks, but it provided some relief, and some would be better than none.

"Miss Dubois," called an edgy voice as I passed the stairs, heading for the door out to the pool and surrounding woods. I stopped and looked up, but didn't see anyone. My vantage wasn't the best, and I backed up a few steps and sawMrs. Parrish descending the stairs.

"Yes,Mrs. Parrish. What is it?"

"Can we have a word?" she asked, as frigid has ever.

"Sure," I said, knowing I couldn't really refuse her, not without causing a problem, and it seemed I had done way too much of that lately.

She rounded the bottom of the stairs and walked over toward me. The normal grace of her movements was still present. Each step smooth and measured under the skirt that flowed down to the ground, which just added to the illusion that she floated across the floor instead of walked. Her shoulder movements accentuated the steps, providing the only physical evidence that she was even moving. "I want to let you know, I appreciate your help with Amy, but it isn't necessary."

If that wasn't a back-handed compliment right across my face then I wasn't sure what was. The words were as sharp as the tone they were delivered in. I paused a moment before answering to avoid mirroring her tone, with a slightly harsher response. The pause worked, and using my best acting skills, I put on the most pleasant face I could, which was the complete opposite of how I felt, and delivered a polite, "Oh, it is no bother. I really enjoy it." What was the advice from Mrs. Tenderschott? Kill them with kindness?Mrs. Parrish didn't keel over in front of me, so either that was bad advice, or I wasn't kind enough.

"Perhaps I didn't make myself clear. Your assistance isn't necessary."

It was obvious that Mrs. Parrish didn't subscribe to the same advice. There was no kindness in that dagger shot. So, since my first attempt didn't work. I decided to do it my way. "You did, but like I said. I really enjoy it." I could have asked, but I didn't want to. I had just spent an hour hearing how I was a problem, and didn't have the appetite to hear another person join in the chorus.

"Well..."Mrs. Parrish seemed lost for words behind her normally blank expression. "You don't need to bother yourself with helping any further."

"It's no bother," I stated directly, but still trying to keep a pleasant expression on my face. Doing this was harder than I thought. Maybe I didn't give Mrs. Tenderschott enough credit.

"Miss Dubois, let me be frank with you," she straightened her posture even more than it already was.

"It's about time." I let it slip, and it caught both of us off guard.

"I don't believe you are the best of influence on her, and I would appreciate it if you stopped all contact."

"Well at least you didn't call me a danger." That one even shocked me. It seemed suddenly I had lost control of my mouth.

"That too,"Mrs. Parrish shot back, striking me right through the non-beating heart. "I can't trust you around someone like her. You might lose control. Not to mention the attention you have attracted to the coven. She is my responsibility to protect, and I cannot do that with you around." She leaned in and asked, "Have I made myself clear, or do I need to speak to Mrs. Saxon on this?"

"Crystal." I stood there trying to return the glare she was giving. If only I had eyes that could. An awkward silence settled in over us like a wet blanket. "Is there anything else?" I asked, wanting to end this encounter as quickly as possible.

The only response I received was a quick spin on her heels, and the sight of the back of her blonde head walking away from me and back to the stairs. I watched as she ascended and through the door on the second floor.

Once the door closed, I let go. Slouching, and stumbling back against the boy's staircase. My bottom thudded on the floor, and I just sat there. The weight of everything that had been dumped on me in the last hour squeezed tears from my eyes, and nothing could stop them. No matter how much I tried. Even the voices of my friends coming down the hall couldn't pause them. I ran out the door to avoid being seen. I didn't stop at the edge of the woods, and sped through them as far as I could, blasting through the low brush and sending a trail of fall foliage up in the air behind me. I felt and sensed every animal I passed, but they were the furthest thought from my mind. Only the salty smelling air of the cove brought me to a stop. There I found a nice quiet spot under the overhang of a rock, where I couldn't bother or put anyone in danger, and I sat and thought, hoping for divine intervention to arrive in the form of answers. Maybe a bolt of lightning would hit the sand and write out the answers for me. I sure didn't have any.

17

I spent the rest of the afternoon and into the early portion of the evening out there, only moving when the sun changed the angle of the shadow I was using for my cover. No matter how much I searched the answers never arrived. No, that's not right. Many answers arrived. None of them were the right one.

The beauty of the spot sent me dreaming of taking Nathan and finding a spot just like this to live our lives together. To leave all the problems behind and just be happy. Something that I realized I only felt in fleeting moments, which always involved him. And there were a few moments in which I honestly believed that would solve everything, but there was one detail I had brushed over, me. I was the source of all problems. My presence was what was causing problems between Mrs. Saxon and the council. My presence pulled danger and the coven in orbit with each other. My presence would do the same with Nathan, and then it would be up to me to keep him safe. Could I? I wasn't so sure. Hell, I wasn't even sure if I could keep myself safe.

The moonlight added to the glistening beauty of the sea spray in the cool night as a wolf howled in the woods behind me. It was Martin, I was sure of it. He and the rest of the dog pack were probably out on their patrol. I let go of the questions enough to pay attention to the living world around me. I felt them, all of them. Everything from the smallest squirrel, the few birds that have yet to migrate south ahead of the coming winter, and two large werewolves roaming close to the cove. I didn't need to feel them. The smell gave away the location of Martin and Robert.

"Larissa, are you okay?" Robert called from up above me on the bluff that overlooked the cove. At first I didn't want to answer them, and I didn't have to. I could sit right here and let them pass by. An attractive option, after the day I had been through.

"Larissa?" Martin's voice called. He was further down the bluff. From where I sat, I could see him walking down the bluff away from where I still sat, under the rock.

"Do you see her?" Robert called to Martin.

"No, but I am sure she is out here," responded Martin. He turned and was walking back in my direction. For a moment I felt he was looking right at me, but his gaze moved on after a moment. The dark shadow of this rock had saved me from being seen, but a gnawing inside threatened to expose me. They were out here looking for me. Could I really be the type of person to just ignore that?

Pushing away all the thoughts of disappearing for the moment. I inched out from under the rock and stood out in the open.

"There you are!" Robert screamed, as he jumped down to the beach. A feat I thought only a vampire could perform. He rushed to me. "Are you okay?"

"I'm fine," I said, brushing the sand off my jeans.

"We were worried your favorite vampire might have snatched you after you were gone for a while," Martin said, after he performed the same feat, and landed just a few feet away from me with a light thud in the damp sand.

"Then I got really concerned when I could smell you, but couldn't see you. I thought you were hurt or dead," added Robert.

I shook my head and explained, "I just needed a moment with my thoughts." Then what he said hit me. "You smelled me?"

"Yep, and it's quite disgusting. I'm not sure how you guys can stand your own smell." Robert nudged me on the shoulder with his fist. "And you thought we smelled bad."

"Let's head back home. The others are worried."

On the way back, Robert suggested a race, but Martin shot that down in quick order. I think he enjoyed the leisurely walk through the woods in his human form. Robert chided him a little that he was afraid of losing. He attempted to do the same to me, and claimed he was faster than any vampire, but I pushed off that challenge to a later date. My competitive streak gave a little fight and wanted to test out his claim, but I wasn't in the mood at the moment.

We didn't talk much, as a group, but Martin told me that Mrs. Saxon came to find them before they headed out on their nightly patrol and told them I left some time ago and never returned. I apologized to both Robert and Martin for being a problem and causing them to come look for me. Tally another mark on the scorecard for how many ways I could cause trouble. Even when I wasn't trying to be a problem, I still managed to. Maybe that was my greatest talent.

Both were magnanimous about it. "We were coming out here anyway," said Martin.

I half expected Mrs. Saxon to be waiting at the door when we returned, but she wasn't. No one was. It was just us walking into an empty entry way, just after nine. Robert and Martin headed up their side of the stairs, and with nothing else to do, I headed up my side, when the next disappoint of the day sent my shoulders slumping. I had missed my nightly date with Nathan, which involved story time with Amy. That probably pleased Mrs. Parrish. While I was out at the cove, I not only lost track of time, a problem for my kind, but even more worrisome, I hadn't even given it a thought. Not that Nathan wasn't in my thoughts; quite the contrary.

My feet paused short of our door, and I thought about walking back down and going to apologize to Nathan, but I knew that action would result in something less pleasant, and I wasn't in the mood for any lecture from either him, Mrs. Saxon, or anyone.

That was why dread filled my mind when I heard my own name. I turned around to see Jack ascending his side of the stairs. "You okay?" he asked, loud and clear to me, but to anyone else it would be nothing but the sound of the wind blowing outside.

"Yes," I replied in the same way. The low tone didn't help with the lack of confidence in which I said it.

"You don't have to lie." He pointed to his head. This didn't annoy me anywhere near as much as it did the first time he did it. Actually, it didn't annoy me at all. There was something almost comforting about knowing someone else knew how I was feeling since everyone seemed to either dismiss it, or tried to get me to avoid it. "If you ever need to talk, you know where I am," he said with a smile with one hand on the door handle to his hall. Then he disappeared behind the door, but I could still hear his voice, but not with my ears. It was in my head. "One day at a time Larissa. Give your problems the time to solve themselves." It would appear that Jack had learned a new trick.

After dismissing any further consideration of walking down to apologizing to Nathan and facing whatever lecture Mrs. Saxon might give, I walked in through my own door and down the hall. It was silent and empty. Some might even call it desolate, which matched how I was feeling. The yearning to turn back and go seek the comfort of his embrace still pulled, and even at times seemed to be worth the cost. I opened my door, with the thought in my head that the bill would come due for what I had done. I didn't know it would be sent via same day delivery, and it would be due upon receipt.

"Larissa Dubois, what the hell were you thinking?" Jennifer was giving a master class in how to project anger and frustration through her voice. "Let me rephrase the question." She got up off of my bed and walked across the room in my direction. "Were you even thinking? Do you know how dangerous it is to go out there alone?"

"I know! I know!" My hands punched up at the air above me to punctuate the exclamation. I stormed past her to my bed, subconsciously channeling my inner teenager. "It was stupid. I admit." There was no reason to fight it. It was, and I hoped by throwing myself on that sword I could avoid repeated points about how idiotic it was, and we could move on to whatever the next point was.

"You have a dangerous person after you. Any of his goons could be out in those woods just waiting to find you alone, perfect for the pickings. Right now, your best... your only protection is this coven."

"I know, and it won't happen again." And I hoped this wouldn't happen again. There was nothing else I could say on the matter. Just agree, and hope she would let it go. I wanted to see her face for any sign that she was accepting this, but I couldn't break my stare from the floor.

"What were you thinking, anyway?"

"I wasn't."

"Don't give me that." Jennifer's tone had lost its edge, but still stung. "What drove you to take off like that? It's so unlike you."

"I needed to think," I confessed, and thought there wasn't any harm in admitting to that. Though I felt a sudden uncomfortable vulnerability and reached for the pillow on my bed. I sat back against the headboard. Knees pulled up, squeezing the pillow against my chest. Both hands had a death grip on my flimsy shield.

"Think about what?"

A heavy and uncomfortable silence was my answer. The sounds of Jennifer's steps were a welcome rescue from the weight of it, even though it meant she was walking closer to me. She sat on the foot of the bed in a stiff move. Her back straight and stiff, and she rotated at the hips to face me. Even she felt uncomfortable in this setting, and had forgotten her own training.

"You know you can talk to me." It was a statement, but it sounded more like a question.

"There is just a lot going on, and it seems like I am causing problems," I said, keeping things as vague as possible. Not that I didn't trust her. If there was anyone here that I did, it was Jennifer. She started out as a teacher, and had now become more of a sister. What I wanted to avoid was any further lectures. The same reason I didn't go see Nathan. There wasn't anything anyone was going to tell me that I didn't already know.

"The council meeting?"

My eyes finally rose to meet hers, and I let out an exacerbated, "Yep."

"More questions about the Nortons?"

"If it were only that," I blurted, surprised I let it out.

Jennifer leaned forward, bracing herself up with her right arm on the bed. The bed didn't give under her hand, telling of the truthfulness of her pose. I wasn't going to hold this against her. She was trying. "What was it now? More concerns that you are somehow dangerous?"

I nodded, and then added, "and because of me, they are now questioning Mrs. Saxon's ability to run the coven."

A laugh, a very natural sounding one at that, was not the response I was expecting. "Is that what this is about? Larissa, you don't need to worry about that. Rebecca and the council have gone round and round on many things, and it is always the same threat. We will remove you if you don't… It's a tool they use. Don't worry about it. What was it this time? Let me take a guess. Your presence and how dangerous you are puts everyone here at risk."

"Yes. They said we were lucky to survive the first attack."

"And they are right. We were, but it's not the first, and won't be the last threat to come after anyone here. Plus, it is not particular to this coven. Every cove is under some type of threat. It's just part of our lives. Remember, we have talked about this."

We had. It appeared to be a repeating theme from Mrs. and Mr. Bolden, and Mr. Helms. Heck, that was the primary rule of Mr. Helms' class. While I thought I had a firm grasp on the threats, I now questioned if I did. I made a note to talk to Edward about it, who I was sure would give me some answers. Hearing the reminder, didn't make me feel any better though. There was a fact that Jennifer had avoided, and I felt that was the correct word for it, avoided. I seemed to be the magnet for that danger at the moment. If I weren't here, that danger wouldn't be. It may come around some other time, but that would be a different danger, and at a different time.

"So, what were you going to do?" Jennifer asked, but then shock exploded on her face. "You were going to run away, weren't you?"

Again, I let silence be my answer. It was noncommittal either way, though I knew which direction she would take it. It was the direction I would if I were in her position.

"Larissa!" She jumped up off the bed. The fact I didn't feel the mattress spring back told me she wasn't really sitting there. "That would solve nothing. In fact, it would make things worse. Throw that thought right out of your mind." Jennifer walked toward me, and reached out. At first I leaned back harder against the headboard, unsure of what she was trying to do. Both of her hands reached for my shoulders and grabbed them before I could move. For a moment I expected a quick shake based on her expression, but it never arrived. Instead, her fingers attempted to rub my shoulders. "Right out of your head, and never think about that again. We are all family, okay?"

"Okay," I agreed. She spoke to me as a parent might, and I almost answered yes ma'am, even though I was actually older than her.

"Now come on. You get to pick the music tonight. You need to de-stress with the rest of your family." She let go and headed toward the closet, with a few looks back at me to make sure I was following. From half up the stairs, she asked, "Plus you couldn't leave Nathan, now could you?" She kept walking, and I followed her up. I didn't have the heart to tell her that my relationship with Nathan was another issue the council had with Mrs. Saxon, and I didn't plan on leaving without him.

18

"Larissa, when I told you we would protect you. I didn't just mean from external threats. It also meant from those inside our world as well. This coven is your family, and we stand together. If I ever thought you were a danger to anyone here, I wouldn't have let you stay here or roam around freely like everyone else, but I do. I trust you. You have never given me a reason not to trust you, and I don't believe you ever will. You strike me as a very responsible and mature person." Mrs. Saxon backed up, and relaxed a little. Which I appreciated. She cast a long and heavy shadow as she leaned over me while I sat on her white couch. "Until a few things have settled down, I do need you to follow the rules that were set. No wandering out or leaving. Got it?"

"Yes ma'am."

"Good," she said, and walked away from the sofa satisfied.

She was until my bad habit reared its ugly head. "I can't believe she told you," I mumbled.

Mrs. Saxon performed an amazing and shocking pivot on the heel of her high-heels. The look on her face was less than amused. "I am glad she did." When she stepped toward me, I knew I was in for another lecture, and again it was my fault. "Look, I understand what you were thinking, but running away was the absolute wrong solution."

"But I didn't run away," I said, pleading a point that was just a technicality. I hadn't run away, just out to the cove to think. She knew that. It was in confidence that I told Jennifer what I had considered while I was out there.

"No, you didn't, but you were thinking about it," she responded, frustrated in tone and expression. Her gaze was intense, and her foot tapped on the floor at a furious pace. Then it all stopped with a single sigh. No tapping. No glare burning a hole through me. She sat on the end of the couch, several cushions away from me. "Larissa, I am not going to talk to you as a student, or even a young teen anymore. You are an adult, and I am not just using this as a psychological ploy many parents do. You are an adult, and you need to work with me here. You have done nothing wrong. You are not a threat to anyone. You are not a problem to me or anyone either. Let the council finish whatever this is, and they will see it too. Running, like you were considering, would only paint you guilty in their eyes of whatever they believe this is. As hard as it is to hear them say these things, just as they say grin and bear it. Someone has already told me this too will pass."

Even though I was listening to her, and understood every word she said, I still had to snicker. My reaction produced a moment of surprise that was followed by a snicker of her own. "I did it again, didn't I?"

"Yep, twice." Several of us had started our own version of a drinking game a few weeks ago. There was no alcohol, or anything being drank, just a score being tallied. At the end of the day, whoever had heard the most cliché's from Mrs. Saxon throughout both her English classes and her Spells class, won. Of course, that meant the witches had an advantage over the others. Mrs. Saxon greeted the news of our contest with a humorous smile, and then it was on. There was a drop in her use of them, but a few still slipped out from time to time.

"Well, it doesn't make anything less true. Now get to class, and next time you get these strange thoughts going through your head, talk to me. You may be older than me, but I have more experience in the dealings of the Council of Mages." She sat there, just looking at me, as if she were waiting for a response, but she didn't ask a question. It didn't take long until this moment was reclassified an uncomfortable silence. Which was the worst type.

My master escape plan? To do what she had just told me to do. I got up and headed out the door to class. While I dreaded the lectures from both Jennifer and Mrs. Saxon, I had to admit I felt a little better. Nothing was solved, and if anything, there were more challenges, but they weren't mine alone. And those I thought I was a problem for, were really my allies working to help. That relieved some of the weight I felt pressing its burden down on me. Not that there was a bounce in my step. There was still a long way to go before that happened, and I had just enough time before class to check on one of the puzzle pieces that might lead to that.

I slipped inside the library and promptly called out, "Edward."

Just as prompt as always, he appeared. "Good morning Miss Dubois."

"Morning Edward. I wanted to check in on our little project."

"I imagined you might. So far, I have found 1,184 references to the name Norton, but upon cross referencing all mentions of the name, except two, were witches or humans, and none of them shared the name Thomas or Marie. The only two references that did, were the two pictures you have seen."

The news wasn't what I wanted to hear, but it was what I thought I might hear. That didn't stop me from feeling or sounding disappointed. "Thanks Edward."

"Miss Dubois. You only asked me to research and report back, so it is not my place to do analysis, but I would be remiss if I didn't mention to you that the lack of mention most likely means they were not involved in what you believe they were. In my review, there were over two hundred altercations and incidents between Jean St. Claire's Coven and the Orleans' Coven during the time period you asked me to

"No," I said and reached up to try to meet his lips again. This time instead of speaking, he turned his head ever so slightly, but I took what he gave me and kissed his cheek before I apologized again.

"You were, weren't you?"

"No, I wasn't," I said, as I let go and backed up. He was no longer looking at the other wall, and as much as I normally enjoyed being the focus of his gaze at this moment I would prefer his pained eyes were back on the wall. It wouldn't feel that hurt like I would.

With the sound of others coming down the hall, I reached out and did something with Nathan I had never done before. I yanked him by the arm, against his will, and forced him down the hall and through a door I had never gone in before. After I slammed him against the backside of the door, both hands pressing his shoulders back against it, I spent a second, or maybe two, looking around at what appeared to be some kind of art studio of various shapes sculpted out of stone. An accelerated thumping in Nathan's chest told me he was shocked by my action, and a protest built inside his opening mouth. I didn't let it escape. "Not without you."

Well, that ended any protest he was planning to make. His mouth abruptly shut, and a new shock overtook him.

"I just felt like I was causing everyone trouble being here. I was putting everyone at risk of being hurt or killed if Jean made another attempt, and then there is your mother. The council, those that run things, were questioning her judgement and ability to run the coven because she let me stay here. To be honest, there wasn't a positive to me being here, except you." I put in a dramatic pause to let that sit with him for a minute before I continued. I really wanted him to understand that. We were big into the holding of each other, but my favorite was kissing. Though I had to hold myself back. What we weren't great at doing was expressing our feelings in words. Neither one of us had ever told the other how we really felt, and absolutely never used the 'L' word. Something that I felt was a war of wills, and I wasn't going to lose, but if he couldn't read between the lines, I might have to surrender my position. "Every thought I had of getting out of here had you coming with me. That was the only option I considered. I would not leave without you, but I am not going anywhere." I let go of the firm grip I had on his shoulders, and gave him a quirky little smile, "Call it just a moment of being an overdramatic teenager."

He finally melted and pulled me in for that embrace I so craved, and for a reason I couldn't explain, it felt warmer than it ever had before.

We walked out hand-and-hand. Our appearance coming from the door raised a few eyebrows, and a comment from Laura, "And what were you two doing behind that closed door?" I squeezed Nathan's hand and hoped he got the message. I was going to handle this.

"Wouldn't you like to know?" I remarked as we walked in the classroom's door.

review. Of those entries, not a single one was missing the names of those involved. There is simply no mention of them."

It would be great if my brain would accept that as the truth and move on. It would be even better if the council accepted it, but I was in no means an expert on how they worked or how they thought. I was barely that when it came to myself, and I knew enough self-doubt had lived in my brain for the last several weeks that even the truth presented by Edward still had question marks behind it. Maybe the only truth I would have accepted was that they were involved. That was the easiest of all. Or it seemed. Even when I considered that, the question of why, and if they had a good reason resonated around in my head. There always seemed to be more questions. "Thanks for looking Edward."

"My pleasure Miss Dubois," then he disappeared, as did I.

I backed out through the door and headed to class. Or that was the intention, but I saw an obstacle standing in the way. One that normally would be welcomed, but that expression on Nathan's face this morning leaning against the wall outside the classroom and waiting on me was anything but. He was hurt. His eyes only cut in my direction a few times. The rest of the time he was focused on the opposing wall. I knew this was coming, this would be the third, and probably the most dreaded of all the lectures. This one would be emotionally charged on all sides, and I needed to diffuse it before it blew up in my face. We had the hall to ourselves for the moment, so I took the opportunity to rush up to him and wrapped my arms around his waist. "I'm sorry."

I felt my connection with him the moment I felt his warmth, but it didn't take long to notice something missing. This was a one way connection, and it hadn't been returned. His arms still hung loosely down at his side, holding his books, not up around my shoulders pressing his books in to back where they needed to be, so I said it again. This time muffled by his chest. "I am so sorry."

God, I hated silence. All types of it, and it seemed I had been forced to suffer through each one. Just this morning there was the awkward silence, and now the empty silence, which hurt the worse of all. It meant something was missing, and not just sound. Something you longed for. Something that defined you. Something that was now gone, leaving a hole. That is what I felt. I gripped him harder, hoping to fill that spot, but it wasn't something I could. He had to help and meet me halfway.

In a move of desperation, I looked up at him and made an awkward attempt to bat my eyes, and reached up to let my lips meet his, hoping I could force it out of him. My lips were almost there. They could feel the warmth of his breath against them when he spoke, instead of leaning down to meet me.

"You were going to just leave?" I could hear the pain in his voice, as his words punched me in the gut.

What eyebrows hadn't raised earlier, raised when I opted for a new seat in Mrs. Saxon's English class. The one right next to Nathan. It was his idea. Something about it being harder for me to get away when I was sitting next to him. I didn't mind.

That was the way we were for most of the morning classes. My escort up to the afternoon classes only let go of my hand after a firm request, "You promise not to run?"

I answered that request with a kiss, which I thought would be answer enough, but his hand didn't let go of mine. As I pulled back away, he used my hand to yank me back closer, and asked again, "You promise not to run?"

"I thought I answered you." I accompanied that with a wide smile, or as wide as I dared give. I still hadn't ever shown Nathan my fangs, and surprisingly he hadn't asked. In fact, other than that one time he asked me what it was like to be turned, Nathan never made any references to my being a vampire.

"That wasn't the answer I was looking for," Nathan said sternly.

"I won't run. I am not going anywhere." Only then did he let my hand go. "I will see you tonight for our normal date."

"You have a lot to make up for." Nathan grabbed me, and before I knew it, he was kissing me, and I melted.

The rest of the afternoon went like a normal afternoon, which meant as abnormal as possible. Today's assignment in Mrs. Saxon's class, teleportation. Which fascinated me. I wondered if that was the trick that I saw Gwen do from time to time during Mr. Helms' class, but as Mrs. Saxon demonstrated it didn't look the same. Also, she explained this wouldn't come naturally to anyone here, and some may not even be able to master it. She was right. By the end of the class, only Jack and Lisa managed to make something disappear, and Jack was able to bring it back. Lisa still didn't know where her ball had gone by the time class ended. My first attempt didn't exactly work. The ball just flickered, but then on the second attempt, poof it disappeared, and never appeared. When we reached Mrs. Tenderschott's potion class, Jack confessed to me he didn't know how he brought it back.

Jack asked me a few times how I was doing and reminded me that he was there if I needed to talk to someone. I thanked him, but when I realized how it sounded, I surprised him when I added, "I really mean it. You would be who I would come to." I punctuated it with a pat on his back. It was a truthful response. The fact that he would know how I was feeling and what was going on in my mind made him the perfect external sounding board to talk to. Could be a useful ability for a psychologist or therapist if he ever pursued life as a human.

Things were progressing well in Mr. Helms' class. Walking in, I saw his motto posted high on the wall and remembered that two others has basically quoted it to me earlier. Maybe I should adopt it as my credo? Something about that seemed almost a given since someone everywhere had questions or problems with me. I wasn't sure if that also drove the extra focus I had in class. My performance was unmatched today. Even drawing comments from Mr. Helms, Tera, and of all people Gwen. "The perfect balance of vampire speed, and leptokinesis." After class, I had to stop in the library and ask Edward what that big word was. He explained it meant control over the world at a molecular level. What a fancy word to explain heating air until you had a ball of fire to throw.

I watched the clock like a hawk while I waited for the hands to show seven thirty. I could have thought of a digital clock, but there was something about the ticking of an old fashion clock that was soothing during the silent moments I spent in my room. Which was mostly when I was doing my homework. I once tried to listen to some music while writing an essay, and realized my mind was too easily distracted with all the other stuff rolling around in it. With the music added on top of that, the essay wasn't being written. There was no essay for me to write tonight. Just more geometry and studying for a history quiz. I left the geometry for Nathan to help me with, though I was sure he was going to quiz me on history as well since I told him more than once it was my weakest area. A statement that drove Nathan to make the commitment to make sure I passed the course. I didn't have the heart to break it to him that I was getting it now.

When the clock finally hit that magical time, I ran out my door and down the stairs. Not caring if anyone saw my eagerness. When I hit the stairs, I stopped dead in my tracks, or rather froze in my tracks. There was a chill in the air, and snow. Snow was falling there in the entry, with a light layer of it covering the last of the leaves that were piled on the floor below. The walk down the stairs and out to the pool was a journey of wonderment as I craned my neck up to see where the snow came from. It didn't really come from anywhere; it just appeared up high around the ceiling and fell as flurries to the floor.

"What is with that?" I asked Nathan from halfway up the path.

"The first flurries of the season. Thanksgiving is this week. Remember I told you the leaves turn to snow then. It will be a regular snowstorm after that and throughout the winter, before disappearing in the spring. Just like out here. We will probably have our first snow fall in the next few weeks."

"Wild." I leaned down and kissed Nathan before he had a chance to stand up.

"You think that is wild, just wait for Christmas. Snowmen, candy canes, a large tree, and a life-sized gingerbread house."

If I were any other place, I would think he was joking. I sat down, and spread out my books, putting my Geometry book and homework on the top. Of course, I didn't physically touch the book as it opened and turned to the right page, keeping my hands below the table so he didn't see the movements to add a little to the impressiveness to the trick.

What was the response I received? A very unimpressed, overdone, yawn that included a full stretch of both arms back behind his head. Well, if that didn't impress him, then maybe this would. I made a quick flourish of my hand and the air around us sparkled. His chair squeaked against the concrete of the deck as he jumped, and I wasn't even halfway done with the trick. As the sparkles disappeared the pool, the coven, and the woods all vanished. Replacing them were the turquoise waters of the Greek islands. We had a perfect view of them crashing against the white limestone cliff we were atop, with a quaint white villa around us. "I believe the Greeks were the fathers of geometry," I said nonchalantly, adding my own very much overacted yawn.

Impressed might not be the right word. Nathan leaped from his chair and walked around; each step an exploratory one. He even bent down to touch the craggy limestone that was beneath his feet. An act which produced a few nervous seconds for me. I had only discovered this ability a few hours ago in my room. I was feeling a little of the stress setting back in and wanted to see the cove. I remembered something I had read about glamour, the ability to change what someone sees, and gave it a shot, and poof, I was at the cove. Well not really. Over the next few hours, I had visited the cove, my home in Virginia where the Nortons lived, my home in New Orleans, and the lilac fields that I loved to lay in as a small girl. It was amazing, it actually felt like I was there. I could see and smell everything. Even the sweet soft smell of the lilac carried in the wind on a cool summer's evening. What I never did was touch anything.

I watched as his hand touched it and rubbed across it. His fingers moved slightly up and down tracing the rough surface, and knew it was a success when he stood up slowly looking at the palm of his hand with little particles of white lime dust on them. "Oh, mom isn't going to be happy about this. You aren't supposed to leave the coven. That was your agreement."

I got up and walked up behind him. His body jumped at my touch, but settled as I wrapped my arms around him. "Trust me," I whispered, and placed one hand over his eyes.

"Oh, I don't know about..." he started to protest, but stopped as soon as I pulled my hand away letting him see the pool, the deck, and the coven.

"We never went anywhere. It's called glamour. I read about it in your mom's text. I can change what someone sees and perceives, but none of it is real. Like, for example." I let go of him and waved my hand again, sending a shower of sparkles over us. When they hit the ground, we were standing in a familiar magnolia lined dirt path. "This is where I grew up."

"The farmhouse in New Orleans?"

"The plantation just outside of New Orleans," I corrected.

He walked down the path, little puffs of dirt under each step just like I remembered during the really dry periods of the fall. As a little girl it made me feel fast to leave a trail of that behind me. As I learned to master more of my skill, I used it to produce a lot of it to look more like what a car or the truck we had would have produced. He stopped at the porch steps with one foot in the air. Almost unsure if he stepped down if he would step through the wooden step or step up on it.

"Go ahead. I already did just to test things. The best I can figure, what you see is as complete as my memory can make it. By the way, I don't know what you would have found if you had walked much further back on the cliff. That was just an image I created in my head. What was inside the villa I hadn't thought about yet."

His foot landed on the step, and the board let out the familiar creak. Then his next step landed on the porch with a light thud. I rushed across the porch to open the screen door. It was my home. It was only appropriate that I was the one who invited him in.

I gave him the grand tour of the place, starting with the parlor that was off to the left, and the kitchen to the right. Even though this was my illusion, I still geeked out touching everything just to feel the texture. Nathan did the same. We were kids in the candy shop of my memories. My fingers lightly brushed up the length of the stair railing as we went up to my room. Every little nick and character mark in the wood was the key to a door unlocking another memory in my head. Amy ran through the wall and down the stairs toward us with her story book for our reading time, and her stoic escort standing behind her.

I sent another shower of sparkles over us, and my old home dissolved, and my new home appeared. Amy hit Nathan full force hugging his legs. She gave me a sidelong glance until I leaned down and held my arms out for her. She pouted her way over before wrapping her arms around me. My arms squeezed her lightly, and I gave what I hoped would be my last apology for a while. "Sorry I missed you last night."

"I thought you left," she said with a sniff.

"Just needed some time to think," I replied. "I wouldn't go anywhere without you, squirt." I picked her up and walked over to our chairs and had a seat. "So what story is it tonight?"

A cough from a lounger on the other side of the pool interrupted Amy's deliberation over the choices of stories we had. I looked up from the book and saw Mrs. Parrish pointing at Nathan while she shook her head. Painfully I understood her meaning.

"Hey Amy. Nathan looks all alone over there. Why don't you go sit in his lap while we read?"

My suggestion drew a quizzical look from both Amy and Nathan. I quickly cut my eyes toward Mrs. Parrish, sending Nathan's rolling, and an encouraging "Go on," sent Amy over to the other side of the table while I mouthed a question toward her chaperone. "Better?"

There was no reply. Just her normal icy and stoic glare. The same glare that continued all the way through Nathan's reading of "Beauty and the Beast," or what I consider our love story. It was still undecided which of us was the beauty and which was the beast.

Promptly with the end of the story, Mrs. Parrish was on the move to retrieve Amy and take her off to bed. I watched her expression as Amy walked around the table to me to give me a hug and say goodnight. I gave her a kiss on the forehead and sent her on her way.

"Did you see that look she gave you?" Nathan asked.

"Yep." I saw it and felt it. It was a hostile, I don't want to meet that woman in a dark alley, kind of look.

19

A couple of days passed after my attempted, or thoughts of, escape, and the concerns that drove me out to the cove that day lost a little of their shadow, and a little of their weight. The concern of being a problem had worn off, and I was feeling that belonging again, with both groups. I was still a prisoner, in a manner of speaking. Before I was put on house arrest I had never even thought about leaving, ironically. Now because there was an order, I felt the presence of the virtual handcuffs. Jennifer told me to just accept it as the price, an unjust one, to end all this and have things return to normal.

Lisa, Tera, and I spent a good portion of the free time after class, and after my story time dates with Nathan, to work on teleportation spells. The one skill that still seemed to evade most of us. With the one lone exception Jack, and that turned into a challenge. One that even persuaded Queen Gwen to work with me without trying to set my hair on fire. The challenge. Each side had ten balls. His were red, ours were yellow. Of course, they just appeared when they were needed. Targets were placed along the pool deck, in the pool, and just on the edge for the woods. All easily seen from the balcony. The aim of the game, make each ball teleport and reappear at that target. The closest to the actual target won the point. The only rule. No other magic could be used. The balls had to disappear and reappear at the target. We couldn't make them reappear somewhere else and then move them through any other means.

We all knew we were in trouble the first night. After twenty minutes of even trying to get a ball to disappear, Jack yelled down to us he would go first to show us how it was done. Damn it, if he didn't put his right on the middle of the target furthest away from all of us. After another couple of minutes, finally one of our balls disappeared. That was progress. We just didn't know who did it, or where it went. I knew it wasn't me. My attempts only caused it to fade. I had yet to make one completely disappear. I was watching mine fade for the third time, when Gwen's normally annoying high-pitched squeal broke my concentration. I didn't cut her a curt look this time. We were both on the same team, and when I looked out of the balcony, there was one yellow ball a few feet from one of the umbrella tables on the pool deck. The closest of all targets. Nathan and Martin ran to measure the distance to the table.

"Four feet, eleven inches," yelled Martin as he and Nathan scurried back inside. Neither wanted to be out there with balls possibly falling from the air, or worst reappearing inside them. Before it began, Jack dropped one in front of Martin and yelled fetch, which resulted in a swift middle finger.

Another half an hour later, our second one deposited itself in the middle of two targets. Gwen wouldn't tell us which one she was going for. Jack on the other hand had placed all ten of his inside of a foot of each target. We were miserably behind with really no way of catching up.

The second night went a little better. Tera had somehow discovered the secret, which she wouldn't share with anyone. She wasn't as proficient as Jack, but she was better than Gwen which created a little of a rift among our alliance against Jack. She made sure not to dominate things, but didn't hesitate to show off when it was her turn. Once even going for the same target Gwen did, but besting her by ten feet, putting it just inches from the center. What came closest to putting her over the edge was when one of mine finally completed the whole trick. It not only faded, but reappeared close to where I visualized, earning a "Not bad for a blood sucker," from Jack. I knew he meant it as a joke.

By the third night, news of our little game had gotten out and now Mrs. Saxon, Mrs. Tenderschott, and Mr. Helms all attended our balcony competition. Mr. Demius never left his residence for anything, adding to the mystery and the stories told of him and his world of the dark arts. So far at this moment his only student was Lisa, but Mrs. Saxon told me I would join them for a class next month.

Each of us now had a good handle on the skill. Which was to say, we could all make something disappear and then reappear somewhat close to our intended target at will. Some were better than others. To even things up, we split up in two teams. It was Jack and Tera against Lisa, Gwen, and me. My membership on her team was at Gwen's request.

We also had a good crowd up above on the vampire's deck, and it was easy to say who their favorite was, even if that meant Apryl would have to cheer for Gwen. A point Brad rubbed in a few times.

Nathan and the rest of the werewolves were the official score keepers. Even Steve and Stan got into the act as score keepers. Stan originally had a different idea on how to take part. He wanted to be a target himself, quickly changing into a rock with a red target on top of it to show us he was up to the task. We were getting better, but weren't completely confident that he would be safe, so we had to disappoint him and just make him master of a tape measure. Suspiciously absent was Amy and Cynthia, Steve's sister. I knew Mrs. Parrish was behind that.

In the game of best two out of three, Jack and Tera mopped the floor with us. The second game only went to us thanks to a few lucky placements by us right on the target instead of yards away like most of our attempts. It seemed the loss stung Gwen more than Lisa or me. We were simply happy with the progress we had made.

Later that night on the deck, my new trick had become a little of a party trick, with everyone asking me to move something or other around on the deck. I entertained a few, but after that I started refusing the challenges saying my witch powers were tired. A comment that received more than a few odd looks.

"Is that how it works?" Laura asked.

"Yep, and I can feel my meter was on 'E.'" Jennifer hid her giggle behind her hand. It wasn't really that much of a stretch. Every spell and every trick took concentration, and even though I physically didn't get tired, my ability to hold focus for that long did wane, and I was reaching that point now. I had one last trick in me, and that would be it for the night. I turned on the music, with a little light show.

20

Mr. Markinson was halfway into his lecture on the kinematic equations when Mrs. Saxon knocked on the door. The minute her head poked in through the door, my heart sunk. I knew who she was here for, and I got up and headed to the door before she called my name. Silence escorted me out of the room, with the thought about how just when you felt good, life likes to turn on the cold shower, and I had a feeling this was going to be frigid.

"Sorry about this Larissa. I wasn't given any warning," she said as we walked toward the ritual room. If her expression wasn't enough to tell me she was concerned, the tone of her voice and the pace of her walk drove it home with an exclamation point.

"What do they want?"

"It's not a they, and I am not exactly sure," she responded, rather annoyed. Once we entered and pushed through the curtain, I knew exactly why she was annoyed. Standing there in the center of the room was Miss Sarah Julia Roberts, all prim and perfect.

"Hello, Miss Norton," she sneered.

"It's Miss Dubois, and what do you want this time?" I stopped right where I was and crossed my arms. Seeing her alone was surprising and frightening all at the same time.

"A few of us were talking, and we have decided to try a different method to get to the truth. A more invasive method."

"What if I don't want you poking around inside my head anymore? You have seen all there is to see."

"Then we would be left to conclude that our fears are true, and you are hiding details of your relationship with the Nortons."

"There is nothing to hide." It almost sounded like I was pleading, and caught myself throwing my arms down when I said it, which I quickly corrected, and recrossed my arms, tighter than before. I wanted Miss Roberts to see me as a large boulder. Immovable, and uncrackable. If she pushed me the wrong way, I might roll back on her.

"Yes. Yes. That is what you have said all along, and that is what you may believe. You may not even be aware of what they were doing, but that doesn't make it any less dangerous."

"What makes me dangerous?" I boomed, echoing around the chamber and even surprising myself. I wanted to seem strong, and a bit pissed off, but not hostile. That was over the top and needed to be toned down a little, but it was hard. That mass of frustration inside was hitting a critical temperature, and it soon would take on a life of its own as anger. Master Thomas had told me the answer to that question, but I wanted to hear them own up to it.

"We have been all through this before. No need to rehash it now," she replied coolly.

"No," interjected Mrs. Saxon. "Larissa asks a valid question."

"Mrs. Saxon, your opinion has no value in these proceedings, and your allowed presence is just a courtesy. Need I remind you that your own judgement in these matters has come into question?"

"No, you don't, and while I believe this will fall on deaf ears as you have already made up your own mind, my judgement is based on what I know of the person herself. If the council would take a moment to get to know her, you would see what I see."

She looked right at me, ignoring Mrs. Saxon all together, and stated, "We know the person, what she is, and who raised her. We know all that is needed. Now shall we proceed?"

Miss Roberts stepped toward me. Not showing any of the fear she once did in my presence. I let her come, at first, but when she was a few feet away, I stepped back to create more space. With that step, I felt my body coil up, and my legs flexed. Kudos to Mr. Helms. His training had kicked in, putting me in a defensive posture without even having to think about it. My enemy is everyone and everywhere.

"I am going to call Mrs. Wintercrest," screamed Mrs. Saxon.

"You do that," Miss Roberts responded with a cackle. "She is the one who sent me."

She was calm and cool on the outside. Her arms were held out a little, ready for whatever I might send her way. Her insides were a different story. Her heart raced. Maybe she was here looking for a fight. Maybe it was adrenaline in response to my stance. Maybe it was fear. It's impossible to tell the difference. Each create the same response in the physical body. Racing heart. Sweat. Oh, to have Jack's ability to sense emotions, not that I would ever admit my jealousy to him.

"Master Thomas then."

"Go ahead," Miss Roberts challenged with her focus firmly on me. I wasn't sure who she was responding to. I had no intentions on making the first move, but if she did, she was getting a response. "Miss Norton, we can do this the easy way or the hard way. Either way is fine with me." Her body crouched slightly. So slight, that I may have been the only one able to perceive it. It was accompanied by a long slow exhale.

With no other choices, and Mrs. Saxon frozen there watching these proceedings, helpless to stop it, I made my move. I relaxed my body and stood up straight. Vampire straight. No slouching. "Miss Roberts, if you see no wrongdoing by the Nortons will I have yours and the council's word that you will let this go and accept me as a sister?" I knew I was pushing the olive branch a little with that last bit, but I saw an opening, and hoped that by reducing the tension of the moment I could lull her into an agreement that she might normally have resisted.

"I can speak for the council, that those concerns would be put to bed," she said, also relaxing her posture.

I noticed she ignored the sister part, but that was okay. I wasn't too sure I wanted to be her sister anyway. All I wanted was for them to leave me alone, and if I had to endure one more probing, it would be worth it. So, I agreed. "All right then."

"Larissa, you don't have to. Let me consult Master Thomas on this matter first."

"No, it's okay Mrs. Saxon. I have nothing to hide, and this ends it all, then why wait." I turned to Miss Roberts, for confirmation, and a little jab. "Right, Sarah?"

There was a look of disdain at hearing her own name cross my lips.

"So how do we do this?" I asked clapping my hands together. "Do I drink something? Stare into a magical mirror? What?"

"Hold out your hands," requested Miss Roberts. I did and watched her hands timidly approach mine. She was doing her best to control the shake, but I could see it, and then felt it when they gripped mine.

There we were, standing in the center of the all-black ritual room, being looked down on by those fat cherubs—who I was going to one day take care of when no one was looking—holding hands with someone who seemed to dislike me more than Gwen, and what do I do? I crack a joke of course. "Should we sing a song or something?"

She was not amused. "This will use dark magic, so try not to scream." She began mumbling to herself, in a language that seemed to lack a lot of vowels. I waited for the room to disappear behind some kind of cloak of darkness or cloud like seemed to always happen, but the room stayed there, steady. It was us that was disappearing. It started with our hands, slowing fading out, then it progressed up our arms, and body. I looked up at her face, her eyes closed, just as it faded away too.

This was different. Definitely different. I didn't find myself in a dream like state, or with anyone else there. I was nowhere, and I was alone. "Hello?," my voice echoed in the chasm that was this space. It was its only answer. I could move and walk, but there was no place to go. Just dark emptiness everywhere, and the feeling around me was getting to me.

I waited and waited. Every moment that passed, let the emptiness around consume me and suck any feeling of existence out of me. Every source of happiness and hope pulled out by the big vacuum of the universe. I tried to remember good memories. Those from my childhood, but those disappeared as soon as I remembered them. The quiet afternoons with the Nortons, and again, they flew out of existence before they even materialized. One source of happiness and hope remained, and I was afraid to even think of it out of fear of losing it, but it was too late. I couldn't remember what Nathan looked like, then soon I couldn't even remember his name. Any remembrance that there was someone was gone.

I came back to the room, still holding her hands, but now on my knees on the floor. Overcome with the emptiness, and just a shell of who I was. If only I knew that was the best I was going to feel for the next few days.

"I found what we were looking for," Miss Roberts announced.

"Then now you can leave Larissa alone, you can see she is not the danger you think she is," challenged Mrs. Saxon. There was hope and relief in her voice, but I knew from how proudly Miss Roberts had made her report, something was wrong. She didn't strike me as the type that would readily and happily admit when she was wrong about something.

"You misunderstand Mrs. Saxon. It is exactly like we believed."

Mrs. Saxon let out a disbelieving, "What?" I was with her in disbelief but unable to verbalize it or react. I was just there, a shell.

Miss Roberts released my left hand and it flopped to the floor. "Come join hands with us and I will show you." She reached out for Mrs. Saxon who seemed both eager and timid about doing so.

"Larissa, is there anything?" she asked.

I knew what she meant by her partial question, and all I could muster was a shake of my head. There was nothing. Nothing I could think of or remember that could even be construed to be what Miss Roberts was looking for, but that didn't mean I didn't remember it, or misunderstood it. Maybe I was naïve.

Mrs. Saxon reached down and grabbed my hand. I was still looking down at the floor and couldn't see either woman's face, but I could imagine Miss Roberts with that arrogant smile, and Mrs. Saxon trying to hold it together. I also didn't know when she finally joined hands with Miss Roberts, but I knew when the spell took hold propelling me back into the darkness.

This time the darkness didn't last. It quickly dissipated leaving me looking at a scene that was both familiar and unfamiliar. I recognized the kitchen in my home with the Nortons. Not that we used it often. It was more of the room that we passed through to get out the backdoor, and maybe sat around at it as a family to talk a few times. Unlike most families, we didn't gather around it for a nightly dinner. There was no need. That was why what I saw reignited the fire inside me. I was still reeling from the toll the first visit took. Something had been taken from me during that trip into my memory. Now someone was trying to put something back.

"Bullshit!" I yelled as loud as I could muster. It came out as a hoarse cough. I did it again, "Bullshit!" and felt a strange sensation following that exertion. I was weak, and fading fast, but that didn't stop me from standing up where I was, and looking around to find Mrs. Saxon and Miss Roberts. I turned right at her, and pointed. "You bitch! This never happened." My hand beckoned at the image in front of us. There I was, sitting there in a blue jumper, something I would have never worn, sitting at the table doing what looked like homework with Mrs. Norton, dressed in a white wool sweater she wore often.

"We haven't even started," Miss Roberts said smugly.

I mustered all I could and looked her right in the face. "You don't need to. We never did this." I turned to Mrs. Saxon. "Ever." I walked over to the table, and ripped the papers out from under myself, and threw them in the air. "There was never anything like homework. My studies were all lessons we covered through reading or on the chalkboard in my room." I put my finger right in Miss Roberts' face, "You are making this up."

The false memory started playing. Mrs. Norton looked at me from across the table and said, "Larissa, I want you to remember, you are better than everyone else out there. You are special. Never let anyone hold you back. Don't forget you are meant for remarkable things."

"Great things," said a deep voice that struck right through the heart. I hadn't heard it in weeks, and just the sound brought a single tear to my eye. The sight of him walking across the kitchen and leaning over me, filled both eyes. "And, when the time is right you will be ready. We are going to make sure of it."

"Do we need to see more?" asked Miss Roberts.

My reply probably wasn't what she was looking for. "That depends, have you created more?"

"Miss Norton. These are your memories. This one is proof of our concerns, but let us continue." The kitchen disappeared, and we were outside in our backyard that was framed by tall bushes from the edge of the house to the edge of the woods. This was all wrong. Not that Mrs. Norton and I were never out in the backyard, but she made a rookie mistake. The sun was out way too much for our liking. We would never have been out here with it this bright. It was overcast days, or early evening and nights that were the only times we ever ventured outside, and what was that thing in the middle of the yard? Some kind of mannequin. I watched as Mr. Norton pointed out the neck, the chest just over the heart, and then made a running pass, leaping, and yanking the head of it clean off in a single move while flipping before he landed on his feet. I was about to scream at Miss Roberts when I saw me running at the same dummy, now with its head replaced, and mimicking what Mr. Norton had done. I turned around to both Mrs. Saxon, and Miss Roberts before the other me ever landed on the ground.

Before she even knew it, I had my hand wrapped around Miss Roberts' neck. "Would you like for me to show you what I would really do to that dummy?" I growled and let my fangs show, as I edged just on the boundary of control.

"Larissa, are you saying this isn't true?" Mrs. Saxon asked. Her voice dripped with doubt.

"Not an inch," I spat. Everything around us disappeared and we were right back in the black room, with the spying cherubs.

"Let me go," croaked Miss Roberts. I felt the vibration of every syllable in my hand. Against my better judgment, I released my grip, and she slid down to the floor, and stumbled backward away from me.

21

I sat in my window fuming over what had transpired. That overdone Hollywood witch bitch had fabricated memories, my memories to make her case. This wasn't even a case of stretching the truth, or taking something out of context, which I felt they may have been able to do if they were that hellbent on proving their point to be true. I had no clue they would go to these lengths. Worse yet, there was nothing I could do about it. No protest, nothing I could do to show them the truth.

Mrs. Saxon said she would speak to Master Thomas who seemed to be more reasonable, and somewhat on my side. He had even mentioned to Mrs. Saxon in confidence, which she broke to calm me down, that to him it was a "so-what" if what Mrs. Wintercrest and Miss Roberts felt was true really was. If I had been groomed, or not. I was still who I was, with the potential to do what I wanted to do.

He was just one person. One out of twelve. Could he sway the others? I didn't know. I didn't even know if I could trust him, yet. I could trust Mrs. Saxon, but even though I promised to let her handle it, I knew her reach would be rather limited. Those members of the council that appeared to be more outspoken than others, didn't seem to trust her. The only thing that was certain in my head was, I couldn't just sit around and wait. I needed to do something. Something to prove to everyone what the real truth was, and there was only one person who could help.

I felt broken sitting with Nathan that night. He knew something was wrong, and was aware that there was another visit from the council. I told him to expect me to be off anytime they visit, which he seemed to understand and said his mother was the same way. With what I had observed, I understood why. These were not nice, everything-is-great sessions. These were, someone screwed up and we want to find someone to burn at the stake meetings. I doubted that they physically did that, but I didn't know. What I knew was I felt like I had been metaphorically burned at the stake. I could still feel the sizzle. It took everything to hold back tears as I gave Amy a kiss on top of the head after our story time. I couldn't even take pleasure in the look of disdain from Mrs. Parrish as I did it. My world was too weepy for that kind of spite based pleasure. When it was time to say good night to Nathan, I held on longer than I had before, and didn't hold back.

"Whoa, what was that?" he asked breathlessly.

"Just wanted to show you how much I love you." I caved in the battle of wills. It needed to be said. With what I was about to do, I wasn't sure I would ever see him again.

My confession appeared to not only catch him off guard but also delight him. Inside, I begged, please don't say it back. Hearing it would only make it harder. Of course, life had a way of picking the hard path where I was involved, and he said it. "Larissa, I love you too." Then we kissed again, and again I didn't hold back. I let all of my emotions flow. Hands, lips, everything working to devour him. I didn't care who, if anyone, saw. It sent him leaning back against the staircase in the grand entry, just inside the door to the pool. This was where we normally said our goodbyes, but tonight I had a different plan, and I walked him back to his door, hand-and-hand, with the biggest smile I could muster. At the door, there was another sweet kiss, before I watched him go inside. I stood there for a moment, and let two tears slowly trace down my cheeks to my chin, where I wiped them away. Then used the anger from earlier in the day to drive my resolve and headed straight for the door.

For the first time since I arrived, I stepped back out on that dilapidated porch. With all the beauty and grandeur of the inside, it was hard to accept how it looked on the outside. I trekked through the weeds and past Mrs. Saxon's long black car, again a stark contrast to the state of the property it was parked at, and headed down the street. I knew where I was going, just not quite sure how I was going to get there. The one benefit, it was night, and no one was out. That meant I could run.

Every city had a bus depot or train station. Well not every city. I knew the train station was over an hour away in another city. That was where Mrs. Saxon picked me up, but there had to be a bus station here. Usually those were in the center of the city, or close to it. Now, if I only knew where the center of Ipswich was. I roamed around for about an hour before I spied something odd on Peatfield Street. A train station. Well not really, it was more of a commuter rail that picked up and dropped off in Ipswich, but that was it. It was definitely the end of the line, not continuing beyond the platform, but to me it was the start of something.

A quick check of the map, and a public terminal showed me that the train sitting here was the Newburyport/Rockport line, and it was leaving in 20 minutes. Its first drop off was in Chelsea. From there I could figure out what was next. I approached the conductor who had his hand out for a ticket, and I just waved my hand making what looked like one appear in his. He welcomed me onboard, and I stepped on and moved to the last car, and sat in the last row.

There was no sleeping this time. I sat and waited until we moved, with only me and two others in this car, probably because of the late hour. Out the window I watched with tears of regret as Ipswich faded away in the distance, giving way to a lush green countryside. I knew what I was leaving behind, but I knew that future was limited unless I could find what I was looking for.

About forty minutes later, the train pulled into the station at Chelsea, and I waited until the other two passengers in this car made their way out before I stood up and did the same. I crossed into the first car, and about jumped out of my skin. I was busted. I knew it the minute I saw four faces glaring back at me.

22

"You promised," Nathan said. His face was just inches from mine giving me a clear view of the disappointment in his eyes. His chiseled jaws twitched. He said nothing else, or waited for me to speak, before he turned and walked out of the train car.

"You okay?" asked Laura.

"What are you doing here?" I asked looking at Laura, but my head turned to Jack who was in the seat across the aisle from Laura with Rob.

"You probably already guessed it," Jack sheepishly confessed. "I was coming down the stairs when you slipped out."

"But why? Why didn't you just let me go?" I asked, knowing he probably meant well, but this was something I needed to do. Not something I needed to drag others into.

Nathan stopped at the forward door of the train car and turned. "Because you still don't get it. It is not Larissa against the world." He stormed back toward where I stood in the aisle. "We don't keep secrets, and when we need help we ask. No matter what it is. That goes with that word you used earlier." He turned and stormed off leaving us on the train car.

Laura reached out and touched my shoulder. It was stiff, but the sentiment behind it was clear. "Larissa, we are all family. We help each other, no matter what it is."

"All of us," Jack said doing the same, but his touch had a little more emotion behind it.

I looked down at Rob who had been uncharacteristically quiet. He looked back quizzically, and shrugged. "It just sounded fun." Jack smacked him up against the head, and Laura and I walked to the front of the train car and then stepped off.

Nathan was standing out there waiting for us. It wasn't crowded, but it wasn't desolate. There were a few people milling around the platform. We fit just as a group of friends heading somewhere. "So now what? We assume you are heading to find Mrs. Norton."

"We take that train, there, to Boston." I pointed across the platform to the SL2, which was loading.

"Then we need to hurry," Nathan urged. "We need to get tickets and on board before it leaves."

"Not necessary," said Jack. He walked right up to the porter and used the same trick I had at the station in Ipswich. We watched as the porter counted five red tickets and then waved us on to the train car.

"Oh, I am not comfortable with this," Nathan said squeamishly.

"Then stay," Jack said, as he stood by the stairs allowing Laura and myself to enter first. Rob followed us, and eventually Nathan gave in and joined us.

Nathan and I took two seats next to each other. The rest were in the rows behind us. My eyes met Nathan's when he sat. "No lecture, please," I begged.

For a moment, a look of disbelief flashed across his face, and I thought he was going to get up and go join Jack two rows back. I would have understood. I made a promise, and I broke it. Something I hadn't done with Nathan before, and I didn't know how he would take it. He slumped down in his seat and pulled up the collar on his brown leather jacket. "How long until the next stop?"

"About twenty minutes," I answered. "Then another train from there for eight hours. That will take us right into Woodbridge. The station is about a twenty-minute walk from our home."

He sighed, and sank a little lower in his seat, leaning toward my side. I took that as a good sign. He could have leaned toward the aisle. I slid down a little too and leaned close to him. I wasn't sure if he wanted to be that near me at the moment. He didn't move as I nestled right on the edge of my seat, inches from him. His eyes were closed, but his entire face frowned.

"I am sorry," I whispered.

"It's fine," he mumbled. I sat there and listened to his breathing until we pulled into Boston.

There wasn't much talking after we changed trains. Everyone but Laura and I slept on that leg of the trip. We both sat next to the windows. Not that there was much to see outside. It was dark, and thanks to the overcast conditions, there wasn't even moonlight to help.

"So, what do you hope to find?" Laura asked, speaking right through the gap between my seat and the window.

I turned around to face her and looked through the gap. For a moment I thought I saw a blonde woman peeking down the same gap from a few rows back. Then Laura's face appeared, and I replied. "I honestly don't know. The best case, would be to find Mrs. Norton and have her come back with us, so she can tell her side of things, and help clear all this up." I shuddered as I thought about the worst case. "Or we find nothing. I don't know. I just know I had to do something." She moved back away from the gap, and I saw the blonde again. Our eyes locked, and she jerked out of the way. I dismissed it as just a nosey-nelly, and turned around.

"So, if we find nothing, what will happen?"

"I don't know. I honestly don't know." I didn't. I didn't have a clue. My mind didn't even have a starting point to make any dramatic leaps from. What I was sure of is Mrs. Saxon wouldn't be able to make this go away like she said she could, with or without Master Thomas' help.

23

The train pulled into the station into Woodbridge just after the sun came up. It was overcast, but seeing the orange glow over familiar countryside highlighted the hope I felt for the day.

I waited for the train to stop before rousing Nathan up. Like his mother had woken me up on a train several weeks ago, I stood over him and gave him a light shake on the shoulder. Laura was doing the same to Jack. There was a bit of laughter when she woke up Rob. I wasn't completely sure what it was, but I heard something about, "drooling like a dog in his sleep."

Nathan got up and walked off yawning. I took a big whiff of the air. Not that I needed the air to breathe, I wanted to smell it. The smell of the honeysuckle combined with the smoke from the factories to our south were exactly what I needed to smell. Some of the locals complained about it in the paper, saying it was sour. The putrid industrial presence overpowered the sweetness of the local fauna, but I wasn't after a pleasant smell. I was after one that to me said home.

"Food. I need food," proclaimed Rob as he walked off, prompting a look from Laura and myself. "What? It takes a lot to drive this awesomeness." My few days as a human reminded me of that feeling, and while I didn't need to stop, I needed to think of the others. "Plus, remember what today is," he added.

Laura and I looked at him blankly until Jack said, "Thanksgiving. We are going to miss Rene's turkey and dressing."

"And Mrs. Tenderschott's pumpkin pie," Nathan added, still rubbing his eyes.

Hearing them talk about it reminded me of the feasts my mother cooked up. The smells were intoxicating. Just the memories of them were strong enough to make my mouth regret my current state.

"All right, we can stop. There has to be a store or restaurant around here some place," I said looking around. This was my town, but I was just as lost as the rest of them. I never left the house. Not once except when we took trips. Over all the years, I never thought that was as curious as I did now, and I had a feeling I now knew why.

"There," Jack said, pointing at a convenience store, where a man in a red plaid shirt and overalls walked out holding a Styrofoam cup of coffee, I could smell it from here.

"You going to handle it?" I asked looking at Jack. He seemed to know what I meant, but so did Nathan who interjected, reaching into his back pocket, and pulling out his wallet.

He waved it in the air, and said, "Let's do things the old fashioned way."

Laura and I stood across the street and watched them disappear into the store. A tall blond, in jeans and a white button-up shirt followed them in. She was one of many people that did, but what got my attention was how she looked over in our direction. No one else did. No one else had a reason to.

"I could go for a snack myself," Laura said as a few locals walked across the street from us. I turned to look, and prepared myself to grab her, but she quickly added, "Just joking. I hadn't thought about Thanksgiving in a while, but I still remember it from... well, before. The few things I miss about being a human."

"I remember it too, but do me a favor. If you feel the need for a little feast, pick Jack." Laura tried to hold it in, but they burst out with laughter, before adding, "Nope, too tart for my taste." That had us both rolling.

We calmed down and I looked around at my town. This was an area I had never seen before. To me it was the perfect slice of America. There weren't many people out this morning, being a holiday and all. But what was out drove beat-up pickup trucks. Many were probably more than a decade old and had thousands and thousands of miles on them. Each served as both a work truck, and a family vehicle. That was just how life was around here. I was admiring the church bell tower in the distance. I had heard the sound of the bell many times, but this was the first time I had seen it.

"Oh my god." I turned around and saw the source that caused that reaction from Laura. While Jack and Nathan emerged with what one might expect, a breakfast sandwich in a wrapper—I could smell the bacon—and a drink, Rob had four, and a package of donuts that he was already mostly done with. He was an eating machine, and was discarding the package and breaking into the first of the sandwiches when they finally reached us. All we could do was shake our heads, and he shrugged in response.

While the others munched, and Rob pigged out—that was the only term to accurately describe the feeding frenzy we were witnessing— I led them through the still relatively quiet streets of my home town. It felt odd being here again after all that had happened. That feeling ramped up when we turned on our road, just as empty as I remembered, with only a few houses on it. Ours was about a mile or so down the road, around the curve that was just coming into view.

"So, not a lot of people live out this way, right?" asked Rob, with a full mouth of food.

"Yep, I feel it," I responded.

"Me too," added Laura with a look around behind her.

Nathan and Jack both cast a curious look behind them, before Jack asked, "What is it?"

"We are being followed," I said. "Since we stepped off the train." Originally I had dismissed the feeling. Others were on the train, having someone head a similar direction might be odd, but not completely out of the question. Feeling someone follow us all the way out here, that wasn't even possible.

"Is it a vampire?" Nathan asked. "Could it be your mother?"

"No," said Rob gruffly. "It doesn't smell like one."

I could tell he was getting annoyed by the feeling and about to phase for a confrontation. "Down boy, I will handle this. Everyone keep walking down to the bend in the road." The others continued as I ducked into the woods on the side of the road and waited.

My wait wasn't long until I heard the footsteps of someone walking on the edge of the road. The soles of their shoes grinding against the dirt and pebbles pushed to the side by the passage of cars. I could tell it was just one person, but one was enough. There was still a slim chance that it was one of the residents that lived down this road, so I waited until they passed, giving me a good look at them. When they passed, it was that same blonde that I watched follow the guys into the store, and that same blonde that was eavesdropping on my conversation on the train. I waited a split second to ponder if I recognized her from anywhere, maybe a council member that had been waiting for me to do something stupid, but I came up blank.

I stepped out and followed her slowly for a few steps just to make sure I didn't recognize her. I didn't, other than from the train and the store. What I recognized was how she was walking and watching the others walk in front of her. She was now looking around, and had slowed up. I think she had realized I was no longer with them. That was enough for me. I sped up and had her suspended above the ground by her neck before she even knew I was there. Her shriek sent the birds fleeing from the woods. The others turned to run back to where I had our little intruder in my grasp.

"Let me go," she pleaded in a deep and hoarse voice. I had no intention of doing that until I knew who she was, and why she was following us.

"Who are you? I demanded, with a little squeeze, which produced another squeal as I forced the air from her throat.

"You're hurting me," she yelled. Her arms and legs were kicking, but I wasn't letting go. Her eyes locked on Nathan when he reached us. "Nathan, help me." He was as surprised as the rest of us when the deep voice of our mysterious woman trailed off to one that sounded like a little girl. "Nathan, please." Then she said something in that voice that caused my hand to open. "Larissa, stop you're hurting me."

She dropped to the ground and fell backwards, landing on her butt. The five of us stood around her while the woman squirmed and jerked, almost like a convulsion, and then changed from being a woman in her thirties to a very familiar little girl.

It was a race between all of us to see who was down to help Amy first. She was okay, but continued to cough, and I felt bad for the red handprint that was still around her throat. I pulled her off the ground and cuddled her against my chest. "Amy, I am so sorry. I didn't know it was you."

She responded by wrapping her arms around me and burying her head into my chest. I knew it wasn't the warmth of my body she was after, it was me. I let the embrace linger, hoping it would make up for what I had done to her. Once her grasp on me loosened I leaned her back and asked, trying to be as stern as possible, "What are you doing here?"

Nathan knelt down next to us. "Amy, you shouldn't be here little girl."

Her tear filled big blue eyes looked up at both of us, and her little girl voice broke my un-beating heart. "You left me."

All I could do was hold her tighter to try to chase away any of the hurt we caused her. I stood up still holding her. While I had been so focused on me. My world. Finding answers to my questions. I had ignored what my world really was, and what it had become. It was now Amy. It was Nathan. It was everyone, and even though my presence brought danger, it was my actions that absolutely hurt them.

I buried my head against Amy's and said, "I'm sorry. I won't leave you again." I let that sit for a minute while I tightened my embrace, hoping I wasn't hurting her. I couldn't hold her tight enough to make the disappointment in my own self go away.

"Hungry?" She nodded her head, which prompted me to walk over and grab one of the two remaining sandwiches Rob had in his paws, and handed it to her. He gave a surprised, but quiet, "Hey!," but dropped the protest and smiled when I handed it to Amy.

24

"Mom!" I yelled when I entered the door carrying Amy on my hip. There wasn't a response, and the house had a stale stuffy smell to it. Like a room that had been closed up for a while, which it probably had. I did a quick look in to the library and the living room, and there were no signs anyone had been there, but plenty of signs that someone had left in a hurry. The paper my father was reading still lay on the floor next to his chair right where he dropped it.

I put Amy down in my old favorite chair in the library so she could finish what was left of the breakfast sandwich. She was clingy, and didn't want to let go. I found I had to peel her arm from around my neck. To help comfort her, I knelt down next to her and told her where we were. "Just sit here in my favorite chair, and finish your breakfast."

"This is your favorite chair?" she asked wide-eyed.

"Yes, you are in my home. So, you are safe now." That seemed to ease her, and she sat back in the chair and chowed down.

"Not what I was expecting," remarked Jack.

"How so?" I asked, turning to see him walking through the library and studying the various titles. The others were doing the same. I wasn't sure what they were expecting. This was my home, and from what I knew, and saw in movies and shows, a very modest home at that. Nothing special, but nothing horrible either.

"Seems so human," answered Jack.

"We keep the coffins in our bedrooms. They would spook any visitors we had if we left them out in the living room." I left that to sit and marinate in the room as I moved on to the hallway and up the stairs. A quick check of the bedrooms turned up nothing except memories. Like a time capsule of my life before everything went to hell.

When I came back downstairs Rob walked over and leaned in close to me. "You were kidding about the coffins, right?"

I just ignored his question and headed down the hall to the kitchen, but not expecting to find anything. That was why I froze right at the door, and both hands gripped the door frame to steady myself. My sudden stop had caught Nathan off guard, and he ran into me. There was something. Something that wasn't there before, sitting in the middle of the kitchen table. The place Mrs. Norton always left any notes for me when she was out running an errand.

"What's wrong?" he asked.

"A note," I gasped.

"Where?"

A hand broke free from its death grip on the door frame and pointed at the table. Then the other hand let go as well. This allowed my legs to take control, and I sped across the kitchen. My arrival was not graceful. I hit and slid the table against the wall with a bang that drew the attention of the others. When they arrived in the kitchen, they found me sitting at the table with a white envelope in both hands. I just stared at it, looking at the paper it was made of, feeling the texture. I knew she had touched this with her own hands. There was no doubt she left it for me. Slowly I opened the flap with my audience of friends looking on and removed the folded piece of paper that was inside. The paper had scalloped edges. I knew it was from her favorite note pad.

Larissa,

I hope by the time you find this that you know the truth of who you are. We never meant to hurt you by not telling you. We only wanted to protect you. In case you don't know. You are Larissa Dubois, a witch from New Orleans. Your family ran a foul with a very bad and powerful vampire named Jean St. Claire. He took your father, and attacked you and your mother, killing her, and left you for dead. Thomas and I knew what they were going to do, and followed to see if we could stop them, but we were too late to help your mother and father, but we weren't to help you. You were almost dead, and there was only one thing we could do, so Thomas turned you. I want you to understand, we had no other options, and at that time it seemed like the right one. A way to not necessarily right a wrong, but to correct it the best we could. If we hadn't, your body would have died. We had no way of knowing that action would have the ramifications it did. By turning you into a one of us, you became exactly what Jean wanted, and Thomas and I vowed to do everything we could to keep you safe from him. We moved, and formed another life, living as humans, and doing our best to avoid attention. How they found us? I don't know. I have thought about that a few times in the three days since I put you on the train, but I can't figure it out. We have had no contact with anyone from our old life, and those that we met, knew nothing of that life. I guess how really doesn't matter. They did, and they now know you are still alive. We never wanted you to have to face this threat. I am going to try to make it right somehow, I just don't know how yet, but that is my pledge to you, on Thomas' memory, you will be safe.

If you are reading this note, it means you left the coven I sent you to. Go back now. That is the only way to guarantee your safety, and that is my number one priority.

Your mother,

Marie.

I dropped the paper and wept. Each tear of grief of not finding her, was mixed with a tear of relief. I could finally put one fear at ease. They did not murder my mother, and most importantly to me, they saved me the only way they could. I was still worried about her, and maybe a little more so than before. What was she going to do to make this right? She couldn't confront Jean St. Claire by herself. That would be suicide. The flow increased a little, and I felt Nathan's hand rub my shoulder. I stood up, and buried my crying face in his chest. My tears barely touched his shirt before Rob burst through the kitchen and out the backdoor, tearing it off the hinges on the way out. Laura and Jack followed him, just slower.

"I smell a vampire," Rob growled. He was crouched down in the center of the yard. "Stay back."

"Of course, you do. Three of them lived here," Jack said.

"No. It's out there." He pointed to the woods, my woods.

"There must be something there. He is really freaked out," stated Jack.

I stepped forward and Laura joined me. Rob held his arms out attempting to block our path, but we both pushed by easily. "Nathan, go watch Amy, please." I glanced back quickly to make sure he did. He went sprinting back into the house, and I returned my focus to whatever Rob felt was out there.

We approached the edge of the woods, with Rob close behind us. He was tense. Each breath an inhale that rumbled in his chest, before being forced out in quick and violent snorts. Even on this overcast morning, the woods were very dark thanks to the thick canopy created by the pines and evergreens. If there was a vampire hiding that would be the best place.

"Could it be her?" Laura asked.

"I hope so," I answered, and had to fight the urge to rush in and look. There was no doubt in my mind if it were, she would have come out at the first sound of my voice. Then again, what if she didn't hear me? I hadn't said much outside the house. "Mom! Is that you?" I screamed.

A few birds scattered high above us in the trees. I had probably disturbed their breakfast. Other than the flapping of their wings against their chest, there wasn't any other sound. No response from Mrs. Norton. I looked at Laura and shook my head. There was no way she wouldn't have heard that. We both stepped back, bumping into Rob. Then the three of us took another step back. It was on the third step, that two figures emerged in the darkened woods.

Rob phased into full werewolf and growled. Laura crouched, and my body did as Mr. Helms had trained it. We dug in, and the figures continued forward. It wasn't until they reached the edge of the woods that enough light hit the figures to illuminate the two pale faces of male vampires, dark hair slicked back, and fangs on full display. Both wore black suits and appeared to not be too frightened by our presence.

"We thought you might return," the taller of the two said. "Now stop all this silliness and let us take you home."

"You destroyed everything I ever called home!" I answered. To ensure they knew that was a no, I let two balls of fire fill each of my hands, ready to throw.

They stepped forward, unfazed by my display. Rob leaped forward and landed between Laura and me. He let out a deep throaty growl. The moist heat of his pants blasted my arms.

"Don't boy," the short of the two said with a creole accent. "Haven't enough people died because of you Larissa?" He looked down at his sleeve on his jacket and then brushed off the pine needles that clung to the fabric. "Your mother and father to start. Then there is Thomas, and let's not forget Marie. Tsk Tsk."

Each name pushed a sharp stake through my being, but the last one penetrated deeper than the rest, and I felt an intense storm bubbling inside. One that was reflected in the size of the balls of fire in my hands.

"No one else needs to die. Just come with us and end all this silliness."

"She is not going anywhere," barked Laura.

"Oh child, you aren't ready for what you are stepping in to. You may be like us, but you will never be one of us," the taller one taunted, and then stepped forward again.

Rob growled, and was about to leap at them, but I beat him to the punch sending both balls of fire right at the taller vampire's head. He ducked the first one, but the second one landed, lighting his hair on fire. To my, and everyone else's, surprise, he stood there, hair ablaze like nothing happened. It gave him even more of an ominous look and produced a gasp behind us.

"Let's not let it come to this –", started the short of the two, but I cut him off with a quick push sending his body crashing through the base of a tall pine. The tree cracked and fell. I turned my attention to his flaming friend, who had rushed at me when I made my attack at the other. Laura and Rob hit him before he could reach me, sending him tumbling backwards through autumn's discarded pine needles. The flames in his hair lit a small patch of it on fire.

"Fine then," he remarked as he stood up, brushing the straw off his suit. A column of smoke behind him. He rushed at me, trying to use his speed, but I had him flying in a different direction before he reached me. I heard another crunch off to my right and saw the shorter one crashing through the walls of Mr. Norton's workshop. I looked back at Jack and said, "Thanks."

He had barely landed before Rob was on him. His jaw snapping at any part of the vampire he could find until it sent him flying across the yard and into Jack. With a whimper followed by a growl, he was up again on all fours. Jack pushed up to his feet as well, but held his side.

The shorter of the two emerged from the crushed workshop wall and strolled, pridefully, back to his partner in crime. Laura and I squared up in front of them, but again their response was words, not action. "You don't really want this to continue, do you?"

"We can do this forever," remarked Laura.

"Her first," remarked the taller one, and then they both appeared distracted by something behind us. "What do we have here?" he asked. I looked back and saw Nathan standing on the steps outside the back door. His pulse raced as panic leaked from his body. It was palatable to all of us, and it seemed to mesmerize them.

They both sped for him, knocking me down while I looked back at him. I grabbed one of them as he passed. His body thudded to the ground. Before he moved, I wrapped both arms around his head and twisted. "Brother, please," he croaked. I gave it a little more of a twist, just to get the attention of his friend.

Laura stood behind me, and Rob moved between him and Nathan. Jack was back on his own two feet, still nursing his side, but was ready to attack. He was surrounded, with no way out. I was about to give him the option to walk away when he knelt down and grabbed a handful of dirt and stones from the back patio. It was an odd move that confused me until I saw a stone flying at me. I ducked, but heard the yowl let out by Rob, and saw Jack fall. Then Nathan fell back against the door. I saw Amy's mouth move through the window before I heard her high pitched, "No!"

A large bear broke through the window and rumbled across the yard striking the surprised vampire, sending him to the ground with three large claw shaped cuts in the back of his suit. It turned for another pass, but this time he dodged it, and grabbed ahold of it by the neck and went for a short ride until he wrestled the beast to the ground. He was squeezing its throat with a great force.

"Amy, change back!" I screamed.

As she did, the beast shrank, and she fell out of the vampire's grasp. Laura sprinted across and grabbed her before he had a second chance. We were in a stalemate, battered, but not yet beaten, and both vampires looked rather stoic and almost amused by each challenge. The taller one was now pissed off and looking for someone to take it out on. He was ignoring Laura and me, and focused more on the three more vulnerable ones of us. Nathan, Amy, and Jack. Rob limped over between them, but he didn't seem to be in any shape to put up a fight. I gave his friend's neck a little twist to get his attention.

"Brother, please," the shorter one croaked in my grasp.

"Yes, brother. Please," I mocked, wanting to keep his full attention on me and no one else. It worked for a second, as he glanced back at me and then at the others. "Remember it is me you want." I reached up with one hand and pulled out the charm to hold it on full display. "Remember?" I asked while I dangled it. That bait did the trick, hook line and sinker.

"Sorry brother," he said as he walked toward me. "It's what master wants."

"Jack, get them out of here," I yelled. My request received a very confused look and appeared to need more encouragement. "Now!"

In a flash, we were back on the patio around the pool outside the coven, and I quickly realized how that happened, and the frightening truth that came with it. "What the hell Jack?"

"This is the only spot I could remember. I guess all the times playing the game out here," Jack said sheepishly, clutching his side.

"No, I meant for you to get everyone out of the backyard. Get them someplace safe, not..." I stopped, with shock soaring through my thoughts. "Have you ever done that with anything living before? Anything at all?"

"No," he said.

23

"I don't have to tell you how stupid this was, now do I?"

I knew Mrs. Saxon's question was a rhetorical one. The answer was a resounding no, and I knew it before it I ever stepped out of the front door. I just didn't expect the others to follow and join in, raising the severity of the stupidity to monumental levels. "You don't. I just.." I wanted to explain, but I knew it would just be a waste of my voice. The looks on the faces of Mrs. Saxon and Master Thomas confirmed it.

"Larissa, I told you to let me handle things. You need to learn to trust us," she said. "I am not as inept as they make it appear, plus we have friends." She motioned to Master Thomas who nodded. "You agreed to not leave the coven, but you did it anyway."

"I didn't know they were going to follow," I interjected.

"They will be dealt with, and I will ground Nathan for a bit, but they are not the concern of the council at the moment. You are. You agreed to not leave while this was being worked out. Your actions have now put us in a tough situation, and it will have consequences. You need to prepare yourself for that during their next visit."

"What will they do?" I asked.

"Larissa, I wouldn't worry too much about that," said Master Thomas. "They will sit on their big podium, lecture you, and threaten over and over, and say everything they can to make you feel bad about yourself, and maybe confine you to the coven, which you already were, but nothing else. The true punishments are saved for true crimes. Worst case, under normal circumstances, you would have extended this little inquest of theirs a little longer, but you are in luck."

I looked up from the spot on the floor I had stared at for the last several minutes, finding it more comfortable to look there than the faces of those I had disappointed. When I looked at Mrs. Saxon, her eyes were narrowed.

"I think I have found something that will help extinguish some of the heat they have put on you, and I have called the council here, for an emergency, an impromptu meeting."

"When?" Mrs. Saxon asked, startled.

"As soon as they can get here."

"What did you find?" I asked.

"You will have to wait to find out," he said with a smirk. That both confused me and also gave me a little hope. Now it was my turn to add to that hope. I reached back and pulled the white envelope from my back pocket, and held it out for Mrs. Saxon.

"What is this?" she asked, holding it un-opened in her hand.

"Read it," I said.

Master Thomas stood up and joined Mrs. Saxon in reading it. Smiles emerged on both of their faces as they did. They now knew what I did. They now knew what part the Nortons played in all this, and why they did it. Whether it would answer the questions from the council was still to be seen, but I had to hope. It was all I had.

"She wrote this with her own hand?" asked Master Thomas.

I nodded, and mouthed a painful, "Yes." When I first read it, I felt my pain, but later as I thought about it I felt her pain. The pain and loss she must have felt when writing it, and one sentence in it haunted me more than any others. What was she going to do? She wasn't there. Had she already done something? I shuddered at the possibilities of what she could have done rolled through my head.

"Good," he said, seemingly pleased. "This helps. This helps a lot Larissa. Thank you."

There was a knock at the door, and a slim redheaded man in a black full three piece suit entered. "Master Thomas, they are here."

"Thank you Seville," he said. Then he looked in my direction, and asked, "Mind if I hang on to this?" The feeling of distress must have been evident on my face because he added, "I promise to give it back to you after."

"You might want to hurry. They don't seem all that pleased," Seville said from the opened door.

"I doubt they will be very pleased by what I have to say anyway, they can wait for a few moments." He folded the envelope and put it in the breast pocket of his grey tweed coat, and took a moment or two to pull at his clothing to straighten them out. I did the same, not knowing if I needed to or not.

"Ladies, shall we?" he asked, motioning for the door. I got up and followed Mrs. Saxon to the door. Master Thomas followed me. "Let me do all the talking."

I entered the ritual room first and came face to face with the eleven members of the council standing on the floor, not up on their traditional pedestals, waiting for me. What Seville, whoever that was, had said was right. They were not pleased. Actually, they all looked down right pissed off and Mrs. Wintercrest made sure that was known when she went on the attack at her first sight of me.

"Miss Norton!" she seethed. Her voice cracked under the strain of her emotion. "You were to remain in the coven, but defied our order. What do you have to say for yourself?"

"She has nothing to say, nor does Mrs. Saxon before you ask," said Master Thomas from behind us.

Mrs. Wintercrest turned her attention to him, and marched over to where he stood, much to my relief. "Then what do you have to say for yourself?" she asked, accusingly.

"I have a lot to say," he said and walked right passed her toward the center of the room.

"Master Thomas," she erupted, and marched after him, but he continued to ignore her.

"My fellow council members, I appreciate you coming on such short notice..."

"You will address me and explain yourself right now. Why have you called us here, and why have you stood up for her?" Mrs. Wintercrest said with a look of sheer disgust in my direction.

"My Council Supreme, he was attempting to. Master Thomas continue," interjected one of the Mr. Demius lookalikes.

"Maybe we should dismiss the formalities and just get to it," Master Thomas said, and then he called out, "Edward."

Right on cue, Edward appeared in the room, and greeted the members of the council. "Council Members."

Several of them bowed in his direction. "There was something about this little inquisition that has rubbed me wrong from the beginning. Both the questions and discussion that occurred out in the open in true council meetings, and those that have occurred outside appeared to lack any true substance, true truths."

There was a little eruption of steam from Mrs. Wintercrest, while the rest of the council and even the cherubs above seemed interested in what Master Thomas had to say. Even Miss Roberts seemed curious, though it was hard to tell behind her resting bitch face that was always present.

"There is no denying Miss Dubois is a unique creature, and much each of you have said is true. Being a witch who is immortal is an extremely powerful combination, but I continued to ask myself the same question she asked of us. What has she done to cause us to fear her, or fear what she may become? Do you know what answer I found? I found it wasn't what she is now, or what she may become that is disturbing to some of us. It was who she was that caused at least one of us to be concerned. One of us researched her background before we ever met her for the first time. I would contend that person was being responsible and doing their due-diligence. That was how it looked at first glance, but a deeper look exposed a different focus."

"Master Thomas, how does any of this change the fact that she left the coven against our direction," Mrs. Wintercrest pointed out.

"It doesn't. She left after agreeing to not do so, but I believe she only did because we gave her no choice. Some of us, myself included, have questioned her in such a way she felt no other option than to take up her own search for truth to answer our own questions. I blame us for her indiscretion and not her."

"That is absurd..." started Mrs. Wintercrest, but Master Thomas reached into his breast pocket and whipped out the white envelope cutting her off mid-word.

"Shall we review our findings?" He asked with a wave of the object.

Mrs. Wintercrest watched it move and appeared to tremble, and her hand attempted to snatch it, which drew mumbles from the other council members. I leaned to Mrs. Saxon and asked, "What is that about?"

"I don't know," she said, never taking her eyes off the display.

He opened the envelope, and then threw the paper into the air. A light illuminated it, and right there before us appeared my kitchen. Mrs. Norton sat at the table wearing the same black pants, and blue sweater she wore the last time I saw her. Her hair was a mess. Then her voice read the letter.

The pain I heard in her shaking voice tore me up, and the tears flowed. Every member of the council except one, watched me stand there and cry, and unlike before when I wanted to appear strong, I didn't care anymore. I couldn't fight what I felt even if I wanted to.

Their looks of disdain melted away right before my eyes as the image of Mrs. Norton disappeared. Master Thomas caught the note as it fluttered down, and then handed it to me. I clutched it close to my chest with one hand and wiped away the tears with another.

"That was a note she retrieved just today, written by the woman she believed was her mother for all of those years. I ask, is there any among you that sees anything in that relationship other than a woman caring for a child, and doing the best she could to protect her?"

Another murmur broke out among the council members, and Master Thomas let it continue, walking back toward Mrs. Saxon and me. He looked rather smug standing there with his back to the council. When he heard several distinctive footsteps, his head bounced with each step, but he kept the same smug look. He held up a finger and whispered, "ignore it."

"This still doesn't answer the true question we have been asking..." Mrs. Wintercrest started. Master Thomas spun around, and again interrupted her, drawing her ire in his direction.

"Her character? I agree. The letter doesn't tell us who Larissa is, but then again, I barely know her. If only we had someone here who knew her family." He meandered across the floor to Mrs. Wintercrest. "But we do, don't we? Your family was from the Orleans' coven, and your family knew the Dubois quite well didn't they? In fact, if my research is correct," he pointed at Edward, and Mrs. Wintercrest quickly covered her mouth, "they passed your own grandfather over to be head of that coven and a member of the council for Mr. Dubois, who he turned it down. Isn't that true?"

"Um... well... I guess. I am not sure," she responded while her expression melted away, as did her strength.

"I think we owe it... No that is not right." He turned back and looked at me. "Miss Dubois, would you allow us to get to know you again as a member of our community?" He winked.

"Yes, I would like that," I said confidently.

He spun back around, with a game-show host smile, and his hands out. "Any objections? From anyone?"

At first no one spoke, but then Mr. Francis Davis said, "I look forward to it." Many of the others agreed, and afterward I spent about an hour shaking hands and speaking to the different members of the council. Each offering both an apology and encouragement. Some, such as Mrs. Claire Chevault from France, offered congratulations of recovering my memories. The oddest reaction of all came from Mr. Juan Signorn. He told me he liked the spunk I showed and offered to help me work on any spells if I needed it. I graciously accepted it, remembering what both Mrs. Saxon and Mrs. Tenderschott told me about the council being great allies.

The two reactions that weren't surprising was the distance that Mrs. Wintercrest and Miss Roberts kept. They stayed to themselves in a far corner of the room.

Master Thomas stayed behind after the rest of the council left. He even sent his assistant, Mr. Seville on telling him, "I will be along shortly."

"Edward, it's always a pleasure."

"Likewise Master Thomas," and with that Edward disappeared.

"I believe that is the end of that," he said with a little dance.

"It still seems Mrs. Wintercrest and her sidekick aren't fans."

"I doubt they will ever be, but they won't be a problem. See, after the last visit, I noted something about Mrs. Wintercrest's arguments about you. There were never any facts or events to back up her fears. It seemed personal, so with Edward's help, I did a little of my own research and do you know what I found? Mrs. Wintercrest's grandfather was a member of the Orleans Coven before they ever moved to the one in New York. They moved because of your family. It's really ironic when you think about it. The concern she had about you being groomed to take power, and yet her family moved because they were passed over for Supreme in the coven, and weren't even part of the trusted circle or considered for the council, but that was your father, and your mother was offered a position, but she refused. She is afraid of you. Afraid that you will be as powerful as your parents, and will one day challenge her. Miss Roberts, well, she will do whatever she has to kiss up to Mrs. Wintercrest. She has designs on being her replacement."

"Why didn't you bring that out in front of the council? That would have possibly been grounds for removal," Mrs. Saxon brought up.

"It would have been, but if we removed a Council Supreme every time they did something petty, we would change them more frequently than you can imagine. It wasn't worth it, but now you have some leverage over her, and worse yet, she knows you have it. Think of it as a get out of jail free card." He reached out for my hand, and I met him halfway. "Larissa, it's been a pleasure. I look forward to watching you develop. If you ever need anything, don't hesitate to give me a call."

"You too Master Thomas."

He wagged a finger and reminded me, "It's just Benjamin. No master." With that, he was gone, and Mrs. Saxon and I shared a congratulatory hug, and I felt her let out a huge exhale. With it no doubt was a lot of concern and stress. That weight had left me as well, or some of it had. I still felt some pushing down on me, and that was the question of where was Mrs. Norton?

With all that I had been through Mrs. Saxon decided to start Nathan's punishment tomorrow, giving us one more story time out on the pool deck with Amy, at least for the next week. Though we didn't really read any stories tonight. Amy and Nathan ate thanksgiving leftovers, while I watched, somewhat jealous, and then we took turns holding Amy while we all just talked until her bedtime. After Mrs. Parrish gathered Amy, it was just us, and there wasn't much left to say except, "Sorry."

"You can stop apologizing. Just stop taking on the world." He pulled his chair around to my side of the table and put his arm around me. "You are part of something much bigger." He leaned over and kissed me on the cheek.

"Is that all I get?"

"Well, you did get me grounded," he sniped back, and turned to look at me. That gave me the perfect opportunity to move in for what I wanted. I moved slowly to relish the feeling of his breath on my lips just before they touched. We were just about to have a moment when for the second time in a few weeks a scream interrupted us, sending us running inside. This was a masculine yell filled with violent and malicious intent. My heart raced thinking about Jean St. Claire. He hadn't paid me one of his little voodoo enabled visits recently. Had he chosen to pay me one in the flesh?

Just like before, heads were sticking out of doors to see the source. Instead of looking down at one of the halls, this time they were all looking up at the boy's landing on the fifth floor, the vampire floor. There was a second primal yell from behind the door, with a few loud bumps and bangs. I heard Mike and Jeremy's voices and the voice of Mr. Bolden. I couldn't go up there, but I was worried for my friends, and ran up my side of the steps to find Jennifer. If Jean, or one of his minions was over there, they would need help. She wasn't in her room, nor was she up on the deck. I rushed out again, where Nathan and the dog pack stood on the ground floor looking up at the source of the commotion, the witches were still on their own landings, and Steve and Stan had become brave enough to step up next to the door on the fifth floor. They couldn't open it, but that didn't stop them from listening through it. They jumped with each bang and yell.

"I haven't heard anything like that since Mr. Bolden had to break Mike," Martin said from below.

"What?" I asked.

"You know. When they found him and brought him in," he explained.

Jennifer emerged through the door, just as another loud bang shook the building. She cringed at the sound as she shut the door in time to muffle the next one. She looked at the crowd that had gathered and announced, "We have a new student, you will all get the chance to meet in a few days."

Up to Next - Coven Cove Book 3—BloodLust

1

"I thought I was going to join Lisa in class." I looked around the empty classroom that seemed like it was right out of a gothic horror movie.

"Not all dark magic is the same. Different witch. Different magic. Different class," replied Mr. Demius. "We need to find out what kind of witch you are." He said while putting away several large leather-bound books. By the looks of the wear on their covers, these were old, which didn't surprise me, considering what he taught.

"Mrs. Tenderschott already did that."

"Um, yes. Her crystals," he mocked. "I am talking about true magic. Come up here to the front of the class." He motioned for me to walk down the stone steps. I half expected to find some cherubs up on the walls; maybe perched over one of his many stone archways, but there weren't any. Good! It was just us, and six empty tables. Three on each side of the central stairs. At the front, the desk that I assumed Mr. Demius used during class resembled an altar, but not from any religion I recognized. Dark wood, much like the ritual room, and old iron accents.

"Let us dispense with the pop culture magic that is taught down the hall. There is a lot more to this than throwing fire, making things grow, and pushing things around. You come from a time when magic was different. It was truly special. I need to see how much of it you were introduced to." With a wave of his hand, five flaming symbols appeared in front of my face. "Miss Dubois, do you recognize any of those?"

I studied the symbols closely. Each burned deep inside me with a familiarity that was hard to shake. I just couldn't place them. Had I seen them in Mrs. Saxon's class, or maybe in some of my reading that I had done under Edward's supervision? Something I hadn't told Mrs. Saxon about yet, though I doubt she would mind someone making use of the library. At least somebody was. The more comfortable I became, the more I wanted to stretch my wings. I walked closer and looked at each symbol one at a time. That was when it hit me out of nowhere. A single memory of my mother and the same five symbols floating in the air with flames radiating out from them. My mouth echoed her words. "The five elements of the world."

"Almost," he replied with a bit of a surprise, but it still came out as disappointed.

"Wait!" I exclaimed as my head attempted to process the memory and the lesson she gave me. Before I answered, the door opened and in walked Master Benjamin Thomas and one of the several Mr. Demius look-a-likes from the council: dark clothes, black stringy hair, and all. Even down to the way he carried himself when he walked. Each step was careful and deliberate, while leaning slightly back to ensure he was always looking down his nose at everything and everyone. The original didn't seem too surprised by the interruption as he reached to greet Master Thomas.

"Larissa, good to see you." He joined me in front of the symbols.

"Good to see you too, Master Thomas." I still couldn't make myself call him by his first name only. It had nothing to do with age, in which I was his senior. It was respect for his position in our world. Behind the symbols, the two dark lords were sharing a less than friendly greeting.

"I didn't tell Leonard I was bringing him," Master Thomas leaned over and whispered to me. "They have a bit of ah, um, a history."

I could tell, but didn't ask what it was. I was too busy absorbing the news that our own dark lord's name was Leonard.

"I didn't know you were coming today."

"I wouldn't miss this for the world. So, do you know what these symbols are?" He asked, and the other two dark figures joined us on the floor in front of the symbols.

"The five elements of the magic world," I responded, repeating the words my mother said in my memory.

"I knew it," Master Thomas celebrated with a clap of his hand. "She remembers."

"Who showed these to you?" Mr. Demius asked.

"My mother."

"That would make sense," added our guest. "Much of that area was stuck in the old ways until just recently. The more important question, does she know what they mean? And I don't mean the traditional meanings. I mean the magical meanings."

All three sets of eyes focused right on me. The only things missing were a spotlight and goofy game-show music with a clock ticking in the background. I tried to ignore them, but couldn't ignore the urge to look back over my shoulder at them from time to time. In between glances, I studied the symbols, hoping to hear my mother's voice cutting through the silence in my head. Either from her finding some way to talk to me from the great beyond, or from a memory.

The first symbol was a triangle with a line across the middle of it. I knew this one. I was certain of it. It was right there on the tip of my tongue, and it didn't appear I wasn't going to get any help from my mother on this one. The way I thought about it, half the work in remembering what this was had already happened. I remembered the symbols and what my mother called them. There wasn't any doubt in my head that she covered a few of them in that same session. Now if only I could recall that memory. I could see us standing there in the parlor. Well, she was standing, and I was sitting on the French settee we had. I loved napping on that when I was small enough to fit. Not because of the settee, but because of the breezes that came in through the windows behind it. My mother displayed the symbols in the air just as Mr. Demius had, but there were more, a lot more. What did we do after she showed them to me? She would have gone through them one by one, wouldn't she? Like any teacher. They don't just show you the alphabet and say go. They show it to you and then start with the first letter. What was first? Then, again, it hit me. This time it wasn't her voice, it was my own. "This is fire." I looked back for confirmation and saw three hopeful faces. I was at least partially right.

"What can we use it for?" prompted Mr. Demius.

I finally understood what they were after. Now if only I could remember what we used each item for. I turned my attention back to the symbol for fire. Of course, it was fire, but that symbol was not used to create fire; thank you chapter one of Mrs. Saxon's book of spells. There had to be a deeper meaning, a more magical meaning.

"Change?" I answered, remembering her words as she explained it.

"Bingo!" Master Thomas exclaimed with another clap of his hands. "Larissa, fire is the agent and energy for change. It can both destroy and create."

"Did your mother tell you this?" our guest queried.

"Sorry Larissa. You must excuse my manners," interjected Master Thomas before I could answer. "I forgot to introduce you to Mr. Theodore Nevers. Our master of the dark world and resident geek of everything old."

"A pleasure to meet you, Larissa," Mr. Nevers said. He never attempted to reach forward and still kept his distance. A common reaction the first time anyone met me.

"Nice to meet you, and yes, I remember her telling me that, but that is about all, I think," I answered, unsure. The search was happening behind my eyes, and so far was coming up with lots of blanks with only a few flashes of information.

"I am willing to bet she showed you more. You just don't remember, yet," Master Thomas stated while appearing to do a little celebratory dance. "Let's see if we can get it out of you."

I wasn't in the mood for anyone to go poking around in my head. Since my last trip with Miss Roberts, no one had. My thoughts had been my thoughts, and I liked it that way.

"I want you to picture that symbol in your head, feel it, and let it be one with you, all while you imagine standing on a patch of green grass," instructed Master Thomas. I must have looked at him like he had two heads by the way he returned my look. "Trust me," he encouraged.

"All right," I agreed, though I was still a little unsure. I closed my eyes and tried exactly what he said. I imagined it just as he told me to. The fire left the symbol, and it drew itself over and over in my head. Faster and faster. It was hard to focus on the second part of his instructions while the symbol danced in and out of existence right in front of me. I had to force myself to think of standing on green grass. That was when the flash happened in my head, and I heard a loud whoosh around me causing my eyes to spring open just in time to see a line of fire expanding out from me, leaving behind it a layer of green grass on the floor.

I bent down to touch it and pulled on it. A few moist green blades broke free in my hands, blade, root, dirt, and all. I let it sit on my open palm while I asked. "Is it real?" I had to be sure.

"Yes, it is real," answered a smiling Master Thomas.

Mr. Demius bent down in front of me and yanked at a larger section until it broke free. He lifted it up, showing me the stone floor below. Even he appeared to smile as he displayed this for me to see.

This was something. Something new and extraordinary, but then I remembered. I had done this before, once, with my mother. While I tried to remember what it was I created, I watched as Mr. Demius stood up with closed eyes, and a flash of fire rolled down him and expanded out, removing the grass and leaving the stone floor clean.

"It can also destroy just as easy," he said, just as I remembered what it was.

I held out both hands, and before I could consider if this was wise or not, I thought of the symbol again, and then what my nine-year-old self wanted almost a hundred years ago. There was a similar flash, and I didn't need to open my eyes to know it worked. I felt its webbed feet on the palms of my hands, and the fluffy fuzz of a baby duck tickled my fingers.

I smiled when I opened my eyes, and resisted saying, "Ta-da." The faces staring back at me were filled with terror, and I checked the duck to make sure I didn't create some demonic creature instead. Who knew if my other dark side would have any effects?

"Larissa, you can create life?" Mr. Demius asked, his voice quavered.

"Did I do something wrong?" I panicked. Based on the faces that stared back at me, I felt I had. Like I had broken some rule or now I was the one with two heads.

"No," Master Thomas replied hastily, though his expression and tone were not convincing. He stepped forward and looked at the duck. "May I?" I nodded, and he took the duck from my hands.

"Larissa," he said breathlessly, while one hand held the duckling, and the other caressed its fuzz. He was like a boy on Christmas morning. "You need to understand, what you did is something that... is extraordinary." he passed the duck to Mr. Demius, "It's not something many can do."

"Any," interjected Mr. Nevers.

"I have heard stories of others," Master Thomas said, addressing his fellow council member. "There have been, and are others, and one was your mother. I read a few accounts of it when I was looking into your background to understand Mrs. Wintercrest's interest. I had no idea it would have passed down. Did she teach you how to do that?"

"Sort of," I said, remembering more and more every moment. "She taught me about that power of creation, and I tried it over and over, challenging myself each time." When that part of my mind remembered the rest of the memory from my nine-year-old self, I saw my mother's reaction and shuddered. "Oh god!"

"She was not pleased when you did it before, was she?" asked Master Thomas.

"No, she was angry. One of the few times she ever was angry with me." I bit my lip as I remembered why and looked at the cute innocent duck in Mr. Nevers' hands and knew the cost.

"Do you understand why?" Mr. Demius asked.

"To create a life, you have to take a life." I answered, my voice shook remembering the lesson my mother taught me.

"That's right," stated Master Thomas. "The universe has a balance, and not even witches can change that balance."

"Nothing to worry about, dear child," Mr. Demius said. He spun his hand around quickly and opened a portal to a pond that was out in a sunny meadow. He stepped through and put the little duckling down. "He will flourish here with his brothers." Just as he said that the duck waddled down to the water and swam across the surface and joined a group of six others. My last view of it before the portal closed was the adult duck grooming its fuzz. "We need to see what else you know, so we can properly train you on how to deal with these gifts. How about these?" He wiped his hand across the air, erasing the four flaming symbols, and replacing them with two of his own.

I walked forward to the first one. It was one I had seen recently, in the runes Mrs. Saxon put on the doors to keep Jean St. Claire from getting in. My finger pointed at it and traced its shape. "The sun," I started, and then corrected myself. "The solar cross. That is for protection."

"Good," cheered Master Thomas. "Do you know how to use it?"

"Yes, it can be used in two different ways. Written in runes," which I didn't really know before now, but felt it was safe to make the assumption since I recognized it in the runes Mrs. Saxon had written on the floor of the ritual room, and around the doors to try to keep Reginald out. Its usage in spells was what I was surer about. My mother had taught me that, though I never really used it for protection per se, but I did use it once to keep Charles Snyder out of my room when he made me mad when I was ten. A move he complained about to his mother. If I remembered correctly, my mother just smiled.

"That's right," Mr. Nevers said, sounding surprised. "How about the other symbol?"

BloodLust – Available as a Paperback on Amazon and Barnes and Noble.

Stay In Touch

Dear Reader,

Thank you for taking a chance on this book. I hope you enjoyed it. If you did, I'd be more than grateful if you could leave a review on Amazon (even if it is just a rating and a sentence or two). Every review makes a difference to an author and helps other readers discover the book.

To stay up to date on everything in the Coven Cove world, click here to join my mailing list and I will send you a **free bonus chapter** from "The Secret of the Blood Charm".

As always, thank you for reading,
David

ALSO FROM DAVID CLARK

The Miller's Crossing Series

The Origins of Miller's Crossing
Amazon US
Amazon UK
There are six known places in the world that are more "paranormal" than anywhere else. The Vatican has taken care to assign "sensitives" and "keepers" to each of those to protect the realm of the living from the realm of the dead. With the colonization of the New World, a seventh location has been found, and time for a new recruit.

William Miller is a simple farmer in the 18th century coastal town of St. Margaret's Hope Scotland. His life is ordinary and mundane, mostly. He does possess one unique skill. He sees ghosts.

A chance discovery of his special ability exposes him to an organization that needs people like him. An offer is made, he can stay an ordinary farmer, or come to the Vatican for training to join a league of "sensitives" and "keepers" to watch over and care for the areas where the realm of the living and the dead interaction. Will he turn it down, or will he accept and prove he has what it takes to become one of the true legends of their order? It is a decision that can't be made lightly, as there is a cost to pay for generations to come.

The Ghosts of Miller's Crossing
Amazon US
Amazon UK
Ghosts and demons openly wander around the small town of Miller's Crossing. Over 250 years ago, the Vatican assigned a family to be this town's "keeper" to protect the realm of the living from their "visitors". There is just one problem. Edward Meyer doesn't know that is his family, yet.

Tragedy struck Edward twice. The first robbed him of his childhood and the truth behind who and what he is. The second, cost him his wife, sending him back to Miller's Crossing to start over with his two children.

What he finds when he returns is anything but what he expected. He is thrust into a world that is shocking and mysterious, while also answering and great many questions. With the help of two old friends, he rediscovers who and what he is, but he also discovers another truth, a dark truth. The truth behind the very tragedy that took so much from him. Edward faces a choice. Stay, and take his place in what destiny had planned for him, or run, leaving it and his family's legacy behind.

The Demon of Miller's Crossing
Amazon US
Amazon UK

The people of Miller's Crossing believed the worst of the "Dark Period" they had suffered through was behind them, and life had returned to normal. Or, as normal as life can be in a place where it is normal to see ghosts walking around. What they didn't know was the evil entity that tormented them was merely lying in wait.

After a period of thirty dark years, Miller's Crossing had now enjoyed eight years of peace and calm, allowing the scars of the past to heal. What no one realizes is under the surface the evil entity that caused their pain and suffering is just waiting to rip those wounds open again. Its instrument for destruction will be an unexpected, familiar, and powerful force in the community.

The Exorcism of Miller's Crossing
Amazon US
Amazon UK

The "Dark Period" the people of Miller's Crossing suffered through before was nothing compared to life as a hostage to a malevolent demon that is after revenge. Worst of all, those assigned to protect them from such evils are not only helpless, but they are tools in the creatures plan. Extreme measures will be needed, but at what cost.

The rest of the "keepers" from the remaining 6 paranormal places in the world are called in to help free the people of Miller's Crossing from a demon that has exacted its revenge on the very family assigned to protect them. Action must be taken to avoid losing the town, and allowing the world of the dead to roam free to take over the dominion of the living. This demon took Edward's parents from him while he was a child. What will it take now?

The Jordan Blake Paranormal Mysteries

Sinful Silence (Book #1)

Amazon US

Amazon UK

He is the FBI's only paranormalist...
...She is america's favorite television medium.
Together they are more than the supernatural world bargained for.

Jordan Blake is the FBI's only paranormalist, a position that costs him more than a little credibility with the other agents. Throw in his girlfriend Megan Tolliver, the darling, and impulsive, host of the top cable paranormal show, "America's Medium", and he doesn't stand a chance of ever being taken seriously. But that doesn't stop them from turning to him when they come across something that the natural world can't explain, such as the mysterious death of a coed in Richmond Virginia. They sent Jordan up to just consult on her autopsy, but her spirit begs him to dig further. With Megan's help, they uncover a ring of evil that spreads up to the highest reaches of government, and cost several young women their lives to keep them silent. What is the old saying, dead men tell no tales? Well that is true, unless you have someone who can speak to the dead now isn't it? Together the hunt down those responsible and try to stay out of the way of their only true adversary, an entity who says he is the source of all Evil in the world.

The Dark Angel Mysteries

The Blood Dahlia (The Dark Angel Mysteries Book #1)

Amazon US

Amazon UK

Meet Lynch, he is a private detective that is a bit of a jerk. Okay, let's face it he is a big jerk who is despised by most, feared by those who cross him, and barely tolerated by those who really know him. He smokes, drinks, cusses, and could care less what anyone else thinks about him, and that is exactly how the metropolis of New Metro needs him as their protector against the supernatural scum that lurk around in the shadows. He is "The Dark Angel."

The year is 2053, and the daughters of the town's well-to-do families are disappearing without a trace. No witnesses. No evidence. No ransom notes. No leads at all until they find a few, dead and drained of all their blood by an unknown, but seemingly unnatural assailant. The only person suited for this investigation is Lynch, a surly ex-cop turned private detective with an on-again-off-again 'its complicated' girlfriend, and a secret. He can't die, he can't feel pain, and he sees the world in a way no one ever should. He sees all that is there, both natural and supernatural. His exploits have earned him the name Dark Angel among those that have crossed him. His only problem, no one told him how to truly use this *ability*. Time is running out for missing girls, and Lynch is the only one who can find and save them. Will he figure out the mystery in time and will he know what to do when he finds them?

Ghost Storm – Available Now

Amazon US

Amazon UK

There is nothing natural about this hurricane. An evil shaman unleashes a super-storm powered by an ancient Amazon spirit to enslave to humanity. Can one man realize what is important in time to protect his family from this danger?

Successful attorney Jim Preston hates living in his late father's shadow. Eager to leave his stress behind and validate his hard work, he takes his family on a lavish Florida vacation. But his plan turns to dust when a malicious shaman summons a hurricane of soul-stealing spirits.

Though his skeptical lawyer mind disbelieves at first, Jim can't ignore the warnings when the violent wraiths forge a path of destruction. But after numerous unsuccessful escape attempts, his only hope of protecting his wife and children is to confront an ancient demonic force head-on... or become its prisoner.

Can Jim prove he's worth more than a fancy house or car and stop a brutal spectral horde from killing everything he holds dear?

Game Master Series

Book One - Game Master – Game On

This fast-paced adrenaline filled series follows Robert Deluiz and his friends behind the veil of 1's and 0's and into the underbelly of the online universe where they are trapped as pawns in a sadistic game show for their very lives. Lose a challenge, and you die a horrible death to the cheers and profit of the viewers. Win them all, and you are changed forever.

Can Robert out play, outsmart, and outlast his friends to survive and be crowned Game Master?

Buy book one, Game Master: Game On and see if you have what it takes to be the Game Master.

Available now on Amazon and Kindle Unlimited

Book Two - Game Master – Playing for Keeps

The fast-paced horror for Robert and his new wife, Amy, continue. They think they have the game mastered when new players enter with their own set of rules, and they have no intention of playing fair. Motivated by anger and money, the root of all evil, these individuals devise a plan for the Robert and his friends to repay them. The price... is their lives.

Game Master Play On is a fast-paced sequel ripped from today's headlines. If you like thriller stories with a touch of realism and a stunning twist that goes back to the origins of the Game Master show itself, then you will love this entry in David Clark's dark web trilogy, Game Master.

Buy book two, Game Master: Playing for Keeps to find out if the SanSquad survives.

Available now on Amazon and Kindle Unlimited

Book Three - Game Master – Reboot

With one of their own in danger, Robert and Doug reach out to a few of the games earliest players to mount a rescue. During their efforts, Robert finds himself immersed in a Cold War battle to save their friend. Their adversary... an ex-KGB super spy, now turned arms dealer, who is considered one of the most dangerous men walking the planet. Will the skills Robert has learned playing the game help him in this real world raid? There is no trick CGI or trap doors here, the threats are all real.

Buy book three, Game Master: Reboot to read the thrilling conclusion of the Game Master series.

Available now on Amazon and Kindle Unlimited

Highway 666 Series

Book One – Highway 666

A collection of four tales straight from the depths of hell itself. These four tales will take you on a high-speed chase down Highway 666, rip your heart out, burn you in a hell, and then leave you feeling lonely and cold at the end.

Stories Include:

- Highway 666 - The fate of three teenagers hooked into a demonic ride-share.
- Till Death – A new spin on the wedding vows
- Demon Apocalypse - It is the end of days, but not how the Bible described it.
- Eternal Journey - A young girl is forever condemned to her last walk, her journey will never end

Available now on Amazon and Kindle Unlimited

Book Two – The Splurge

A collection of short stories that follows one family through a dysfunctional Holiday Season that makes the Griswold's look like a Norman Rockwell painting.

Stories included:

- Trick or Treat – The annual neighborhood Halloween decorating contest is taken a bit too far and elicits some unwilling volunteers.
- Family Dinner – When your immediate family abandons you on Thanksgiving, what do you do? Well, you dig down deep on the family tree.
- The Splurge – This is a "Purge" parody focused around the First Black Friday Sale.
- Christmas Eve Nightmare – The family finds more than a Yule log in the fireplace on Christmas Eve

Available now on Amazon and Kindle Unlimited

A big thank you to my beta reading team. Without all your feedback, books like this one would not be possible. Thank you for all your hard work.

The Secret of the Blood Charm © 2022 by David Clark. All Rights Reserved.
All rights reserved. No part of this book may be reproduced in any form or by any electronic or mechanical means including information storage and retrieval systems, without permission in writing from the author. The only exception is by a reviewer, who may quote short excerpts in a review.

This book is a work of fiction. Names, characters, places, and incidents either are products of the author's imagination or are used fictitiously. Any resemblance to actual persons, living or dead, events, or locales is entirely coincidental.

David Clark
Visit my website at www.authordavidclark.com

Printed in the United States of America

First Printing: January 2022
Frightening Future Publishing

Printed in Great Britain
by Amazon